Esme's Gift

elizabeth foster

PRAISE FOR *ESME'S GIFT*

'With a well-developed whimsical world and heroes you can cheer for, this series has more than earned its place alongside *Nevermoor*.'
Julian Barr, Author

'Thrilling and exciting … a beautifully creative fantasy world, coupled with an equally as creative magic system, all backed up by a fascinating gang of characters.'
Jean, Goodreads

'*Esme's Gift* is much more action packed than *Esme's Wish*, but still doesn't lose the enchanting feel. Fans of *Harry Potter* will love this book for its similar themes.'
Sorcha, Goodreads

'*Esme's Gift* took me for an absolutely amazing ride! I highly recommend this series!'
Chelsea Taylor, Goodreads

Published by Odyssey Books in 2019
www.odysseybooks.com.au

A Cataloguing-in-Publication entry is available from the National Library of Australia

Series: Foster, Elizabeth. Esme Series; book 2
ISBN: 978-1-925652-83-3 (pbk)
ISBN: 978-1-925652-84-0 (ebook)
Keywords: Young adults, Fantasy, Mystery

Cover artwork by Furea (www.fureadesigns.com)
Map artwork by Christopher Foster

In memory of my mum and dad. All the love.

What would an ocean be without a monster lurking in the dark? It would be like sleep without dreams.

—Werner Herzog

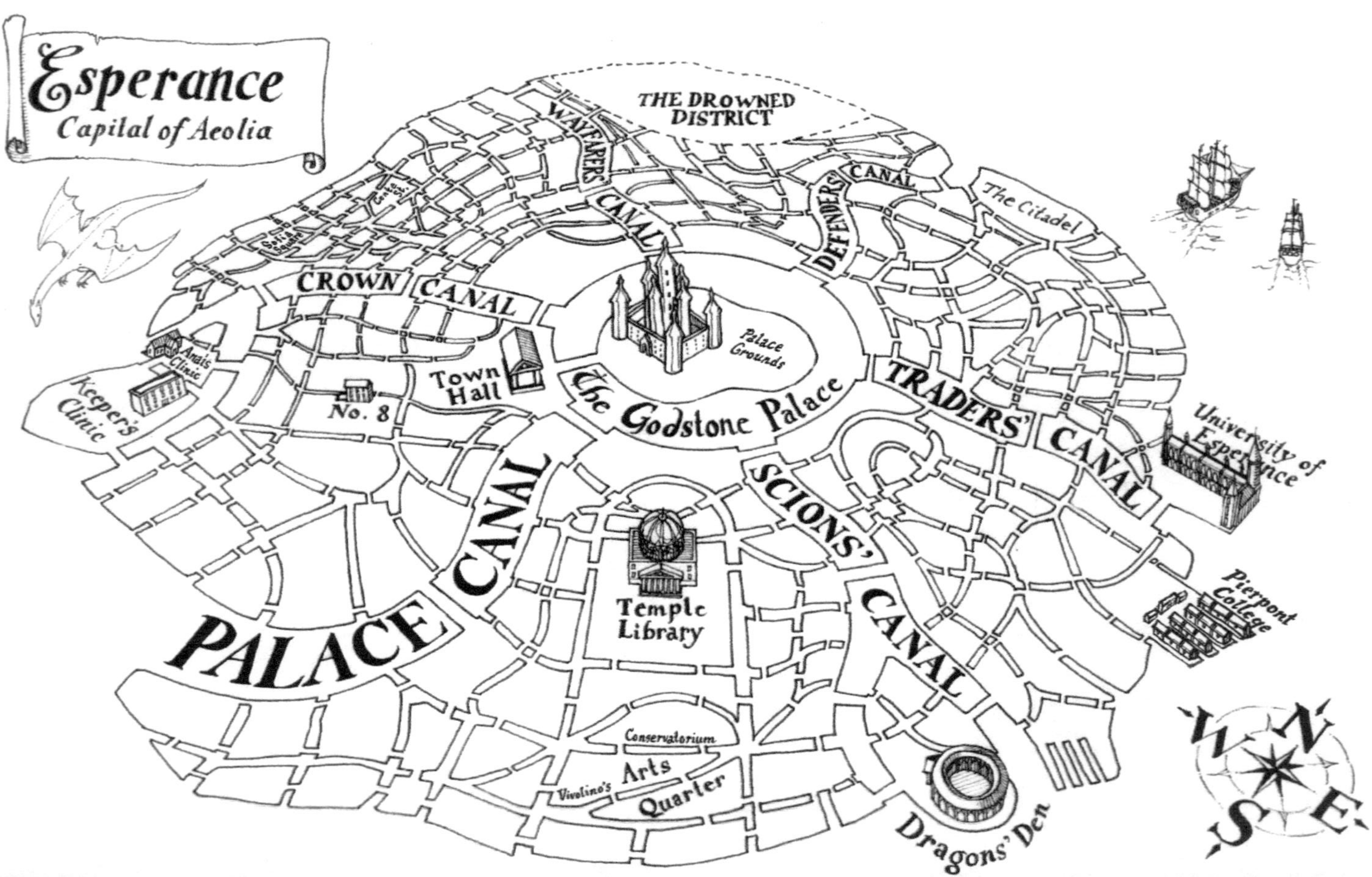

Esperance
Capital of Aeolia
THE DROWNED DISTRICT
WAYFARERS' CANAL
DEFENDERS' CANAL
The Citadel
CROWN CANAL
Palace Grounds
Anais Clinic
Keeper's Clinic
Town Hall
No. 8
The Godstone Palace
TRADERS' CANAL
University of Esperance
PALACE CANAL
SCIONS' CANAL
Temple Library
Pierpont College
Conservatorium
Violino's Arts Quarter
Dragons' Den
W N S E

Welcome to...

PIERPONT COLLEGE
1989 Student Diary

Name: Esme Silver   Form: 5th

TIMETABLE

MON	TUE	WED	THU	FRI
Maths	History	Maths	Biology	History
Biology	History	Free!	Maths	History
RECESS				
Art	PC	Biology	Art	Art
Art	PC	History	Free!	Art
LUNCH				Internship
Biology	Sport	PC	Maths	with
Biology	Sport	PC	Maths	Augustine

GUIDE TO SCHOOL GROUNDS

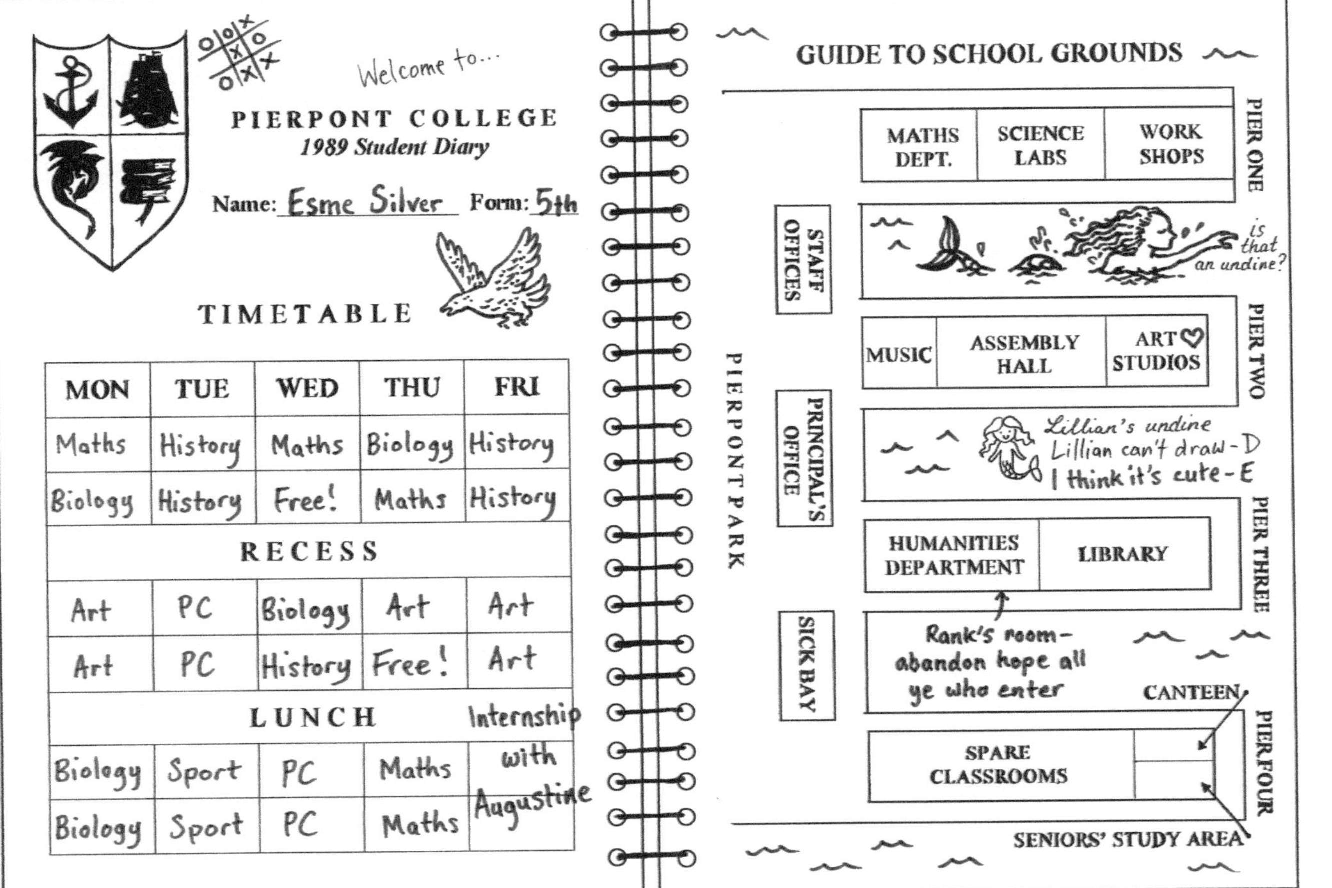

Chapter One

As fifteen-year-old Esme Silver lurched off the ferry and onto the water-lashed wharf, she swayed as if she were still at sea. Torrential rain pounded the wooden treads underfoot; winds gusted so forcefully, they threatened to sweep her sideways off the dock. It was as if Picton Island, the place she'd called home all her life, was punishing her for abandoning it.

Except Picton Island didn't feel much like home anymore.

Her heart was back in Esperance, the glittering capital of the parallel world of Aeolia. Esme had spent the past several weeks there, searching for her long-lost mother Ariane. And against all odds, she'd succeeded. Her mother was alive, but in a trance, confined to bed. Now Esme faced a challenge that seemed even more insurmountable: convincing her father that Aeolia was real.

For the whole trip here, she'd fretted about how her father would respond to her news. Now her stomach was as knotted as the twist of storm clouds over Picton Village.

It was only early afternoon, but the sky was so dark it could have been dusk. Shielding her face with the hood of her rain jacket, Esme turned left, skirting the village, a collection of near-identical cottages that clung to the hillside as tenaciously as their inhabitants clung to their closed-minded ways.

Her pace quickened as she passed the church in which her father had remarried earlier that summer. She could still hear the scandalised murmurs of the congregation after she had flung up her hand in objection to the proceedings:

'*Selfish child, ruining Penelope's special day …*'

'Ariane's been gone for seven years. She's not coming back …'

'What is wrong with that girl?'

That day was a raw bruise that had yet to heal. Esme hadn't been able to stay silent that day, because letting her father marry Penelope would have been a tacit acceptance of her mother's fate—a fate inscribed on a cenotaph within the church grounds.

In memory of
ARIANE MAY SILVER
Beloved Wife of Aaron and Mother to Esme
1950—1981
Lost at Sea

Further up the hill, the blue light of the police station blinked at Esme. She was sorely tempted to venture inside and take down her mother's tattered missing person's poster, still pinned up on the bulletin board:

Name: Ariane Silver. Age: 31. Last known whereabouts: Spindrift Island, December 2nd, 1981. Appearance: Long, straight, dark brown hair; medium height; slight build; blue eyes.

Along with the rain peppering Esme's cheeks came a chilling thought: *What if there's a notice in there for me, too?*

Name: Esme Silver, read the poster conjured up in her mind. *Age: 15. Last known whereabouts: Spindrift Island, January 14th, 1989. Appearance: Long, curly, light brown hair; medium height; slight build; blue-green eyes.*

At the crest of the hill, the village fell out of sight. Picton Island vaguely resembled a beached whale, with the southern harbour forming its tail. Esme and her father lived on the island's isolated northern point, where wild grass caressed the black cliffs of Splinter Bay.

As she hurried north along the whale's back, the familiar blue-and-white lighthouse—and her father's cottage beside it—came into sight. A warning pinged with each raindrop, and each muddy step closer. Was her father even there? For all she knew, the cottage might be deserted. Maybe her father had finally been bullied into moving back down to the village.

Aaron Silver was Picton's lighthouse keeper and ranger. He loved his job, but his parents had never forgiven him for refusing to work for the family fishing fleet. They wanted him back in the village, at any cost—and so did Penelope.

She picked her way around the last of the puddles and unlatched the cottage gate. The letterbox attached to the picket fence was stuffed full of mail, all addressed to her father.

Wait—one letter was addressed to her.

Just as she was about to open it, a feline form butted up against her.

'Reuben!' she cried, scooping her beloved cat up in her arms. 'I missed you so much.'

Reuben sunk a claw into her arm in retaliation for her long absence, then retracted it and snuggled into her embrace, limp with relief. She carried him to the porch, where she examined him with care. He didn't look any the worse for wear, apart from another sprinkle of grey in his ageing black coat.

BANG.

The front door slammed open so fast Esme almost dropped Reuben on the porch. Her heart lodged in her throat as she recognised the brown-garbed woman framed in the doorway. It wasn't Penelope. It was somebody much worse.

'Finally,' sniped Mavis, Penelope's odious older sister. 'Come crawling back, have you?'

For an instant, Esme thought she glimpsed genuine relief on her step-aunt's face, but it might have been a grimace.

'I don't want to hear any sob stories,' Mavis barked before Esme could speak. 'I don't want to hear any excuses. Half the summer, you've been gone! The whole village has been out looking for you. Your father's been in an absolute state. My sister too; she's beside herself! We should have finished the move weeks ago, but your *father*'— she made a huffing sound—'has been refusing to leave without you.'

She hustled Esme inside and down the corridor. Reuben followed after them.

The house was an empty shell. Most of the furniture was gone, and the walls had been stripped of all Ariane's magnificent paintings, bar one. Halfway down the hallway hung a rich oil of Odysseus at sea. The Ancient Greek voyager stood at the prow of his ship, intent on navigating the treacherous waters guarded by Scylla and Charybdis, immortal monsters who rose on either side of the narrow passage. Esme tried, but failed, to suppress a snort.

Which one's Mavis and which one's Penelope?

Mavis glared at her. 'Wipe that smirk off your face. With all the trouble you've caused, you won't be smiling again for a long time.'

The living room was bereft of its usual comforts, save the sofa, still facing the fireplace. The room reeked of a woody ferment that only grew stronger as Esme rounded the sofa.

'Dad!' she cried.

Her father lay there—asleep, unshaven, more grey in his hair than ever before. Air skittered out of his slack mouth, a whistle on the tail of each breath. His calloused hand loosely cupped a low glass tumbler. A half-empty bottle of whiskey rested on the floor, and an upturned crate beside the sofa—a makeshift coffee table— was littered with empty glasses and dirty plates.

While Mavis looked on, faintly disgusted, Esme threw down her satchel and tried to rouse her father. Her efforts had no effect.

'What's happened?' she asked her step-aunt. 'Is he ill?'

Mavis sniffed. 'If he is, he's brought it on himself. Or rather, you have. The only reason we haven't moved that sofa out is because he won't get off it.'

She picked up an empty glass off the floor and added it to the mess on the crate.

'You're all he ever talks about, you know. How much he misses you. How much he wants you back again. *You* did this to him.'

Esme opened her mouth to protest. 'I—'

But Mavis was gone. Shortly afterward, Esme heard the front door slam shut. She knew exactly where Mavis was headed— straight to Penelope, to spill the news.

Her eyes drifted to her father's insentient form on the sofa.

You did this to him.

Mavis's words lodged like a splinter in her heart. As she kneeled down beside her father, it dug in even deeper. She pried the tumbler from his hand and shook his shoulder.

'Dad?'

His snoring stopped—then resumed. As she rose to her feet, at a loss as to what to do, the letter from the mailbox fell out of her pocket. She tore open the envelope, then realised, too late, that it wasn't addressed to her.

The scribbly, rain-smudged handwriting read *Mrs Silver*—not *Ms Silver.*

Oh. Her heart did a little sideways step.

Her first, honourable, instinct was to stuff the letter back in the envelope and pretend she'd never seen it. Even though Penelope ignored her to the point of neglect, nobody deserved to have their private life snooped into.

Then Esme noticed the anchor and rope on the letterhead.

That was the logo of the Silver family fishing fleet. The logo on all the stationery belonging to her grandparents. Ignoring the guilt nipping at her, Esme pulled out a slip of paper with only a few words on it.

See you down in the village. Keep up the good work.

Pulse spiking, Esme peered inside the envelope and saw num- bers—*lots* of numbers—on what looked like bank statements. When she unfolded them, her eyes boggled. Once a month, for the past year, substantial payments had been transferred from Aaron's parents to the account of one Penelope Silver.

With dawning horror, Esme replaced the documents and resealed the envelope as best she could. *It could mean nothing,* she tried to reassure herself, slipping the letter back into her pocket. *Those payments could have been for anything.*

But she couldn't get the bitter taste of suspicion out of her mouth. Aaron's parents had introduced him to Penelope. They'd done all they could to encourage the courtship. They had even paid for the wedding.

Moving as if in a troubling dream, Esme gathered up her father's dirty glasses and dishes, and trailed off to the kitchen. It was as derelict as the rest of the house, with half-packed boxes everywhere. She filled the sink with hot, soapy water, and reached for a plate—one she'd never seen before. It was decorated with a fading rose-coloured castle on a lake, and a large crack ran down its middle.

It must be Penelope's, thought Esme.

She dipped it in the suds.

The moment her fingers touched the water, a roaring started up in her ears. Her head began to throb as if a thousand needles were stabbing into her brain.

'Oh no.' She clenched her teeth. 'Not now.'

She tried to let go of the plate, but her hand was stuck to it. Her whole body, in fact, was frozen in place. This had happened to her before: in this very kitchen, at this very sink. This time, she knew what was causing her agony, but knowing didn't make it any less terrifying.

This was her Gift: the power to travel through the memories of water and bear witness to the distant past. Her Gift had a chance of activating whenever she came into contact with water, and where she went—*when* she went—was beyond her control. Her consciousness shifted and she fell into a trance.

When the roaring faded, the vinyl floor under Esme's feet gave way to chequered tiles. She was still in a kitchen, but not her own. This was the sort of kitchen that would have been fashionable back in the fifties.

A booth for four was tucked into one end of the room. A pastel blue fridge stood in the opposite corner. Between them, cabinets hung above a long bench, where a young girl was washing a plate.

The same kind of plate that Esme had just been washing.

Matching dishes were stacked in the drying rack by the sink. The whole set was new; no cracks or chips marred the china.

The room was hot and airless, the child at the sink red-faced and perspiring. She paused to draw a handkerchief from the pocket of her dirt-coloured smock. After wiping her forehead, she turned toward Esme, as if she could sense the latter's presence. As the girl's olive-green eyes stared right through her, Esme reeled in shock. *Those eyes.*

This little girl could only be a younger version of Mavis.

Mavis swung back to the sink. As she resumed scrubbing, a middle-aged woman entered the kitchen, holding the hand of another little girl: a fair-haired girl in a frilly pink dress. Mavis, elbow-deep in soapsuds, began to complain.

'Why do *I* always have to do the washing up? It's never Penelope's turn.'

Without a word, Penelope slid into the booth and started smoothing out the frills of her skirt. Meanwhile, the middle-aged woman cast a critical eye over Mavis.

'Your sister's all dressed up, ready for the party. It's her special day.'

'It's always her special day,' grumbled Mavis.

With a pointed glare, the woman left the kitchen.

Immediately, Penelope piped up in a sing-song voice, 'Last night, when Mummy and Daddy were talking and they thought we were in bed, I heard them say something funny.'

'What?' asked Mavis grumpily.

'Mummy said to Daddy that I got all the best bits of them, and you got all the worst. That I'm the smart one and the pretty one, and no one will ever want to marry you. Daddy … said she was right.' She went back to fiddling with her skirt. 'But don't worry. I'll always be here to look after you.'

Little Mavis had started to shake. Esme glanced over at Penelope, who was watching her sister from the corner of her eye, clinically observing her distress. As Mavis trembled, the plate in her hand wobbled like a wheel coming off a wagon.

'*Noooo!*' she cried as it slipped from her fingers.

On impulse, Esme ran forward to catch it, but her hand passed right through the solid china as if either she or it were made of air. It hit the floor and smashed in two.

'The new china!' Mavis exclaimed. 'I have to hide it.' Her eyes darted fearfully to the door and then helplessly toward Penelope.

Penelope swung around to face her sister. She lifted the hem of her dress, making a pouch large enough for the broken plate.

'I won't tell,' she promised. 'Hide it in here.'

As Mavis thrust the razor-edged shards into the pouch, Penelope winced.

'Ouch! You cut my finger.'

'Sorry,' Mavis cried. 'Don't tell!' she pleaded, at the sound of approaching footsteps. 'Please don't tell.'

Their mother walked in and started rummaging around in one of the high cupboards. While Mavis shrank away, Penelope's tinkly voice rang out from the booth.

'Mummy, can I get a new dress?'

Her mother, peering into the cupboard, shook her head. 'Don't be silly, darling. That one *is* new. And the colour's perfect on you.'

Mavis, twisting the dishcloth in her hands, stared nervously at Penelope.

'But this one's ruined,' Penelope wailed.

'What do you mean it's ruined?' Her mother's eyes darted from the cupboard to the booth, and she gasped. 'Is that *blood?* Penny, you poor thing!'

After pulling a plaster from a drawer, she hurried over to her youngest daughter. Penelope whimpered as her mother bandaged the wound.

'Oh, darling, are you all right?' She finished ministering to her daughter, then examined the dress. 'Oh no, it really is ruined! I'll try to get the stain out, but if I can't, I suppose I can get you another one. How on earth did this happen?'

Penelope's eyes drifted toward Mavis. Her mother followed her gaze, her features hardening.

'Tell me the truth.'

'Mavis threw one of your new plates on the ground and made me hide the pieces. That's how I cut my finger,' Penelope said sweetly. 'Look.'

Like a magician performing a trick, she revealed the plate hidden in her dress.

With a gasp, Mavis sprinted from the room. Her mother stormed after her. Penelope's pale, grey, scheming eyes were the last thing Esme saw before she was rushed back to the present.

The roar in Esme's ears subsided, but her headache remained. She was back in her own kitchen, in the present, and she could move again.

What she had just witnessed only worsened her fears for her father. Just because Penelope was manipulative as a child, didn't mean she'd conned Aaron. But Penelope had been wed before, for short periods, and Esme had often wondered what had broken up her previous marriages. She'd always tried to give her new stepmother the benefit of the doubt.

Still, her suspicions about Penelope's true agenda were rapidly crystallising into something she couldn't ignore.

As she lifted the plate she'd been washing out of the sink, a pulse of pain left over from her Gift shot through her head. The ancient china slipped out of her wet fingers. This time, it didn't just split in two. This time, it smashed to smithereens, obliterating the castle on the lake.

Chapter Two

As Esme tipped the shards of china into the bin, she wished she could banish with them the scene she had just witnessed from the past. She ducked back into the living room to see if the noise had woken her father—no such luck—then grabbed a bundle from her waterproof satchel.

Inside was a loaf of fresh breyberry bread, baked that morning in another world.

Back in the kitchen, she cut several thick slices, brewed a pot of coffee, and piled everything on a tray. After returning to the living room, she set the tray down and stared at her father.

Fear fluttered in her stomach. Her tongue had a metallic taste to it. She swallowed, but the taste wouldn't go away. Leaning over her father, she spoke right into his ear.

'Dad. Dad. It's me, Esme.'

One bleary eye opened. Drool dribbled out the corner of his mouth.

'Dad, it's me. I'm back!'

Finally, her voice managed to penetrate the recesses of his liquor-soaked brain. She helped him sit up, and he blinked at her from a face dirty with stubble. Half-moons of exhaustion hung beneath his eyes.

'Esme? Is that really you?'

His quavering hand met hers, its touch forcing out hot, itchy tears from her eyes. Blinking them away, she wrapped her arms around him. Beneath the whiskey, he smelled of fish and grime and the sea—and sorrow.

When they finally broke apart, he gazed at her with cloudy eyes. 'Where is everyone?'

'Out. Here, I made you coffee, extra strong, just the way you like it.'

He downed two cups, but refused the breyberry bread. When he was down to the dregs of his second mug, his eyes cleared a little. The fuzz in his brain must have, too, because he was able to string more than a few words together.

'I thought I'd never see you again. I went to Spindrift, searched the cliffs, waited for your body to wash ashore …' Esme flinched at the broken expression on her father's face. 'I thought the sea had snatched you away, the way it took your mother. Where *were* you?'

'You didn't get my letter?' she asked in a small voice.

Aaron's black brows knitted together. 'You mean this one?'

He reached into his pocket and pulled out the letter Esme had sent from Esperance. It was crumpled from having been read countless times.

'I found this on the doorstep when we got home from our honeymoon.' He unfolded it and read parts of it aloud, his tone incredulous. '*I'm spending the summer with some people who knew Ariane. Don't go looking, you won't find me.* Really? What else was I meant to do? And this: *If you'd like to write, give your letter to the messenger bird that delivered this one.*' He gaped at his daughter. 'The *messenger bird?*'

'I—' Esme stopped short.

The letter had sounded perfectly reasonable when she wrote it—reassuring, without giving too much away about where she really was. But now that she heard it read back to her, she realised how distressing it must have sounded to him.

'I thought you might have been kidnapped!' Aaron cried, waving the letter frantically. 'Or that this was some kind of sick joke! The only part that sounded like you was …' He glanced back down at the letter. '*Please tell Mavis I'm not missing her at all.*'

'I didn't mean to be gone for so long,' Esme tried to explain. 'I went to Spindrift, just for one night, just to get away from Mavis for a bit, and then …'

Her father wasn't listening. 'I thought somebody might have forced you to write this letter. I even thought you might have lost your mind, like—'

His hand clapped to his mouth. He'd never before come this close to telling Esme what he knew about Ariane.

'Like my mother,' said Esme. 'I already know, Dad.'

His features paled. 'You know … what?'

'I know what you think happened to Mum. I know she was being treated by someone called Doctor Wright from the Garson Sanatorium. I found a letter from him on Spindrift saying she should go on medication. You'd thrown it in the fire, but I pieced the scraps together. I know that everybody thought she was—'

'We didn't think it,' said her father, burying his face in one hand. 'We knew something was wrong with her. She kept talking about other worlds, the way her grandmother used to. Trying to convince me they really existed. Then one day, she told me she'd gotten better, that she'd made it all up, that I could stop worrying. I was so happy—she'd come to her senses at last. Then she said she had to go to Spindrift for a week to prepare for an exhibition.'

His eyes misted over. 'I—I'm sorry you had to find out the way you did. But by the time you were old enough to know, I couldn't bear to think about it anymore.'

Esme glanced toward the corridor. Any moment now, Mavis would return, likely with Penelope in tow. Time was running out to tell her father about Ariane. She couldn't put it off any longer, but she was finding it hard to breathe. The eerily bare walls seemed to be shrinking around her.

Steeling herself for his reaction, she said, 'Mum's alive, Dad. That's what I came back to tell you. I found her. She's … in Esperance.'

Her father went very still.

'No,' he said in an agonised whisper. 'Not again.'

'But she's not well. She couldn't come back with me.'

'No … It's happened to you, too.'

He glanced around the room, like a man on a sinking ship searching for a lifebuoy. His eyes settled on the whiskey bottle.

'Dad, wait.' Esme heaved up her satchel. 'I brought proof. In here, there's a roll of film with pictures of Mum, and a compendium she illustrated, over in Esperance. It's about Aeolia's myths and legends—'

Her father groaned. 'Aeolia *is* a myth, Esme.'

Glass in hand, he was pouring himself another drink. When she tried to pass him the roll of film, he pushed it away and took a deep draught.

'This is all my fault,' his grim lips mumbled beneath whiskey-slick stubble. 'I should have known when you objected at the wedding. And then I left you here on your own … with Mavis, of all people.'

While Aaron was blind to Penelope's faults, he'd always shared Esme's low opinion of Mavis. At least in that respect, his eyes weren't welded shut. Part of her wanted to show him the bank statements she had found, but she couldn't—not now. He was staring at her like she was a stranger, her features blurred through lenses of disbelief.

'Can't you see this is all in your head? Your mother's gone.' He slowly enunciated each word, as if hoping they might leap into Esme's addled brain and fix things. 'Lost … at … sea.'

He squeezed his eyes shut, then murmured in a tar-thick voice, 'Oh, Esme … what are we going to do with you?'

'It's perfectly clear what we need to do,' said Mavis, from the doorway. 'Take her straight to see Doctor Wright at the Garson Sanatorium. In fact, I'll take her for you.'

Esme shot up and swung around, caught off guard.

Mavis, wrapped in her well-worn brown cardigan, entered the room. Penelope, petite and perfectly formed, flitted in beside her. If Mavis, in her drab attire, resembled a moth, Penelope was like a butterfly that had just emerged from its chrysalis. Everything about her shone: her new dress, her sleek fair hair, and her jewellery, especially the enormous diamond that Aaron's parents had paid for, glistening on her manicured finger.

Her eyes lit up upon seeing Esme. Esme, however, didn't think for one moment that Penelope's happiness was related to her safe return—in any way but one. Now Aaron had no excuse not to move down to the village.

'Oh, Esme!' Penelope cried in the syrupy voice she always put on when Aaron was around. 'Thank goodness you're back! The horrors you must have been through. We were all so worried. It's like everything stopped while you were away.'

I'll bet it did, thought Esme.

Mavis caught sight of the envelope in Aaron's hand. 'Is that Es-may's infamous letter? Sent by pigeon post, from an imaginary world?'

'I should have known you'd be eavesdropping,' muttered Esme.

Mavis smiled almost fondly at her. 'It was quite educational. I'm truly amazed at how creative deluded minds can be.'

Esme curled her fingers into a fist, then let them go. After her glimpse into Mavis's childhood, her hatred for her step-aunt had begun to dissipate. Anything Penelope fed Mavis, Mavis believed. Esme somehow doubted Mavis knew about whatever was going on between Aaron's parents and Penelope.

'Now, now, Mavis,' Penelope tinkled. 'Stop it. Give the poor girl a chance to recover from her ordeal. And don't call her Es-may. It's pronounced Es-mee.'

Penelope flashed Esme an ingratiating smile.

'Why don't I take you to Doctor Wright myself, get you checked over? I'm sure he'll be able to take care of you.'

Esme glared at her. 'I don't need to be *taken care of.* Stop talking to me like I'm five years old.'

'But darling,' Penelope simpered, 'don't you see it's for your own good?'

'Dad,' said Esme. 'Say something to her. She's not going to listen to me.'

Throughout the whole exchange, Aaron had remained oddly silent.

'Dad?' She turned toward him.

Aaron had topped up his whiskey glass again. His eyes were glazed over. He was on his way back to that pleasant land where nothing mattered except the next drink.

He blinked up at his daughter.

'Penelope knows what to do. Let her look after you. I can't lose you again.'

After a brief quarrel over which of them should stay to look after Esme and Aaron, the sisters concluded that the two of them could look after each other and prepared to depart. While Mavis struggled at the door with her umbrella, Penelope buttoned up her smart black overcoat and shot Esme a sympathetic smile.

Esme didn't smile back. Her hand was in her pocket, clutching the letter addressed to the new Mrs Silver.

'You should be glad my sister puts up with you,' Mavis grumbled at Esme. She gave up on her own umbrella and seized one of Aaron's from the coatrack.

'I don't "put up with her", Mavis,' Penelope insisted. 'I'm really very fond of her.'

Penelope's voice was so sickly sweet, Esme wondered how her gleaming teeth weren't full of cavities.

'Yeah, right,' Esme said before she could stop herself. 'You've never liked me, have you, Penelope?'

Penelope, who had just opened the front door, turned back round to face Esme. She started to speak in her own defence, but Esme cut her off.

'What about my father? Do you really love him? Or is this just a marriage of convenience … for you?'

Mavis gasped.

'His parents want him back. Back in the village, back in the family business—and they're prepared to pay for it, I suspect.' Esme's eyes narrowed. 'Am I on the right track?'

'How *dare* you!' hissed Mavis.

Penelope, however, stayed silent. Her grey eyes lifted, then flickered to the floor. Too late. In that brief moment, Esme had seen the truth laid bare.

'I've found you out, haven't I?' said Esme. 'Mavis, your sister has you fooled. She has everyone fooled except me.'

She glanced at Mavis and saw something flit across her face too. Fear.

In that moment, Esme felt more desperate than ever for her father, who had lost his heart to Penelope, and for Mavis, too, who was entirely under Penelope's sway.

'Once you've got what you want, are you going to leave my father, too?' Esme goaded Penelope. 'Move on to bigger prey?'

Penelope drew close and whispered in her ear. Her perfume assailed Esme's nostrils like a dark miasma, expelled from a rotting flower.

'Just remember that from now on, no one will believe a word you say.'

Esme took hold of Penelope's wrist. 'If you hurt my father ...'

Penelope shook Esme's hand away. As she retreated toward her sister on the porch, her eyes turned wide and innocent, like those of a doe.

'I love your father very, very much. Anyone can see that—anyone who's in their right mind, that is. Let's go, Mavis.'

As soon as Penelope's back was turned, Reuben sprang forward and dug a claw into her leg. Penelope shrieked, almost tripping down the front steps. Like a bloodhound protecting its master, Mavis lunged at the cat—but Reuben had already scrambled back inside, seeking refuge behind Esme's legs.

Esme slammed the door shut, then slid down onto the floor,

shocked that she had managed to crack Penelope's cool façade.

That brief but damning flicker of avarice in Penelope's eyes … Esme had seen that grasping look before. It was the same expression Dr Nathan Mare had worn when he had gazed upon the fabled Pearl of Esperance.

Mare was the reason Ariane had disappeared, the reason she was trapped in a trance right now. Esme, along with everyone else, had been totally fooled by his reassuring manner, his kind smile, his honeyed tones—right up until she'd witnessed that involuntary glimmer of greed on his face.

When Esme was certain the two sisters were far away, she left the house for the back garden, full of paper daisies and flannel flowers limp from the rain. Behind the blue-domed lighthouse, the ocean cut away beyond the cliffs, streaming off to the other islands of the archipelago. The storm-laden clouds were gone, leaving only ragged tatters behind.

Torn inside, Esme gazed at the lavender bushes her mother had planted long ago.

How futile it had been to try to convince her father of the existence of another world. All she had done was force him to delve into a past he had remarried to forget, reopened wounds that had finally started to heal. It was like pieces of gravel were lodged in her throat, rubbing painfully against each other.

Then she noticed movement out of the corner of her eye.

One of the birds perched on the lighthouse's dome was lifting off: a white sea eagle speckled with grey. This was the bird to which Esme's letter had referred, the bird that had hung around the lighthouse all her life. Her mother had always been fond of it; it had even featured in some of her paintings. In Esperance, Esme had discovered that the uncannily intelligent eagle was no ordinary creature. It was a messenger bird from Aeolia.

It spread its wings wide and circled over Esme before soaring off to the open ocean. It was as if the bird was beckoning for her to follow.

Spurred into action, Esme headed back inside.

As much as it hurt to leave her father so soon, it would be unwise—dangerous, even—to dally here any longer. Penelope would be back tomorrow to take her to see Doctor Wright, and there was a good chance he might recommend an extended stay in the Garson Sanatorium. If she ended up there, in a locked ward, she might never have the chance to return to Aeolia.

Aeolia—where her mother needed her more than ever.

After pouring every last bottle of whiskey down the sink, she emptied the contents of her satchel into another bag and took it with her to the lighthouse—the only place she knew she could leave a message to her father without Penelope or Mavis finding it first.

She climbed the spiral stairs with a heavy heart. On the dust-covered desk on the lighthouse's top level, she searched for a pen and some paper, and began to write.

Dear Dad,

I'm sorry I had to leave so soon. I've gone back to Esperance, to look after Mum. She's bed-bound, and I don't know how much longer she'll last. She needs me by her side.

She needs you, too.

Please, please, look in the bag in the cupboard behind this desk. It's easy to tell that Mum painted the illustrations in that book—you know her style better than anyone. Look at the photographs on the roll of film—some are of her, some are of me in Esperance, some are of us together. And if you hold the shell in there to your ear long enough, you might just hear a siren's song.

I'm going to write to you every week while I'm away. The letters will be delivered by the sea eagle with speckled wings, the one Mum used to paint. If you want to write back, give your letter to that bird and say it's for me. And if you want to come to Aeolia yourself, the way there is through one of the rock pools on Spindrift Island—the teardrop-shaped pool that great-grandma Lucinda used to love so much. Dive to the bottom, touch the shell hidden amongst the reeds, and you'll be on your way.

Esme wasn't sure whether she should add the next part, but ultimately, she thought it would be better for her father to know everything, no matter how much it might hurt him.

There's something else inside the bag. An envelope, addressed to Penelope, full of bank statements. I opened it by accident (really). Your parents are paying Penelope a lot of money—they have been for a while—and I can't help but think it's connected to getting you back to the village. I'll leave you to draw your own conclusions, but I'm worried for you. Moving out should be up to you—not anyone else.
Your loving (and perfectly sane) daughter,
Esme

PS: Ease off the whiskey … and please look out for Mavis.

By the time Esme returned to the cottage, the only noises in the house were Aaron's snores, Reuben's purring, and the whispers of waves far below. The sea's ceaseless refrain slipped in under doors and through crevices, reminding the cottage's inhabitants of their duty to keep the lighthouse beacon burning, to warn ships of the treachery of Splinter Bay.

The sea had nothing to say about treachery of a different kind.

Just before dawn, Esme kissed her sleeping father goodbye.

'I love you,' she whispered, her heart breaking.

Then she slipped a note into his pocket. *Don't forget to check the lighthouse one last time before you leave.*

As she turned away from the sofa, Reuben yowled at her feet.

'I can't take you with me,' she said sadly, lifting him up and snuggling him in her arms. 'I want to, but I can't. You hate getting wet. If I tried to take you through the portal, you'd scratch me to ribbons. Plus, someone needs to be here to look after Dad.'

She let him down onto the sofa and hurried out of the room.

The sun crested the horizon as Esme made her way to the harbour. She spent the next few hours in the churchyard by her mother's cenotaph, sheltered from the scattered rain by the leaves of an ancient oak.

When the ferry was due to depart, Esme raced down to the jetty.

'Off again?' the ferrymaster asked her.

Esme was thankful that he didn't recognise her as the girl who had vanished from Picton several weeks ago. To him, she was just the girl he had picked up yesterday from Spindrift. She nodded, keeping part of her face hidden under her hood.

'You must like it over there,' he said. 'Funny time of year to be going to Spindrift, though. Fish won't be biting for weeks.'

'I don't go there for the fishing,' said Esme. 'My family has a holiday cottage there.'

He smiled and clipped her a ticket. 'If I were you, I wouldn't stop there. You're young. Go see the world while you can.'

Several hours later, when the vicar of Picton Church took a stroll through the grounds, he stopped and stared, dumbfounded, at the damage some ill-bred vandal had inflicted upon one of the cenotaphs under the oak tree.

The date of Ariane Silver's death had been scratched out, and the last line on the tablet no longer read '*Lost at Sea*'.

It simply read: '*at Sea*'.

Chapter Three

Esme sped across the long basalt shelf at Spindrift Island's southernmost point. Charcoal cliffs rose at one end; the ocean fell away at the other. This tiny, wild islet, beloved by fishermen, hung right on the archipelago's fringe, as if straining to escape its tamer brothers and sisters. To the people of Picton Island, visiting Spindrift was like visiting the edge of the world.

The speckled eagle circled above, floating in its own sea of blue.

The teardrop-shaped pool before Esme hid the portal that, several weeks ago, had swallowed her whole and spat her out into Aeolia. It had taken her days to accept that Aeolia was as real a world as her own—days during which she hadn't known if she was dead, dreaming, or delusional.

She crouched down and ran a hand over the pool's icy surface, then waded in, treading water at its deepest point. The chill made her gasp, but she didn't wait to acclimatise. With a deep breath, she dove toward the inky reeds below.

Concealed amongst them lay the shell her mother had christened 'Triton Dreaming'. Iridescent blues, greens, and purples shimmered across its curves.

Esme reached down and touched the shell.

The water ran in silken threads around her, gracing her with one last limpid caress—before going rogue. It was as if a great wave had crashed over the shelf above, stirring up the pool. Currents surged from nowhere, catching Esme in their wild gyrations, pushing her down against the rocky floor.

The floor vanished.

Down she flew, down into the deep, down into the abyss between worlds. Eventually, the current slowed, stranding her in a space devoid of life or light. After what seemed like an age, a pin-prick of daylight pierced the darkness above.

Esme inhaled.

The water turned to air in her mouth: crisp, clean, pure air. Her lungs gulped it greedily. The current returned, just as fierce as before—but this time, it was propelling her upward. She stroked as fast as she could and, with a final thrust of her arm, broke through the water's skin into the sunshine of another world.

Esme had emerged in one of the tide pools on Laertes Island, one of the many isles that bordered the lagoon surrounding Esperance. A bowl of wispy blue sky, feathered with clouds, curved from one edge of the horizon to the other. The ocean's ancient, ancestral voice rumbled nearby.

As she climbed out of the pool, the water began bubbling and boiling again. The sea eagle shot out, shaking fat drops everywhere, before landing beside Esme.

'Could you deliver a letter for me?' she asked. 'To Daniel?'

Daniel Swift, the first person Esme had met in Aeolia, had promised to pick her up upon her return. She dug into her satchel for a notebook, tore off a page, and scribbled a brief letter, which she rolled up and secured with a hair tie.

The sea eagle regarded her with an impassive yellow eye, then took the scroll in its talons and soared off to the north.

Esme followed it via a winding path that led to the other side of the island. When the trees and bushes thinned out to reveal a sandy beach, she stopped short, wonderstruck.

Esperance, capital of Aeolia, shimmered like a mirage on the lagoon's surface. The city of spires and marble and magic called to her across the water, beckoning her to its shores. This place, she realised with a smile, was stealing her heart—the way it had stolen her mother's all those years ago.

She sat down on the sand to dry out, then took out her notebook again. Daniel wouldn't be here for ages, and the city looked so picturesque in the afternoon light …

Esme began to draw: first the topmost tower of the Godstone Palace, then the spires surrounding it, then the domes and roofs of the city below. A hazy reflection formed beneath the city, a mirror image in rapid, horizontal pencil strokes. Time passed unnoticed. As her hand flew back and forth across the page, she grew so absorbed that she hardly heard the faint voice hailing her from the water.

'Hellooooo!'

Esme jumped up, casting her drawing aside. Happiness surged in her at the sight of Daniel in *Talia*, a blue-trimmed timber boat with a carved dragon on its prow. Close to shore, Daniel leaped into the shallows with a tremendous splash.

On the water's edge, he gripped Esme in a bear hug. Esme hugged him back just as fiercely, grateful to be back in a place where people didn't doubt every word she said.

'How's Mum?' she asked as they broke apart.

She searched his familiar features for an answer. Beneath Daniel's spiky brown hair, a tattoo resembling ocean waves splashed down one side of his dark-skinned face.

'She's fine,' he said. 'Not fine, of course, but you know—the same. Not any worse, at least. I saw her today. I just came from the Anais clinic.'

His deep brown eyes roved up and down the beach.

'Your dad didn't make it?'

Esme shook her head.

'He didn't believe anything I said.' She struggled to keep the misery out of her voice. 'He wouldn't look at the compendium, or the photographs. He thought something was wrong with me. He was going to take me to see a doctor, and I was worried I might never see Mum again, or you, so …'

'So you came back early,' said Daniel, studying the tight line of her lips.

'I left everything there, though, with instructions on how to get here. Maybe he'll make it over.'

Daniel squeezed her hand. 'Well, *I'm* glad you made it back here okay.'

Together, they strode into the warm shallows and clambered into *Talia*. They sat side by side on one of the dinghy's benches and gazed toward Esperance.

'To the Anais clinic, *Talia*,' said Daniel.

The boat set off by itself, as if the prow was the head of a real dragon, whose submerged body was paddling underneath the boat, ferrying the vessel on its back.

'I don't know how I ever thought I could convince my dad this place was real. It's not as if I believed in it when I got here.' Esme flushed. 'I thought this lagoon was the river Styx and you were some accursed ferryman.'

Daniel laughed. 'Charon. That's the ferryman's name.' He held out his palm and said with a smirk, 'He demands a gold coin in payment for the trip.'

'*Talia*'s the one doing all the work,' Esme said wryly. She leaned out the side of the boat to skim the water with her fingertips. 'Maybe you should start paying her.'

'We do pay. A yearly fee to an enchanter to keep her running. A rather steep one, too.'

As different as Esme's world was from Daniel's, she found comfort in the fact that the two worlds shared significant swaths of history and culture. The founders of Aeolia had been refugees from Ancient Greece. Over the centuries, others fleeing war, famine, and persecution had found their way here, too, settling the many small islands strewn across Aeolia's vast oceans.

Soon, *Talia* slipped into the cool embrace of Esperance's shadow. Palatial buildings in bronzes, creams, and pinks graced the foreshores, their ornate exteriors mirrored in the waters below. Closer up, though, the cracks began to show. Tiles were missing from roofs, crumbling brickwork was exposed, towers were covered in scaffolding, turrets leaned perilously toward the water. These were the residual wounds of seven years' worth of relentless earthquakes.

Caused, unwittingly, by Esme's mother.

When Ariane stole the Pearl of Esperance, seven years ago, Aeolia's magic was thrown out of balance. Ariane, however, hadn't known that her actions would destabilise the city's foundations. She'd only taken the pearl to prevent it from falling into the hands of Dr Nathan Mare, who had spent half his life searching for the all-powerful artefact.

On the elusive Isle of Mists, Ariane's Gift had activated, forcing her into a trance. And that was how Esme had found her, seven years later: pearl in hand, so pale and motionless she might have been made of candle wax. When Esme and Daniel returned the pearl to Esperance, the quakes ceased. Now it had a new hiding place, far beneath the city.

While the city had suffered, the water, at least, bore no scars. A parade of craft cruised the lagoon: gilt-edged ferries, tall white sail-boats, and gondolas in jewel-like colours—dazzling blues, crimsons, emerald greens. Sea dragons looped above the rooftops, twisting their sinuous forms in concert with the winding waterways below.

As Talia veered round the city's edge toward the west, Daniel cried out, 'Look! Water weavers!'

A man and a woman were standing on a jetty, channelling water up from the lagoon, sculpting it into a perfect rolling wave. Inside the wave surfed a young girl, balancing on a wooden board, her hand skimming the back of the glistening green wall.

'And water walkers,' Esme pointed out.

Several feet out from the jetty, a group of performers were climbing on top of each other to form a human pyramid, with nothing to support their weight but the lagoon itself.

'Is this what it was like here before the quakes?' Esme asked, looking back as the pyramid collapsed and laughter travelled across the water. 'People practised their Gifts out here all the time?'

'Oh, they're just celebrating,' said Daniel. 'Things will calm down soon, once everyone gets used to their Gifts working properly again. If only they knew that you're the one responsible for getting things back to normal.'

Esme shook her head. 'It's better that nobody knows anything about the pearl. And I didn't do it on my own.'

The laughter faded as *Talia* entered the city via the broad Crown Canal and started nosing her way through the narrower waterways that veined the Keeper's Quarter.

'Speaking of Gifts,' Esme said, 'mine activated again while I was away.'

'Really?' asked Daniel, brushing away a fragrant curtain of jasmine that hung from a low bridge. 'What did you see?'

His eyes grew wide as Esme described her vision of Penelope and Mavis as children, then his lip curled as she told him about the letter linking Aaron's parents to Penelope.

'Your poor dad,' he muttered. 'I thought evil stepmothers only existed in fairy tales.'

'Penelope's not evil,' mused Esme. 'She's just selfish, and manipulative. Nathan Mare—now *he's* evil.'

Esme and Daniel disembarked by a small stone bridge. The Anais clinic, staffed by Esperance's finest healers, was situated at the end of a nearby lane. Ivy twisted over the oft-patched walls of the great villa, and its antiquated doors creaked as Esme pushed them open.

Inside, the clinic was white-walled and sparsely decorated: a little like a hospital, but slightly more welcoming, thanks to its high ceilings, timber floors, and old-fashioned wainscoting. Ariane's room was situated on the ground floor, down a long corridor.

'I'm back, Mum!' Esme called as she hurried into the room.

Dark locks spilled around Ariane's face, and the faintest trace of a smile played at the edges of her lips. Esme sighed with relief at the sight of her mother, but the moment's solace swiftly faded. Ariane looked exactly as she had in the alabaster cave on the Isle of

Mists; like she was carved out of marble, part of the rock. Despite the reassuring steadiness of her pulse, there was a transience to her that couldn't be ignored.

Opposite Ariane's bed, a large window overlooked the clinic's garden. Daniel unlatched it, and the hush of the room was exchanged for the sounds of daily life: the twitter of birds in the trees, the chatter of people passing by, the song of a gondolier as her boat swished down the garden-side canal.

A rush of wings announced the arrival of the sea eagle. It landed on the windowsill and cocked its head toward the birds in the garden, as if to establish that this was its territory.

Then the door opened to admit Augustine Agapios, the Keeper of Esperance: Aeolia's foremost authority on magic.

Augustine had a youthful air about him that belied his true maturity and hid the true extent of his knowledge. He was dressed in black robes, his white-blond hair was tied back, and his stride was full of its usual purpose. When Esme stepped forward to greet him, his brilliant blue eyes, a tell-tale sign of his royal blood, pierced hers.

'No luck with your father?' he said, opening the clasps on his case. His sentient divining rod, Willow, flew out and into the palm of his hand.

Esme shook her head. Before she could speak, a cry came from the doorway.

'Esme! You're back! What happened? Your dad—where is he?'

Lillian Lovell, a tall, curvy girl with long auburn hair, dashed in, out of breath. Her mother Miranda followed behind, acknowledging Esme's return with a little sideways tilt of her head and a warm smile. Slight, russet-haired Miranda had been one of Ariane's closest friends in Esperance, and had let Esme stay with her over the summer.

'Dad didn't make it over,' said Esme.

Miranda gave Esme's hand a sympathetic squeeze. 'I'm sorry to hear that.' She placed a pot of lavender—Ariane's favourite flower—on the bedside desk, then leaned over her friend, searching for signs of life.

'There's been no change in her condition?' Esme asked Augustine.

'She remains stable, for now. But her condition is truly beyond our understanding. She's in perfect health, somehow. Her Gift is keeping her physical body in a kind of stasis. She doesn't need food or water. She hasn't even aged in seven years.'

'You're right,' said Miranda. 'Ariane looks exactly the same as she did when I knew her.' Her breath caught. 'Isn't there anything we can do for her? Anything at all?'

She turned to Esme, wringing her hands together. 'You've been in trances like this before, haven't you? Lillian told me that you and your mother have the same Gift. How do you break out of it when this happens to you?'

'I don't,' said Esme. 'I can't. I just have to wait until the vision is over. And when I do wake up, I've got a thumping headache … thanks to Mare.'

Miranda gave her a blank stare.

'Do you mean … Nathan Mare? The Mare your mother knew?'

Augustine nodded. 'Esme and I suspect that Mare's tampering with Ariane's Gift is the reason she is unable to wake.'

Miranda's hand went to her heart.

'Dr Mare … tampered with Ariane's Gift? I remember his trial. I know he was imprisoned for experimenting on people's Gifts, but that all happened a few months after I last saw your mother.'

'Mum wasn't just Mare's friend,' explained Esme. 'She was one of his patients. When Mum was pregnant, she was worried about losing me, so she went to him for help. Whatever he gave her worked, but it also affected our Gifts somehow. Mum got a terrible headache whenever she used hers … and now I do, too.'

Miranda looked horrified. 'How could he betray his patients' trust like that? And under the pretence of saving your life …'

Esme felt a strange twinge, like a flat note striking right after one in perfect tune. She didn't ever want to feel that she owed her life to that man. He had tried to kill her, and her mother, so he could take the pearl for himself. And he was still reaching out to them, ruining them through their Gifts.

'Nathan Mare has always been obsessed with Gifts,' said Augustine. 'Perhaps ... due to the fact that he himself does not possess one. His parents were two of Esperance's most renowned enchanters, and they couldn't bear the shame of having a Giftless son.'

'It's nothing to be ashamed of,' said Miranda, pink spots rising in her cheeks. Esme knew why—Miranda didn't have a Gift herself. 'What happened when they found out?'

The keeper sighed. 'It's a long story.'

Miranda glanced at the slumbering Ariane. 'We've got time.'

The keeper took a seat by Ariane's bed.

'When Mare didn't live up to his parents' expectations, they took their anger out on him. They couldn't see that he was, in fact, brilliant—blessed with an extraordinary scientific mind and an aptitude for medicine. They took him to my clinic to see if I could "fix" him ... and I told them there was nothing to fix. Indeed, I thought he showed such promise that I took him on as my part-time assistant.

'For the years he was under my wing, I told him that my duty— my life's work—was to keep the magic of Aeolia in balance. I tried to curb his youthful impatience, to teach him moderation in all things, to encourage him to cast off the ambition of his parents. I tried to teach him many things, but ...'

He trailed off, stone-faced. Motes of the past swirled around in the room, like deadly germs, come back to infect the present.

'I failed ... utterly. Mare left my clinic, taking all the knowledge I had given him. But he didn't use it to heal, as I had taught. His true aim, all along, had been to enhance others' Gifts, make them more powerful—as if to prove to his parents, and himself, that even without a Gift he could defy the laws of nature. He brewed elixirs that blended magical herbs with harmful chemicals, dangerous medicines with addictive intoxicants, science with magic.

And he prescribed them to his patients without their knowledge or consent.'

Agitated, he rose from his chair to pace the room.

'But that is all in the past. Let's focus on the matter at hand.' He turned to Miranda. 'Tell me, the first term at Pierpont is about to commence, is it not?'

'Next week.'

'Well then. May I suggest, Esme—with your mother indisposed and your father not here to guide you—that perhaps you should consider attending?'

Miranda heartily seconded the idea. 'Yes! I'm sure your mother would wish for you to continue your studies. You can stay with us again, of course.'

Esme blinked. She hadn't even considered the possibility. She couldn't imagine herself back home, enduring another dreary year at Penzance High School. But school here? In a place like this?

'Well?' asked Lillian.

'Well?' Daniel echoed.

Somewhat dazed, she nodded her assent. 'I'd love to. I'll write to my dad and let him know.'

Chapter Four

A week later, Lillian's voice roused Esme from a dreamless sleep, note by note dissolving what was left of the night. Her lilting song, floating up through the now-familiar house at 8 Nestor Street, sounded like a siren calling from the deep—and Esme would know. She and Lillian had met real sirens earlier that summer.

On that visit, Melisande, chief guardian of the sirens' songspells, had told Lillian that she was destined to become a songstress. That was the very Gift Lillian had always desired: the ability to imbue her music with magic and influence the world around her through melody. Since Melisande's prediction, Lillian had been practising her singing twice as much each day, but so far, her renditions of Melisande's songspells, while beautiful, had remained distinctly unmagical.

Esme yawned and sat up in bed, pulling her quilt up around her. This room, in which she had slept most of the summer, overlooked the Lovells' back courtyard. She only had to step out onto the bedroom's small balcony to see dragons flying overhead, or a gondola gliding down the slim canal that rippled by the terraced house.

The week since her return to Esperance had flown by fast. Thanks to Miranda's efforts over the past few days, the room now contained both a wardrobe and a rug, in addition to the bed, desk, and chest of drawers. Her blue Pierpont uniform hung in the robe, ready for the start of school the next day, and her new textbooks sat neatly on the desk. The rest of her things were all over the floor, as usual. Even in another world, she couldn't kick the habit of using her floor as a wardrobe.

Maybe it was Lillian's siren song, or maybe it was the thought of attending school with people who possessed talents out of the ordinary, but the magic of the city seemed to be swirling through the room, and Esme couldn't wait to start the day. She quickly dressed and went downstairs.

Lillian. Lillian. Lillian.

Her friend's name, a song in itself, danced unaccountably through her brain as she descended the stairs. When she reached Lillian's bedroom door, she was surprised to see Miranda there in a dressing gown.

'The strangest thing just happened,' said Miranda, after stifling a yawn and rubbing sleep from her eyes. 'I felt like I did back when Lillian was just a baby. I'd often wake up moments before she did. Like I knew she needed me before she even knew herself …'

Esme went to knock on the door, but before she could, it flung open. Lillian stood there, clutching a thick tome of songspells to her chest. Its rich red cover was worn at the edges, and the title *Incanto of Melisande, Vol II* was embroidered on the front in gold thread.

'You're here!' she cried, her eyes ablaze.

'But *why* are we here?' asked Miranda.

'Don't you see? I brought you here. With that songspell!'

Miranda gasped. 'You—what?'

They followed Lillian into her room, which, like Esme's, was strewn with clothes and shoes and other paraphernalia. The only thing in any semblance of order was the bookshelf, beginning to buckle under the weight of Lillian's songspell collection.

'It was one of the subtler spells,' Lillian explained, flicking through the deckled pages of her songspell book. 'It draws people to you, but only if they're willing to come.'

'Oh, Lillian!' Miranda cried. 'That's exactly what it felt like—an inexplicable tug. Your Gift—it's come!'

'Wait,' Lillian implored. 'What if it's a false start? I have to be sure.'

She placed the book on her music stand, all the while feverishly turning pages.

'This one. I'll try this one. If this works, then …'

As Lillian's clear soprano voice rang through the room, hints of something extraordinary began to fill the air, hints of a place where magic saturated the rocks, the air, the water itself. It took a moment for Esme to place the familiar sensation—then she realised what it was. She felt like she was back in the sirens' cave, with Melisande.

When the subtle energies were at their height, Lillian's unmade bed began to make itself. First, the sheets ironed themselves out and tucked themselves under the mattress. Then the purple bedspread smoothed itself over the top. Finally, the pillow gave a little shake, plumped itself up, and settled into place.

Lillian kept singing, kept the spell going, just to prove that she could—and the wardrobe responded with a deep shudder. Its double doors flew open. The clothes on the floor rose up, then straggled like lost lambs into the wardrobe's embrace.

When the song was over, Lillian stood there, very still, her face radiant. Somehow she seemed fuller, more complete, like a piece of the puzzle of who she was had slotted into place.

'It's really happened, hasn't it?' she murmured. 'Oh, Mum!'

Miranda wiped away a tear. 'I never thought I'd see the day you tidied your room without being asked!'

She sprang at her daughter and hugged her tight. The room was filled with laughter and tears. After the initial excitement died down, Lillian eagerly took up Melisande's songspell book and plumped down on her neat bed.

'You so deserve this,' said Esme, sitting down beside her.

With Miranda behind her other shoulder, Lillian slowly turned the pages.

'I can sing all of these for real now,' she said in amazement.

'I can't understand a word of them,' said Esme, gazing down at the curving letters that looped across each page. 'It's all in siren language, isn't it?'

'Yep. All the ones in this book were composed by Melisande him … her …' she frowned. 'Theirself. Most of the spells in this book are solo, but some can only be cast in harmony—and some are so difficult, they can only be sung by sirens. Sirens always sing perfectly, and they have an incredible range. There are a lot of factors that can affect the success of a spell—the quality of your voice, your timing …'

'So that's why you're always practising,' said Esme.

Lillian nodded. 'Songstresses and bards are often compared to enchanters, since we can do lots of different things with our Gifts. But in my opinion, songspells are much more difficult to get right than enchantments. One flat note can ruin a spell—or give it a totally different effect.'

'I'm glad to hear you talk so sensibly, Lillian,' said Miranda. 'Your cousins got so carried away when their Gifts came in, caused so much trouble. But you won't try any spells you're not ready for, will you?'

Lillian glanced down at the tome on her lap, then met her mother's crinkling olive eyes. 'Of course I won't. I'm smarter than that.'

Later that day, Esme, Daniel, and Lillian wound their way through the cobbled streets of the Arts Quarter, on the hunt for last-minute school supplies. These narrow thoroughfares of uneven stone were used to the tap of students' shoes. Most belonged to the aspiring musicians of the nearby Conservatorium, where Lillian took singing lessons—although Daniel and Lillian recognised plenty of familiar faces from Pierpont College amongst the crowds. Some had stopped to chat, creating little islands in the middle of the lanes, around which students flowed like the water of the adjacent canal.

Daniel peered into his wallet. 'This is looking a lot emptier than before.'

'Mine too,' said Esme. 'It's a good thing Pierpont doesn't charge school fees. I've almost run out of the merles Mum left behind. But Professor Sage wrote and said he'd send me her royalties from the compendium.'

'Last stop,' said Lillian, as they joined the long queue outside *Delfino's: Stationers to Royalty.*

At once, Esme recognised the extravagant 'D' on the sign, embellished with swirls and flourishes. 'Mum must have come here,' she said. 'That symbol … it's on the back of her notebook. The one the sea eagle used to lure me to Aeolia.'

'Smart bird, that one,' said Daniel.

As the queue inched forward, an enormous window display came into sight. The enclosed space behind the glass was filled with water, like an aquarium—but no fish swam inside. Instead, pens, pencils, and notebooks in fluorescent colours drifted lazily through the water. A sign below the huge tank read:

This Season's Waterproof Collection

In the centre of the tank hung a large, open sketchbook. A dozen enchanted markers were scrawling on its pages, frantically outlining a trio of faces.

Esme started. 'Oh my gosh, it's us!'

The pens had already turned Daniel's spiky hair into a forest of technicolour dashes. His tattoo appeared next, thanks to a few deft strokes of blue. The waterproof inks then made fast work of Esme: a mess of pink and red scribbles soon fell in colourful disarray around a heart-shaped face. Her gaping mouth was simply a purple 'O'.

Lillian's head, turned toward Esme in evident amusement, was the only one drawn in profile. After filling in her classical features, a dark red marker started on her hair—only to be butted away by an overzealous neon green comrade, which finished off Lillian's long, voluminous locks.

When the drawing was complete, the sketchbook flipped to a new page, dart-like markers poised impatiently above it.

'Hurry up, will you?' said a girl's voice from behind them. 'Ricard, darling, tell them to hurry up.'

'Yeah, move it,' said a boy's voice.

Esme turned around to see two people awaiting their turn at the window. The boy was tall and muscular with a glossy brown mane. His arm was entwined with that of a slim, pale girl with white-blond hair. The girl regarded Lillian with a look of studied indifference.

'Not used to standing in line, are you, Liza?' said Lillian. 'Poor Ricard, always having to do your bidding.'

Daniel tugged at Lillian's wrist and the three of them moved away. 'Don't bait her,' he murmured.

'Who was that?' asked Esme.

'An enchantress in our year who thinks she's better than everyone else,' said Lillian, loud enough for Liza—and everyone else in the queue—to hear.

Daniel groaned. 'Well, that's got things off to a good start. And I was looking forward to school being better this year.'

'In what way?' asked Esme.

'Lots of ways. You're going to be there, for one thing. And no more cold stares whenever I try to talk to Lillian, no more earthquakes, no more problems with the Gifts! Well, beyond the usual issues. Your Gift will be coming in any day, Lillian!'

'Maybe it's already arrived,' said Esme, shooting Lillian a conspiratorial glance, 'and she just hasn't told you.'

'I would never be that cruel,' Lillian crooned. 'Although I do remember how *someone* forgot to tell me he was fireproof until *after* he'd set himself on fire.' She glared at Daniel. 'You almost gave me a heart attack.'

He shrugged. 'It was worth it for the look on your face.'

They shuffled toward the front door, a substantial affair of polished wood and gleaming brass.

'How can Delfino's be "stationers to royalty"?' asked Esme. 'Weren't the royals all wiped out during the Tyrian Wars?'

'Yep,' said Daniel. 'But this shop's been around four hundred-odd years, and they still like to boast about that one time the queen came to visit. Good memory, though. Dr Rank—the history teacher at Pierpont—will like you.'

'Don't be silly,' scoffed Lillian. 'Rank doesn't like anyone.'

A liveried doorman ushered them through the entrance.

Inside, Esme stopped short, astounded by the store's sheer size. Delfino's had the woody, old-world smell of a library, and just as many shelves, judging by the endless aisles of polished mahogany, each one of which beckoned temptingly toward her.

Before her, revolving on a pedestal, stood a life-size female figure made entirely out of paper. The origami goddess was a tribute to the sea: her eyes anemones, her cheeks blossoming waterlilies, her ears perforated shells, her dress a school of tessellated fish. Every part of her was alive with movement, from her shifting garb to her seaweed hair. A sign below her read:

'*The Spirit of the Sea: courtesy of famed paper charmer, Reo Akitsu*'

Further in, Esme spied the black-haired, bespectacled Akitsu himself, hunched over at a table. He was folding boats from colourful marbled paper, which he then sent sailing into the air.

'You're here!' Esme exclaimed. 'Remember me? Your butterfly helped me find the way to Sofia Square.'

'Ah, yes.' He smiled at her. 'Did you find what you were looking for?'

Esme put her hand to her neck and showed him what she had discovered that day in Sofia Square's jewellery shop: a necklace that her mother had ordered for her, with a tiny pearl suspended above the letter 'E'.

'All thanks to you,' she said, tucking it away. 'Do you work here now?'

'No, my nephew is minding my little shop for the moment. I come here a few times a year to act as Delfino's resident paper charmer. It takes a lot of different Gifts to keep a place like this running … and it helps that they pay quite handsomely.'

Lillian turned up with two shopping baskets. Esme's was soon packed with pads, pens, drawing materials, and envelopes. She slipped in, too, a couple of the exact same sketchbooks in which her mother had drafted her paintings.

At the end of one of the aisles, Esme and Lillian paused in front of a display stand. The name 'Newell' swirled in gold along the caps of several pens in apricot, plum, and peach. When Esme picked one up, a tiny magical light began to trace the letters on the lid.

'Newell fountain pens.' Lillian sighed. 'I've always wanted one of these. They never run out of ink, no matter how much you write.'

'How does that work?' Esme asked. 'I know it's magic, but you can't just summon something from nothing, right?'

'Trade secret,' Daniel said with a wink. 'Although I've heard rumours there's a giant vat out the back of the store, and they just refill it whenever it runs too low.'

'I love that purple one,' said Lillian, checking the price on a card affixed to the stand. 'Yech. Forget it. They're even more expensive than last year.'

'Of course,' Daniel said dryly. 'Can't sell too many, or they'd need a bigger vat.'

A sculpted bronze arm reached out in front of them.

'Excuse me,' said Ricard, the boy who'd told them to hurry up in the queue. He took a pen in each colour, not bothering to check the price.

'For Liza?' asked Lillian.

Ricard stalked off without responding.

'Ricard's from a very wealthy family of enchanters,' Lillian told Esme in an undertone. 'And he's completely under Liza's sway.'

'Well, if we're all done here,' said Daniel, shaking his basket, 'let's go eat.'

Lillian grinned. 'Come on, I'll take you to my favourite café: Vivolino's.'

Chapter Five

Beyond the next bridge, buskers roamed the streets, strumming guitars, blaring out breathy tunes on brass instruments, and singing a cappella. The rich vibrato of a solo violin floated toward the three friends, and as the music grew louder, Esme dug in her pocket for some merles. When they reached the source, however, she dropped the coins in surprise.

The busker was only half-there.

A disembodied leg, hip, arm, and shoulder protruded from the claret-coloured wall. The arm held a violin, across which a bow moved gracefully. The rest of the busker's body, however, was firmly stuck in the stucco.

'The walls around here are vicious,' joked Daniel, as Esme scrambled on the cobbles for her merles. 'Don't ever lean against one.'

A laugh came from the wall.

'Hi, Fern,' said Daniel.

The girl and the wall came apart—or rather, the girl stepped forward, and the wall stayed where it was.

'Fern can pass through anything she wants,' Lillian explained to Esme.

Fern was slight-framed and amber-skinned, a wisp of a girl who looked as though she could float away at any moment. She only seemed tied to the earth by her long fall of straight, glossy black hair.

'What a cool Gift,' said Esme.

There were plenty of times when she herself had wanted to disappear from view, like at her father's wedding. That day in the church, after she'd objected to the nuptials, she would have given anything to melt into the wall or through the floor.

'Thanks, person I've never met,' said Fern.

'Want to come to Vivolino's with us?' asked Lillian.

'No thanks. I don't want to lose this spot. It's busy today, and people are feeling generous.'

Esme threw her rescued merles into Fern's velvet-lined violin case. 'Do you study at the Conservatorium?'

'I hope to, one day.'

'Fern's in our year at Pierpont,' said Lillian. 'Fern, Esme. Esme, Fern. Esme's new to Aeolia—she's starting at Pierpont tomorrow.'

Fern smiled at Esme and then she was gone, embraced by the wall again. Her floating violin, played by an arm and a half, picked up the slow, expressive tune from before. As Esme left, she heard the clink of more coins being added to the girl's case.

'Talk about a wallflower,' said Esme.

'Huh?'

'Ah … back home, that means someone who's shy.'

'I wouldn't call Fern shy,' said Daniel. 'She's just happy in her own company.'

Leaving the plaintive strains of Fern's violin behind, they entered Allegra Square, home to the Conservatorium. The impressively wrought institute was fronted with a long colonnade, marbled muses and graces reposing in its shady recesses. The rest of its grand façade was adorned with depictions of sirens. The fish-tailed androgynes swam up columns, leaped along lintels and arches, gazed over painted pools, and swam together in shoals.

'We'd better go,' said Lillian. 'If we don't hurry, we won't get a table.'

In a well-trodden lane only minutes away stood Vivolino's. Music spilled out through a doorway fashioned in the shape of a double bass. The interior was warm and vibrant, with low lamps hanging over leather booths, and woodcuts of famed musicians decorating walls patterned with rich red flounces.

Lillian quickly snagged a booth. On a small, low stage in the corner, a piccolo trio played a fast and furious tune, the notes chasing each other higher and higher as they flowed out of the tiny instruments. Esme, Daniel, and Lillian were soon preoccupied by the voluminous menu.

'Order for me, will you?' asked Lillian. 'I'll have the pumpkin ravioli.' She shifted out of her seat and disappeared.

'The fish and potato pie, please,' Daniel said when a waiter showed up.

'Same—and a pumpkin ravioli,' said Esme. 'Plus a coffee. Thanks!'

A copy of the *Aeolian Eye*, Esperance's largest circulated newspaper, had been left on the table. Daniel picked it up and whistled. 'Wow. Celia Skye's running for lord mayor.'

'What? Let me see!'

She scooted round beside him and bristled at the headline. Celia Skye, Esperance's Chief Enchantress, had a vast portfolio, overseeing the city's police force and prison system. Ever since she had tried to extract information from Esme by magical means, Esme had been wary of her.

Trevelli's Got the Trembles, Resists Naming an Election Date
By Basil Roth, Chief political correspondent

Esperance Lord Mayor Everett Trevelli is facing increasing pressure to announce an election date, and your faithful correspondent can only speculate as to the reasoning for the delay. With the cessation of the earthquakes that have long plagued our fair city, Esperance is set to experience a renaissance. Perhaps Trevelli hopes that if he holds on to power a little longer, voters will associate this rebirth with his leadership.

Trevelli's image, after all, is in dire need of rehabilitation. He has spent most of his tenure fighting the baseless superstition that he has brought bad luck to the city—despite the fact that he has spent seven years, and a great deal of the city's revenue, repairing the damage caused by the quakes. To his credit, he has not attempted to claim responsibility for the quakes finally ending. The true reason for the restoration of Esperance's fortunes remains unknown.

However, the delay could prove a two-edged sword for the wily Trevelli. Celia Skye, who has just announced her candidature, is already using the extra time to smooth out the edges of her formidable and aloof persona. In recent months, she has been seen visiting the poorest regions of the city, including the Drowned District, which has been neglected by Trevelli's government and is in desperate need of assistance.

In her first campaign speech, Skye announced ambitious plans to raise the Drowned District from the lagoon, using volunteer enchanters from her charity, the Skye Foundation. She also plans to bankroll the rebuilding of the district, promising that her financial aid will continue regardless of whether she wins the election. In her favour, too, is the loyalty of several powerful enchanter families, who can only benefit from her mayorship.

The winds of change, though, blow where they may. Perhaps they will knock down both Skye and Trevelli and uplift another candidate. A reliable source has informed me that respected city councillor, Bernice Chen, is about to enter the race.

Below the article, a cartoon showed Celia in goddess-like robes. One hand pushed Trevelli down into a crevasse, while the other gestured toward buildings rising in the distance. A shadowy silhouette in the background represented the third candidate.

Lillian slid back into the booth and eyed the newspaper.

'It's true, about Bernice Chen,' she muttered, pointing to the shadowy figure in the cartoon. 'Mum's the source. She's friends with Basil Roth, and she told me yesterday that she's going to work on Bernice's campaign. If Celia wins, she'll probably put enchanters into as many key government positions as she can—as if they didn't have enough power already. Mum could lose her job.'

Esme's coffee came, and she diluted the thick black liquid with plenty of milk. She still wasn't used to Aeolian coffee. The piccolo trio moved off stage, making way for a clarinettist. A few minutes into her slow, bluesy song, the food arrived. Esme poked her fork into the crust of her pie, releasing a sauce that smelled divine. She took a small mouthful, savouring the delicate herbed fish.

Lillian barely touched her pasta, instead keeping an eye on the café's performing space. When the clarinettist finished to scattered applause, she left the booth and hurried to the stage.

Esme nudged Daniel, who was still focused on the *Aeolian Eye*. 'Look.'

Daniel lifted his head just as Lillian began to sing.

The powerful, mellifluous language of the sirens drifted through the crowded café. All the patrons stopped chatting to listen. Even the waitstaff and cooks paused from their duties, as Lillian's song-spell started to work its magic. Vivolino's was no longer a café; it was a repository for ancient magic, weaving its way through this small, hospitable corner of the Arts Quarter.

A smile soon wreathed Daniel's features, and Esme's too. She closed her eyes as the spell took her back to her childhood. She was eight years old again, running up the whale's back of Picton Island. Her heart pounded in her chest. The ocean was running too, up the cliffs toward her.

You'll never catch me, she cried out to the waves.

The air was fresh in her lungs, the salt stung her cheeks, the spray wet the cliff edge. It was one of those moments where nothing else mattered; there was no division between who she was and where she was. As the song's notes faded, so did the memory.

A huge round of clapping, from both customers and staff, greeted Lillian as she returned to the booth. A number of Lillian's classmates came up to congratulate her. When the last of them were gone, Daniel turned to Lillian, grinning.

'Your Gift came in! You managed to keep that quiet. When did it happen?'

'Just this morning.'

'Well, it's everything you've ever wanted. Congratulations.'

'What sort of songspell was that?' asked Esme.

Lillian flushed with pride. 'One that lets you relive good memories.'

'That's exactly what happened. I was a kid again, running along the cliffs back home. I felt—free.' She turned to Daniel. 'What about you?'

He smiled. 'Maybe I'll tell you one day.' Then he twisted round. 'Hey, that's someone from school, waving at me. I'd better go say hello. I'll be back soon.'

'But—dessert!' cried Lillian. Three plates of apple crumble and a jug of thick cream had just landed on their table.

'On the house,' the waiter said to Lillian. 'The head chef loved your performance.'

Lillian poured cream on her crumble. 'Well, that was a bit of an anti-climax. I thought Daniel would be ... more surprised, or annoyed, or something.'

'Why would you want that?'

Lillian scooped some apple into her mouth and shrugged. 'Revenge.'

'Huh?'

Esme wondered if she was missing something. There was far less animosity between Daniel and Lillian now than when Esme had first met them. Did Lillian really want to start squabbling with Daniel again? Or was there something else going on?

She leaned over and lowered her voice. 'Can I ask you something?'

'Ask away.'

'You don't have feelings for, ah ...'

Lillian almost choked.

'You think I'm keen on *Daniel?* Don't be daft! We're just friends. Good friends ... thanks to you.' She glanced over at Daniel with a mischievous grin. 'Come on. Let's split his piece of crumble.'

Chapter Six

Early the next morning, Esme, Daniel, and Lillian caught a ferry to the city's northeast and walked through an enormous park, all the way to the edge of the lagoon. Soon, they were standing on a timber boardwalk parallel to the water, facing a place that looked decidedly unlike a school.

Four long piers jutted out from the wooden walkway, and large warehouses ran the length of each pier. With their post-and-beam construction and double-gable roofs, these salt-licked edifices evoked the hue and cry of stevedores, not school bells, stern voices, and chalk on blackboards. Small boats rocked in the water off each jetty: canoes, dinghies, and two-person sailboats, all with dragons decorating their prows.

'Are we here?' Esme asked uncertainly. 'Is this Pierpont?'

'Yep!' said Daniel.

'This … is … awesome!'

When Lillian had said that Pierpont was 'on the water', Esme hadn't thought much of it—after all, everything in Esperance was 'on the water'. She'd been expecting some place more like Penzance High, a collection of drab grey buildings with synthetic grass lawns.

'Before it was a school, this was Esperance's main trading dock,' said Lillian. 'But it was too small, so they built a bigger one'—she gestured southward—'down that way.'

Behind the boardwalk, at the park's edge, three squat white buildings served as Pierpont's administrative offices. The middle building was slightly larger than the rest, its doors and windows picked out in navy blue. It bore an unmistakable ring of portside authority, confirmed by the brass plaque set into the wall.

Harbourmaster's Office

'The principal's in there,' said Daniel. 'Go get your timetable. We'll see you in assembly, on Pier Two.'

As he and Lillian departed, Esme felt like a warm blanket had been lifted off her shoulders. Her first-day nerves, which had been quelled momentarily by the sight of the glittering water, came back in full force.

The blue door opened into a room with a staircase on its right. A receptionist informed Esme that Principal Marisa Aguado was up on the first floor. Slowly, Esme climbed the steps, feeling self-conscious in her scratchy skirt, pale shirt, and midnight-blue blazer.

Atop the stairs, she found herself in a pine-panelled waiting room. On one wall, dwarfed by its own elaborate frame, there hung a portrait of the former harbourmaster. He looked far too stiff and formal for Esme's liking.

'Take a seat, Esme,' a woman's voice rang through the half-open office door. 'I won't be a moment.'

The atmosphere in here, one of well-oiled calm and order, was quiet—too quiet. Esme glanced out the window, watching more students arrive, streaming through the park toward the docks.

Then another student came up the steps: a thin, muscled boy, about Esme's age.

He took a seat opposite. She tried not to stare at him, but his face was so banged up, it was hard not to. A bruise blossomed on one side of his jaw; the other side bore a line of livid scratches. A muscle on his neck twitched on and off. Long blond hair hid his eyes from view.

He lifted his head and stared right back at her. For some reason, his gaze provoked a stab of deep dislike in her. Bruises and cuts should invite sympathy, not enmity—but he wore that same hard expression that so many bullies assume before dealing out their daily quota of cruelty. Whatever fight he'd been in, he'd probably started it.

Keeping his eyes on her, he raked his hair back, resting his fingers on his scalp before releasing them. 'First-day jitters?' he asked.

She shrugged her shoulders in reply.

Despite the conciliatory overture, he smelled of thinly veiled aggression. His long, slender fingers were now moving restlessly on his lap. His hazel eyes continued to regard her, and the longer they played over her, the more she tagged him as someone to avoid.

'Esme?' the principal finally called.

Esme didn't have a chance to close the door before a short, olive-skinned woman with corkscrew curls strode forward to shake her hand.

'Lovely to meet you, Esme. I'm Marisa Aguado.'

The principal wore the slightly harried look of an over-stretched official with too many things to do and not enough time in which to do them. However, Esme could tell from first glance that she was well-intentioned. Genuine warmth and interest radiated out from behind her gold-rimmed glasses. She retreated to her desk, and Esme took the seat opposite.

'Miranda Lovell tells me you've only been in Aeolia for a short while.' Her voice softened. 'She also mentioned that your mother's unwell. I'm very sorry to hear that.'

The principal slid into a dry, rehearsed speech about the ethos of the school, about how they fostered an equal partnership with students, about how their number one priority was a well-rounded education. Then she dipped into a file on her desk, producing a map.

'It shouldn't take you long to learn your way around. The piers that comprise our school are labelled one to four, from north to south. Science and mathematics classes are held on Pier One. Pier Two houses art, theatre, and music. Humanities are taught on Pier Three, next to the library. School sports take place in the park behind these offices. Pier Four is home to everything else, including the canteen, and the seniors' study area.'

She reached into the file for another sheet of paper.

'Here is your timetable for the coming term: art, history, biology, sport, mathematics, and PC. I must inform you that PC won't start until next month.'

PC, Daniel had told Esme, stood for 'Principal's Choice'. All Esme knew about the course was that Principal Aguado designed the syllabus herself each term.

'Do you teach PC yourself?'

'On occasion. Usually, I bring in people from outside—experts in their fields. This term, Argent Brand will be teaching the course. I doubt her name means much to you, but—'

Esme was delighted. Now she understood why Daniel had been badgering her to take the class with him. 'She's the Esperance dragonmaster, right? My friend Daniel is always talking about her.'

'Ah, yes—Daniel Swift. He'll be doing his work experience with Argent in the dragons' den.' The principal scanned Esme's file again. 'And you must be looking forward to your internship with Augustine Agapios. His letter came by jigger just this morning.'

'Sorry—what?'

'Oh, a jigger is an enchanted bottle that we use to send messages along the canals. They're usually shaped like fish.'

'I know what a jigger is,' said Esme. 'I just haven't heard anything from Augustine about any kind of internship.'

The principal waved a paper scroll at her. 'It's right here—he's requested you, personally, to intern at his clinic. I'm not sure if Lillian has told you, but it's a fifth-form requirement to participate in work experience.'

Esme blinked, baffled by this turn of events. 'And you're sure he asked for me?'

Principal Aguado peered over her glasses. 'Yes, it says your name right here: Esme Silver. Augustine must think very highly of you to make such an offer. He often takes on interns from our school, but until now, he's always left the selection up to us. This is a plum placement, reserved for our best and brightest.'

Esme found herself taking a sudden interest in a fishbowl on the principal's desk, glad that her report cards were stuffed in a cardboard box back on Picton. They had disappointed her father for years. '*A student of great promise, not reflected in her uneven grades. Esme needs to apply herself more.*'

The principal pushed herself up off her chair.

'A rather rushed introduction, I'm afraid, but the first assembly of the term begins shortly. I'm sure Lillian can give you a tour and help you find your way to your classes. My door is always open, of course.'

She waved Esme out and called for the next student.

'Seth? Come in, come in. Time is getting away from us.'

The bruised blond boy unfolded his legs and swung out of his chair in one swift movement, like a leopard more used to the environs of a jungle than an old harbourmaster's office. In a few strides, he was through the principal's door. Esme, glad to see the last of him, hurried off to rejoin her friends.

Daniel and Lillian were waiting for Esme halfway along Pier Two, by a pair of open doors. Lillian ushered her into an assembly hall that took up over a third of Pier Two's warehouse. Cross bars and joists underpinned a soaring ceiling, beneath which ran a row of high windows. Their panes spilled bricks of light below, playing hopscotch on the student's heads, all the way up to the teachers on stage. On both sides of the hall hung blue-and-gold banners emblazoned with Pierpont's crest: an anchor, a ship at full sail, a coiled dragon, and a stack of books.

After Esme, Daniel, and Lillian found seats, the assembly started out much the same as back home. Someone dropped a book, someone scraped their chair back, someone sneezed three times, someone yawned.

A nearby first-former erupted into a fit of giggles.

'Take a look at those ears,' she whispered.

It was obvious who the girl was talking about. Esme's eyes went straight to the gruff-looking teacher standing partway down the aisle. His thinning hair made his prominent ears stand out more than they already did. Esme thought she saw them go pink, even though there was no way he could have heard the student.

'Elephant ears,' the girl continued, encouraged by titters from her neighbours.

This time, the whole assembly heard her.

The words 'elephant ears' boomed around the room, as if the child had spoken through a megaphone. Her hands flew to her mouth and she cowered in her seat. The older students burst out laughing.

'Quiet down, everyone,' said Principal Aguado, striding through the double doors. Seth slouched in behind her and disappeared into the back row.

'I see that some of you have made the acquaintance of Dr Percival Rank.' Esme caught a faint whiff of obligation creeping into the principal's tone. 'Dr Rank, the head of our history department, has taken it upon himself to keep assemblies pin quiet at all times. He possesses the Gift of amplifying sound—a Gift that also gives him an acute sense of hearing. Be careful what you say in his vicinity.'

She went up on stage, stood behind a lectern adorned with the school crest, took a sip of water, and began.

'Welcome. I hope that everyone had a relaxing holiday and that you're all refreshed for a busy term ahead. For new students, please be sure to read the school handbook. For returning students, a refresher might also be beneficial.'

She cast a scrutinising eye over the assembly.

'Over the long break, it appears that some school rules have been forgotten. Wearing a blazer over your everyday clothes does not constitute a uniform. Remember, too, that while piercings, dyed hair, and tattoos are acceptable, unenclosed shoes are not, for safety reasons. Please have your uniform in order by the end of this week.'

The principal checked her notes. 'I would also like to remind our younger students that only those in third form and above are permitted to use the school boats. Furthermore, all students, no matter how senior, must disembark the boats if a teacher requires use of them …'

The principal's monotone was making it difficult to focus on what she was saying. Students around Esme were openly yawning. Daniel had his eyes closed.

'Students are not to bully the undines living under the piers. Students are not to hit the undines with boats. Students are not to throw breadcrumbs at the undines. Breadcrumbs are for ducks, not—'

Principal Aguado's words were cut short.

Her mouth was still opening and closing, but nothing was coming out. Her hand went to her throat and she stood there, helpless, blinking out over the sea of faces.

Dr Rank hurried forward. 'Whoever's doing this, stop it at once!'

Principal Aguado coughed, then tried to speak again. All she could manage was a croak. Several students erupted into laughter. The principal drank a whole glass of water while Rank roamed the aisles, looking for the offender.

Daniel nudged Esme.

A dark-haired, round-faced boy a few rows in front of them was trembling. The back of his neck had gone red. He rose up from his seat in slow, jerky movements.

'Poor Vince,' murmured Daniel.

'Vincent Chen!' shouted Dr Rank. 'Were you responsible for that cruel trick?'

Vince's skin was slick with sweat. A wretched noise came from his mouth.

'Urrgghh … I'm so sorry, Miss Aguado. I think it was my fault. My mum has the same Gift—she can mute people just by thought.'

Every syllable of his confession—every breath—bounced off the walls, amplified by Dr Rank.

'That was inexcusable, Vince,' said Rank.

'I didn't mean to do it, I swear! It's never happened before. My Gift must have come in just then. I was just thinking—I'm so sick of hearing the same speech, year in and year out, why doesn't she just shut up—and then she did.' Vince's black eyes darted to the principal. 'I mean, er—that didn't come out right—'

'Dr Rank, that's enough!' Miss Aguado cried. 'He clearly didn't do it on purpose.'

The sound of Vince's anxious breathing faded.

'And everybody else,' the principal commanded, 'calm down, please!' Her voice was almost back to normal. 'Our first Gift of the year seems to have arrived, in rather spectacular fashion.'

Principal Aguado massaged her throat before resuming.

'Please, everybody, as your Gifts begin to arrive, keep your wits about you. If any problems arise, seek a teacher's help. My door is always open. The school rules regarding Gifts are clear. At Pierpont, there are no limits placed on the use of Gifts, unless they endanger other students or staff, intentionally disrupt classes, or are used for cheating in exams.'

She took a sip of water.

'Before letting you leave, I would like to extend a warm welcome to our two new fifth-formers: Seth and Esme. Esme is an otherworlder, and I expect her peers to help ease her transition into an Aeolian way of life.'

Esme, startled, rose in a half-crouch, before quickly retaking her seat. Seth stayed hidden in the back row.

'Everyone dismissed,' said the principal. 'Except for you, Vincent Chen. A word, please.'

The animated chatter of the student body carried out on to the boardwalk.

'What's the chance? His Gift coming right in the middle of her speech like that?'

'Now *that* was an assembly worth going to.'

Only one voice dissented. A girl's voice rang out, clear as a bell.

'I doubt it was an accident—and even if it was, he deserves whatever he gets. An enchanter would never lose control like that.'

The speaker was Liza, in the midst of an adoring entourage.

'You know that's not true, Liza. When your Gift first comes in, anything can happen. Enchanters are no exception.'

Liza smiled at the boy beside her, then brushed the back of her hand against his. 'Did someone say something, Ricard?'

He flushed at her touch. 'I didn't hear a thing.'

'Lillian's right,' said Esme. 'It could have happened to anyone.'

Liza shaded her eyes with her hand, as if Esme was an irritating ray of sunshine. 'Oh, it's the new girl. The principal did you no favours in there.' The menace in Liza's silken words was almost hidden, but not quite. 'Despite what everyone pretends, otherworlders aren't welcome here.'

'What ... what's that supposed to mean?'

'Oh!' Liza blinked in faux surprise. 'Did Lillian not tell you?'

She turned on her heel and departed, her followers trailing after her like the tail of a comet. As soon as she was gone, Esme rounded on her friends.

'What does she mean? About otherworlders?'

'It's not a very common prejudice,' Lillian said apologetically. 'If it was, I would have warned you. It's more the older generations. People our age are usually fine with otherworlders. Liza's just being cruel.'

'Just so you know, people sometimes discriminate against us Thalassans, too,' Daniel said. 'So you're not alone.'

Otherworlder ... It was another label that had been stuck on Esme, like 'troublesome', 'selfish', 'delusional'. But this was something that was true, something she couldn't help.

Out on the lagoon, a gentle breeze teased the water into tiny peaks. Two girls on a keelboat laughed as they sailed in wide arcs, spurred by the wind.

'Hang on.' Esme furrowed her brow. 'Did they just skip out on assembly?'

'They're sixth-formers.' Daniel sounded envious. 'They're allowed to skip assembly.'

'That'll be us next year,' Lillian said wistfully.

As Esme watched the boat speed across the water, she couldn't help but smile. Several fey-like creatures, who looked to be made of pure light, had begun to race the girls. They were undines, cavorting alongside the vessel, leaping in and out of the lagoon like dolphins.

She lingered a little longer, mesmerised by the view, by the sun on the water and the undines' graceful, glistening backs. Despite all the things that were weighing her down—Liza's bad attitude, her mother's condition, the lack of any response from her father to the letter she had sent—she was entranced by her new surrounds and excited for the weeks to come. No matter what trials lay ahead, at least here at Pierpont there would always be some magic to distract her.

Chapter Seven

Esme's first few weeks at Pierpont were memorable ones, not so much due to the jumble of new faces, places, and routines, but because of the wonder that sprinkled her days.

While wandering the boardwalks around each warehouse, Esme would often witness tiny miracles, like a water-walker taking a shortcut to class between piers, or a songstress singing a sheaf of papers she'd dropped back into her arms. Sometimes a wall or door or even a tree would swell and split before her eyes, and Fern's form would emerge.

However, students like Fern, who had mastered their Gifts, were in the minority. New Gifts were exploding amongst the fourth, fifth, and sixth-formers, as suddenly and forcefully as Vince's had in assembly. Many of these invoked utter mayhem.

With the pearl's return to Esperance, a bottleneck had sluiced away. Like a dam bursting, Gifts rushed forth with abandon. More than once, hapless students ended up with sprains, broken bones, and even concussions. A wind-waver's Gift slammed a student to the ground in an almighty gust. A water-weaver's Gift spun torrentially out of control, drenching the seniors' study area at the end of Pier Four.

On one occasion, Esme only just managed to flatten herself against a wall to avoid being skewered by a mathematical compass. A levitator's Gift gone wrong had turned the contents of a geometry set into deadly projectiles.

Fortunately, Liza's dire prediction—'*otherworlders aren't welcome here*'—hadn't proven to be true at all. None of Esme's peers had treated her with any disdain since her enrolment. Instead, she'd found herself an object of avid curiosity. The portals between the two worlds had fallen into disuse over recent years, and the younger students plied Esme with questions, wanting to know how her world was different from their own.

'People really can't breathe underwater over there?' a wide-eyed first-former asked.

'Well, we can breathe underwater with special equipment. That's how we solve problems where I'm from—with science and technology, not with magic.'

'Seems like way too much effort.'

Unfortunately, not all the surprises at Pierpont were pleasant. Esme's history teacher was none other than Dr Percival Rank, who had tortured Vince in assembly, and who seemed hell-bent on using his Gift to make students' lives as miserable as possible. Whenever he wanted to make a particular point, his voice boomed out so loud that Esme's ears rang afterward. And if he ever caught students whispering to one another, he took it upon himself to amplify their private conversation.

As Rank strode into class one morning, he seized upon the voice of a boy murmuring to Vince: 'You've got a *crush ON LILLIAN?*'

Vince went bright red and shrank into his seat. Lillian, next to Esme, glanced over at Fern as if to say, *'I wish I had your Gift right now.'*

A rare, sickening smile creased Rank's pinched face.

Close to the end of class, he heaved a box of books onto his desk.

'This year,' he said, 'I have set individual questions for your major term assignments. This will eliminate cheating, while making marking slightly less banal for myself. If you wish to gain a pass, I expect considered, thought-out arguments, not mere regurgitations of facts. The texts with which I am about to provide you should prove the starting point, not the end point, of your investigations.'

Dr Rank called each student up by name, handing them an essay question and accompanying text. He injected Esme's name with an extra shot of venom.

As Esme left her seat, a drum beat started up: *Thud-Thud. Thud-Thud. Thud-Thud.* Esme couldn't tell where the noise was coming from. She saw only shocked faces, staring up at her. With each step she took toward Rank's desk, the pulse grew louder.

It was a heartbeat: her own. This intimate noise was coming from her, a mortifying realisation that only made her heart hammer faster. By the time she reached Rank's desk, her heart was pounding away like she'd been running from a pack of wolves.

'How dare you!' she said, barely able to contain her fury.

'How dare I what?'

'Invade my privacy with your Gift.'

The drum beat faded away.

'I have no idea what you're talking about,' he said. 'Here.'

He thrust a heavy hardback at her: *The Fall of Mann: A Comprehensive History of the Tyrian Wars*, by Dr Percival Rank.

Esme purposely let the book slip from her hands. It smacked down loudly onto the desk. A strange 'oof' came from him, as if someone had punched him in the oesophagus.

'Take more care,' he snapped. 'Books are precious things, young lady.'

'So are people,' she retorted, snatching her essay question. 'Amplify that, Dr Rank.'

Nods of approval and a few grins greeted her on her way back to her seat. Esme ran her eye down her essay question, not really taking it in the first time.

Then she read it again, realising that it was full of spite.

The long lens of history condemns the infamous otherworlder, Alexander Mann, who was responsible for

*some of the worst massacres of the Tyrian Wars. These
atrocities may not have come to pass had Mann never
set foot in Aeolia. How can we keep our world safe
from barbarians like Mann in the future? Discuss at
length—3,000 words minimum.*

By the time the bell rang, Esme was seeing red. The essay question looked like it was written in blood, rather than ink. While Lillian packed up, Esme muttered: 'I'll meet you outside.'

When the classroom was empty, Esme went straight to Rank's desk.

'Yes, Miss Silver?'

'If you're trying to make a point, why not say it to my face instead of turning it into an assignment question? Tell me, Dr Rank, do you have a problem with otherworlders? How different are our worlds, really?'

Dr Rank smoothed down his only remaining tuft of hair.

'Alexander Mann saw no difference between our worlds, either. To him, Aeolia was merely an extension of his own world, a far-flung province ripe to ravage and exploit. He drove Esperance's royal line to extinction. Many of the city's oldest families were wiped out, including some members of my own.' He shuffled some papers into a folder. 'If you are new to Aeolia, then you should be taught the entire history of our world, including the parts that may not be so … palatable.'

In his tight words and manner, Esme detected a bitterness far beyond Lillian's ability to hold a grudge. 'I'm sorry about your family,' she said. 'But it's not the eighteenth century anymore.'

'Nonetheless, we must always be on guard to avoid repeating the mistakes of the past. Good day, Miss Silver.'

Outside, in the salty air, Lillian and Fern had been eavesdropping at the door. Dr Rank passed them by, his face like thunder. As soon as he was out of sight, Fern gave an impish smile.

'I don't think anyone's ever given him as much lip as you just did.'

'Do you think he's on his way to the principal?' Esme asked anxiously.

'Who cares? If he complains about you, just tell the principal exactly what happened. We'll back you up. Principal Aguado is no friend of Rank's. She barely tolerates him, but she can't do much about it. His family are big donors to the school.'

'How in the world do you know all that?' asked Lillian.

'Sometimes I hang out in the staffroom. Well, I wait in the wall until all the teachers leave, then I chow down on free biscuits and coffee. Sometimes there's birthday cake. It's usually pretty boring, what they talk about, but I can tell you they all despise Rank as much as we do.'

Her words did little to ease Esme's anxiety. 'Why is he even a teacher if he hates his students so much?'

Fern grinned. 'Why don't you ask him next class?'

Daniel, out of breath, rounded the end of the pier. 'There you are!' He hurried toward Esme. 'Come on. It's the first PC class with Argent. We'll be late!'

'You two had better get a move on, then,' said Lillian.

'You're not coming?' asked Esme.

'I've got a free period. I try to avoid prolonged exposure to dragons … and fire.'

She flapped her arms to imitate a dragon as Daniel dragged Esme away. Esme looked back and couldn't help laughing as she ran with Daniel toward Pier One.

The first person Esme set eyes on in PC was Seth, the hard-faced boy she'd met outside the principal's office. He was in every single one of her classes except history. *Lucky him*, she thought. *No Dr Rank.*

There was an empty chair beside Seth, and he glanced up at Esme, as if inviting her to sit with him. Esme ignored him and dove in between Daniel and Vince.

'That was amazing, the way you stood up against Rank,' Vince said.

'Someone had to. It wasn't on, what he did to you, either—eavesdropping on you before class had even started.'

'I wish I could control my Gift better,' Vince moaned. 'Then I might have been able to mute my friend before he could say … er, what he said.' He sighed. 'I think I'll just have to get used to it. Being singled out, I mean.'

'Why's that?'

'Tomorrow, my mum's going to announce that she's running for lord mayor.'

'Oh, your mum's Bernice Chen! I read that rumour in the *Aeolian Eye*.'

'Yep, she leaked it on purpose, to gauge how people felt about her. She wants to make Esperance fairer for people with less powerful Gifts—or with no Gifts at all. She'll be going after enchanters, in particular … cracking down on nepotism, making sure they pay their fair share of taxes.' He frowned. 'All the enchanters in school are going to hate me. More than they already do.'

'I already feel sorry for you—and your mum. She's in for a tough time against Celia.'

Vince shrugged. 'Can't be worse than what's happening to your mum. Daniel told me she's not well.'

Esme nodded. 'She's in a coma. At the Anais clinic.'

'The Anais clinic?' Seth twisted back toward them. 'Things must be really dire if she's there.'

Thanks for that observation, Esme thought.

'Quiet down, everyone,' sounded a voice that brooked no argument.

Argent had arrived. A tall, muscular woman with brown ochre skin, she strode confidently toward her desk and placed down a bundle wrapped in cloth. Her lined, square-set face panned the room, scrutinising each and every student.

'My name is Argent Brand, but you may address me as Argent.

For the rest of this term, I will be instructing you on the anatomy, habits, and history of dragons. But first, I've brought something to show you all.'

Argent donned a thick pair of gloves and unwrapped the bundle. An excited murmur rippled round the room. She'd brought an egg: an egg that looked as though it had survived a volcanic blast. It was blackened, marked and pitted all over, like a fossilised relic.

Esme glanced at her fellow students. Daniel had a soft, pensive look on his face. Vince regarded the egg with a strange mixture of fondness and fear.

'This dragon egg was found abandoned on Laertes Island and has been adopted by our den. As the dragonling inside matures, the egg will grow hotter and hotter. It's only a few weeks away from hatching, so I have to handle it with gloves.'

Dragonling? Esme leaned forward, as transfixed as everyone else.

'Once the egg is closer to hatching, I'll keep it in this classroom and put it under your watch. I'll roster you all on during the day, and I'll take care of it at night. Come on up, have a closer look.'

Once the students were all gathered round, Argent pointed out several miniature craters on the egg's surface. 'These will increase in size until the dragon's birth. They'll provide a useful marker of his or her progress.'

'I like dragons so much better at this size,' said Vince. 'They're much less terrifying.'

'Dragons aren't terrifying,' said Daniel. 'You just have to get to know them.'

'Easy for you to say.'

'So, you're in this class under duress?' Argent asked Vince.

'Yes, I'm only here because Daniel insisted.'

'He did mention that he was bringing someone along under sufferance. I hope you'll come to realise, Vince, that dragons are in fact very wise and highly intelligent beasts.'

Heat came off the egg in waves. Esme could have sworn she

sensed a presence emanating from it—an aura of limitless poten-
tial, far too large to be contained by such a tiny charcoal cocoon.

She had a distinct feeling that she was going to enjoy Argent's
class far more than Dr Rank's.

PC wasn't the only subject Esme had to look forward to. Every time
she arrived at art class, she felt at home. Back on Picton, art had
been crammed into a smelly room beside the gym. At Pierpont,
however, the class took place in an enormous studio at the end
of Pier Two. A low, wide window showcased the lagoon outside.
Inside, the moving water's reflections dappled everything with soft
light. Works from former students hung everywhere, making the
space feel more like a gallery than a classroom. Esme enjoyed being
there so much, she barely noticed the absence of Daniel and Lillian.

She'd pinned up most of her drawings from class in Ariane's
room at the Anais clinic. She was trying to make it feel more like
home, and less like a waiting room for the next world, so she'd
decorated its walls with dragons, sirens, mist-covered islands, and
canal-side cafés. With Ariane's return, Esme's long-suppressed
urge to make art had finally resurfaced.

The only irritant was the presence of Seth, who, on the first day
of class, had claimed the easel right next to her, a space which from
then on oozed with existential angst. Their art teacher, Miss Merrow,
strongly encouraged her students to critique each other's work, and
Seth never missed an opportunity to offer Esme unsolicited advice.

'Needs a touch of colour,' he'd said two weeks in, peering over
her shoulder at her seascape. 'How about some purple?'

'It's a grey, stormy day,' Esme had replied through gritted teeth.
'This is exactly how it's supposed to look.'

'But that corner looks so empty. I'm telling you, add a bit of
purple, and everything will pop so much more.'

Begrudgingly, Esme followed his instructions, and had to admit that the painting looked much better afterward. She'd resolved, from then on, to at least consider his suggestions, even if she couldn't treat him with anything resembling warmth.

Despite getting to know him a little, that warning bell that had rung inside her the day they'd met had never stopped ringing. Sometimes, he didn't show up to class at all, and she was always glad of the break from his ruminating presence.

Somewhat hypocritically, Seth limited himself to a palette of blacks, greys, and crimsons, which he channelled into pure abstraction. His paintings had a sad, savage power to them. Sometimes figurative shapes would make an appearance—a hunched shoulder, a curved back, a clenched fist rising out of the gloom—but mostly he painted a murky miasma of nothingness, surreal vistas that defied definition.

'Seth,' Miss Merrow would sometimes say as she passed him by. 'Don't you want to try something different today?'

He made up for his restricted colour palette by experimenting with different marks and materials. Sticks of charcoal, twigs of varying size, pieces of string, leaves, seashells and eggshells invariably littered his work table.

'That looks finished to me,' Esme told him one afternoon. 'Glue any more twigs on there, and you'll end up with a bird's nest.'

'I like it,' said a girl's voice from behind them.

Esme started. She'd thought she and Seth were alone—Miss Merrow was long gone, allowing them to work through their free period—but the most talented girl in the class, Meera, had stayed behind as well. She had dark brown skin and wavy black hair, and wore a blue-and-gold pashmina shawl over her uniform.

'Esme's right, though,' said Meera, hoop earrings swinging as she scrutinised Seth's artwork. 'It's finished. Don't overdo it.'

Seth nodded, then left to clean his paintbrushes. Satisfied, Meera traipsed back to her own spot. Esme stayed where she was, relishing in Seth's absence, wishing that Meera, instead, had chosen the easel beside her on the first day.

Meera was much more fun to be around than Seth. When Seth was in a black hole of a mood, it sucked in everyone around him, so they steered well clear. When Meera was down, it usually stemmed from her own perfectionism. After being complimented on her artwork, or given some pointers, she would perk right back up.

Without warning, Meera yelped so loudly Esme almost dropped her paintbrush.

'Are you okay, Meera?' Esme called out.

There was no answer.

Esme wandered between easels to the back of the classroom, where Meera's oversized canvases leaned against the wall. Meera was standing in front of her latest hyper-realistic streetscape, gazing at it with a slack jaw.

'Look …' she murmured. 'It's finally happened!'

'What's happened?'

'Just look …'

The painting depicted a narrow lane in the Arts Quarter. Esme marvelled at Meera's grasp of perspective. The lane's brick walls were covered in street art, but none of it looked flat or disproportionate: it was all perfectly foreshortened, stretching toward the viewer. It looked more accurate than a photograph. Actually three-dimensional … almost real.

Esme blinked.

The painting looked *very* real.

So real, in fact, that the clouds overhead were slowly crossing the sky, and the glimpse of the canal at the lane's end twinkled in the sunlight. The only thing that didn't look real was the gauzy blur that swathed over everything, making the lane look as though it was underwater.

In awe, Esme tilted her head to the left. The perspective shifted, allowing her to see part of the lane that had previously been hidden.

'This is incredible … is this your Gift?'

Meera nodded. 'This Gift has run in my family for generations. I had a feeling it would come to me one day, if I was patient.'

'What exactly *is* it? The power to … make paintings look real?'

'Oh, this isn't a painting anymore,' Meera said dreamily. 'It's a portal.'

She dabbed the canvas with her paintbrush. The tip went straight through, creating a circle of ripples in the portal's surface. Seth strode up behind them just as Meera pulled it back out.

'Wow! You're a portalier? Since when?'

'Since … about two minutes ago,' said Meera. 'Wait, ah, I wouldn't do that—'

Seth's index finger had disappeared into the painting.

'A portalier's first portal is always unstable,' said Meera, while he stood there, his finger trapped in the canvas. 'In fact, you really shouldn't go near a portalier's first few *dozen* portals. Who knows where you might end up?'

'It goes to Burner Lane, right?'

'Well, it should, but it probably has a mind of its own.'

'I love Burner Lane. Let's go!'

Before Meera could stop him, Seth ran right through the portal.

Jolted out of her daze, Meera dropped her brush. With a harried glance at Esme, she followed Seth through. After a few restless seconds waiting for them to reappear, Esme drew a breath and sprinted impulsively into the canvas.

She immediately regretted it.

The brand-new portal didn't seem to know what it was. It certainly didn't know what to do with Esme. Inside, it was dark—too dark to see a thing. Her feet weren't touching the ground, and they felt much bigger than they should: like she was a giant, able to stride a mile in two steps. Then she was an ant, so tightly compressed into herself that she couldn't breathe. In the vague recesses of her mind, she could hear something or someone telling her to 'stop it'.

Stop what?

Stop curling up on the ground, said the voice.

But I'm so small. I'm the size of an ant …

'You're perfectly normal-sized, Esme,' said Meera. 'I felt the same way a minute ago. Just open your eyes and you'll be fine.'

With the effort of a planet tilting out of orbit, Esme blinked them open.

The portal had brought her to the exact place the painting had promised: Burner Lane. The alley's long walls were splashed with psychedelic street art: rainbow-tailed mermaids, paradisiacal forests, and an enormous blue-haired Zeus. A painting of the Keeper's Tower wavered over Esme. A dragon coiled around the top, smoke flaring out of its nostrils. The initials MS were hidden in its eye.

'Didju paint that?' Esme slurred.

'I did,' said Meera. 'Are you all right?'

'Moshtly.' She was still quite groggy, and Meera helped her up. 'I'm not sure about him, though.'

Seth was on the ground beside them, curled up in a ball as Esme had been, moaning to himself. 'Why is everything moving? Stop it moving.'

Meera kneeled. 'What were you thinking? I warned you what would happen. And since you were the first one through, you got the worst of it.'

Seth, on his back now, kept trying to bat away things that weren't there. 'Urggghhh ...'

'Where's the portal gone?' Esme asked, looking around.

'I don't know. I think it's faded already. I've heard they don't last very long when the Gift first comes in. Oh, pull yourself together.' Meera dragged Seth to his feet.

He swallowed, straightened up, and spotted Meera's dragon. 'That's yours, isn't it?'

Meera nodded. 'Did you notice my initials in the eye?'

'No, but I can always spot your style.' He almost toppled over, and Meera righted him. 'You're so talented.'

Meera looked very pleased with herself, and Esme looked away. While Meera flirted with Seth all the time, this was the first time he'd ever flattered her in return.

'Paint a dozen more portals,' he said, 'and then we'll go again.'

Meera laughed. 'After what you've just been through?'

'Yeah, it wasn't so bad, being compacted into a single atom.'

'I never know what's going to come out of your mouth, Seth.' Meera looped her arm through his. 'That's what I like about you. Come on, Esme, let's go back to school the old-fashioned way—by foot.'

Chapter Eight

Whenever Esme visited the Anais clinic, after school and on weekends, the sight of Ariane's ephemeral form squeezed painfully at her heart. A whole wall of the room was now covered with drawings. The pot of lavender from Miranda's garden still rested on the bedside desk. Sunlight streamed in through the open window, and the sea eagle was perched on the windowsill. The light, the art, the flowers, and the bird's constant presence all served to make the room much warmer than it had been upon Ariane's arrival.

Ariane's touch, however, was as cold as ever.

Perhaps it was a good thing her father hadn't come here, Esme thought as she tried to massage heat into her mother's fingers. To discover that Ariane was alive, only to find her in this lifeless state … he might think the same thing Esme had when she'd first discovered Aeolia.

That this was the land of the dead.

Nonetheless, she frequently borrowed Daniel's camera and took snapshots of Ariane, to include in her weekly letters to her father. Sometimes she would send him magical artefacts, too—like an origami butterfly from Akitsu's—but no matter what the sea eagle delivered, she received no response.

She missed him so much that she was almost tempted to return to Picton, try to convince him all over again. Then, a few days after Meera painted her first portal, Esme arrived at the Anais to news that dashed all notions of revisiting her own world.

When Esme entered Ariane's room on Saturday morning, the regular contortions of her heart were joined by a flutter of panic. The keeper was there, black robe billowing about, blond strands escaping his ponytail as he paced back and forth.

'What's going on?'

'Somebody tried to break in last night.'

'*What?* Is Mum okay?'

'She's safe and sound. The nurses notified me first thing this morning. It seems that the assailant failed to trespass through the window and fled. There's no sign that anybody managed to get inside.'

As he spoke, he swished Willow to and fro.

'Willow and I are weaving a protective spell around your mother. When we're done, we'll go outside and create a barrier around the whole clinic. You can rest assured that no one will breach these walls.'

Esme crossed over to the window. A long crack floated in the glass, flashing in the light, mocking her naïvety in thinking her mother could ever truly be safe. Hairline cracks splintered out from the larger one. It wouldn't take much, a little jiggle at the most, for the entire pane to fall out and shatter to pieces.

She looked outside. The space directly under the window was paved, and a large puddle had pooled on the flagstones.

How did that puddle get there?

It hadn't rained last night—and the water couldn't have come from the canal, all the way across the garden. As Esme squinted at the water, trying to make sense of it, the sea eagle splashed in and began preening its feathers.

'Who would want to hurt Mum?' Esme asked, before giving voice to her worst fears. 'Could it have been Mare?'

Augustine joined Esme by the window.

'Unlikely. But it could have been someone working on his behalf.'

'But what could Mare want from Mum? She doesn't have the pearl anymore.'

'I've been asking myself the same question all morning. Perhaps she knows some secret about him, something that could finally, permanently, destroy his reputation. Or maybe he just wants revenge.'

'When I saw you here, I—I thought you were going to tell me Mum's condition was getting worse.'

Augustine sighed.

Esme's breath hitched. 'No, don't tell me there's more bad news.'

'I had Willow examine her this morning. While your mother's vital signs are much the same, Willow has observed … a slight weakening in her life force. An infinitesimal shift—one that will take many months to manifest any physical symptoms.'

Esme shook her head. 'No—this can't be the end. There must be something we can do.'

The keeper bowed his head. 'I've spent all my life studying Gifts, but Mare has influenced Ariane's in ways I cannot fathom. Her Gift has become … malicious. It's taken over her whole body and won't let her go.'

An agonising lump rose in Esme's throat. Even in her misery, the wheels of her mind were spinning. A wild idea came to her—if were even possible.

'Is there any way we can get rid of it?'

Augustine looked baffled. 'Get rid of what?'

'Her Gift. If that's what's causing all the problems, can't we just remove her Gift, somehow? Then she might wake up.'

The keeper blanched.

'I'm afraid things aren't that simple,' he said. 'It is … possible … to separate a person from their Gift. But such a procedure can have grave consequences.'

'Grave? How much graver can things get?'

'Infinitely graver. Believe me. If I were to repeat the process of stripping someone of their Gift, recreate the Elixir of Severance, then … things could get much, much worse for your mother.'

'Repeat the process? So you've done it before?'

'I've failed before,' he murmured.

The keeper slumped into a chair. He scrubbed at his temples, summoning the past.

'Back in my youth, when Nathan Mare still worked here, I was contacted by a patient whose fire Gift was spiralling out of control. Or rather, he didn't *want* to learn to control it. He didn't think himself capable. He begged me, day and night, to get rid of it—and for good reason. Left unchecked, his Gift was certain to kill him … and others, too.

'After rifling through the keepers' archives, I stumbled upon the recipe for an elixir designed to remove one's Gift. It was invented by Thomas Agapios, the twelfth Keeper of Esperance. However, the recipe was damaged beyond repair. The archives have flooded more than once. After three centuries' exposure to damp, decay, and mites, only about half of Thomas's recipe was legible.

'And yet …' Augustine closed his eyes, as if to hide the shame in them. 'We proceeded anyway. When we couldn't interpret the ingredients or directions, we made our own slapdash substitutions. It was utter, unforgivable hubris.'

'We?' Esme asked.

'Me … and Nathan Mare. He wasn't then the man he is now. He was a bright, promising young student, too young to know any better. I sometimes wonder if my actions back then helped plant the seeds for his future ambitions, and his ultimate ruin.'

'You were only trying to help your patient,' said Esme.

'Sometimes, good intentions aren't enough,' Augustine said darkly. 'As I discovered when I walked into our patient's room, hours after giving him the elixir, and found him dead.'

Esme froze. Augustine's eyes, misted with grief, met hers.

'From that day on, I vowed to uphold the precepts of my role as keeper. Removing someone's Gift is beyond my capabilities, and I am loath to try again.'

Esme turned away. She was caught in an impossible bind. There was nothing she could do to stop her mother's decline—nothing apart from convincing Augustine to recreate the elixir that had brought him such trauma.

Her shoulders slumped. Then something bumped against her hand, forestalling grief, giving her a window of clarity in which to think. It was Willow. Willow, sparking Esme's memory of the day she'd met Augustine, several weeks ago—the day the divining rod had examined her Gift.

'*Water has a memory of its own,*' Augustine had told her that day. '*It stores within itself the history of all it sees. Through your Gift, you form a kinship with the water's memory. You are able to see all that it has seen.*'

Esme's mind was soon running fast with possibility, with an idea as terrifying as it was hopeful. 'Do you think there would have been water there, when Thomas first brewed the elixir?'

'I'd be surprised if there wasn't. The elixir requires water to make. There's a sink in my treatment room at the clinic, and that room's barely changed since Thomas's time.'

She drew a deep, eager breath. 'What if I were to use my Gift to go back in time and see the full list of ingredients? If I do, could you try to recreate the elixir?'

The keeper, still sunk in woe, began to rise out of his stupor.

'I don't have any control over my Gift at the moment,' Esme went on. 'But if you teach me to use it properly, I could go back to Thomas's time and locate the full recipe.'

The grey pallor on the keeper's face lessened. He blinked, like he'd just emerged from a dark, dusty chamber into the light of day.

'The ingredients for the elixir were rare even back in Thomas's time,' he said. 'Now they may be unobtainable. And I will allow no substitutes.'

'I understand. No substitutes,' Esme echoed.

He packed Willow back into her case. 'Then … yes. If there's a chance I can replicate the original elixir, I am willing to try. Your internship officially begins this coming Friday. While you're at my clinic, I'll do what I can to help you master your Gift.'

Chapter Nine

It was difficult to focus in school the next week, as Esme waited for Friday with a mixture of fear and anticipation. Only in art, PC, and biology did she pay full attention. Her large, airy biology classroom was lined with tanks housing fish of every shade and stripe, collected by her sandy-haired teacher, Mr Donnelly.

Esme had always been fond of biology. Back home, she'd relished any opportunity to learn about the animals that shared Picton Island with her. Her father would often bring injured creatures to the cottage and nurse them back to health: seagulls, fruit bats, stray cats, and turtles amongst them.

At Pierpont, however, Esme was learning about creatures she'd thought confined to legend: sylphs, undines, water-sprites, and shapeshifters.

'I once saw a team of rangers trap a rampaging shifter,' said Mr Donnelly, sitting on his desk. 'A shifter's strength is proportionate to their size, and this one kept phasing between being a dragon and an elephant. You can imagine the damage it was doing.'

'How did the rangers manage to trap it?' asked Seth.

'Well, shifters can't hold large forms for long. So the rangers just let it wear itself out. After a few hours, it turned into a mouse, and they caught it in a cage.' He whistled. 'What a sight that was. The shifter kept trying to change form to escape, but there wasn't enough space. So it became this angry whorl of shimmering quicksilver.'

'Couldn't it have become an insect?' suggested Meera.

'Good thinking, Meera, but a mouse is about the smallest form a shifter can take. As for the largest … no one knows. When we let this one go, it became a tortoise the size of an island.'

'You just let it go?' asked Seth. 'After it went on a rampage?'

'Why not?' said Daniel. 'It was probably some stupid human's fault in the first place. I bet they teased it, or encroached on its habitat.'

'That's exactly what happened, Daniel,' said Mr Donnelly. 'Shifters, like dragons, can be fiercely loyal companions. Cross one, however, and …'

His moustache twitched.

'Well, hopefully you lot are too smart to let that happen to you.'

After class, Esme and Daniel walked to their usual lunch spot on Pier Two and sat on one of the long wooden blocks at the boardwalk's end. Across the water, students sailed out as far as they could without leaving the school grounds, marked by a line of buoys. The air held a bite of cold, and the sky was serene: an uninterrupted panorama of blue, except for three wafer-thin cirrus clouds, floating along like runaway wedding veils.

'Where's Lillian?' asked Daniel.

'She's had a bad cold the past few days,' said Esme. 'Maybe she went to sick bay.'

Within moments, however, Lillian arrived, looking very out of sorts. Judging by her moist eyes and red nose, her cold had gotten worse.

'You look terrible!' said Daniel, through a mouthful of sandwich.

Lillian's face crumpled.

'Sorry,' he said sheepishly, wiping away crumbs. 'What I meant to say was you look sick. Really sick. Maybe you should go home?'

'I'm going to,' Lillian said with a sniffle. 'If I'd stayed in bed, none of this would have happened.'

'None of what?' asked Esme.

Lillian kept glancing back down the pier, as if somebody was following her. She was shivering as though she'd just fallen into the lagoon.

'If something's worrying you, you can tell us,' Esme said. 'What is it?'

The words came out strangely flat, as if Lillian was talking about something that had happened to someone else, rather than to her.

'My music teacher says to never sing when you're sick. That it can twist your songspells, turn them into something else entirely. She was late to class today, so we were mucking around. Trying out different spells. We were about to have a test, so I thought I'd cast a songspell to calm everyone down, help them think more clearly.' She winced. 'I was only trying to help …'

'And?' Daniel prodded.

'At the end of class, everyone handed me … love letters.'

Daniel raised an eyebrow. 'Love letters?'

She hid her face in her hands. 'I was singing so flat, I accidentally cast a completely different spell: Cupid's Mark. On *everyone*.'

'Cupid's Mark?' Esme repeated. 'What does that do?'

Lillian groaned at the sky. 'What do you think? My entire music class is infatuated with me!'

'Oh, no,' Esme breathed.

'Is that your class down there?' Daniel asked, pointing to two dozen students at the pier's other end.

Lillian nodded.

'I didn't realise Vince did music.'

Lillian mumbled something about Vince having a very nice voice, then leaned over the water. 'Maybe I should jump in there … Hide with the undines under the pier.'

'Don't,' said Daniel. 'Your admirers will probably throw themselves in after you.' He tapped a finger to his lip. 'Wait. If you're in total charge of their hearts and minds, you can set whatever rules you want, right? The way Liza does with her lot.'

Lillian stared at him, horrified. 'I'm not Liza!'

'Actually, that's not bad advice,' said Esme. 'Tell them you've got a terrible cold and that the best thing they can do is leave you alone.'

The music class caught sight of Lillian and started marching her way.

'Hang on, is that Ricard leading the pack?' Daniel asked. 'Most girls would kill to have Ricard besotted with them.'

Sculpted bronze Ricard, who reminded Esme of a statue of Prometheus she'd once seen in the city, was overtaken by a starry-eyed Vince.

'This is wrong,' murmured Lillian. 'So wrong.'

When Lillian's admirers were halfway up the pier, they passed Liza and her clique. Liza peeled herself away from her friends and started tugging Ricard's arm. 'What's gotten into you?'

'Lillian,' Ricard called, while Liza wrapped herself around him. 'Your hair looks so beautiful in that light! I've never noticed the red in it!'

'This is a disaster,' moaned Lillian.

Vince reached Lillian first. He tried to hand her a note, but before he could, he was overrun by a dozen other students, all bearing their own missives. Flowers were laid at Lillian's feet, the dirt-covered roots still hanging from them. One girl tied up her lunch with a hair ribbon and offered it as a gift. When Lillian refused to take it, she laid it reverentially on the boardwalk.

'Just in case you're hungry later.'

Ricard, determined to outdo the others, waved a hand in the air to cast a spell. Some of the flowers lifted themselves off the ground, braided themselves into a garland, and floated above Lillian's head.

Lillian bowed over in woe. Ricard smiled, mistaking her reaction for pleasure.

'I'm glad my tokens of affection please you. Take this as the first offering from my armoury of love. My heart, my soul, my all, are yours forever …'

'What in *Hades*,' Liza bellowed, 'is going *ON*?'

'Lillian cast a love spell,' Daniel explained. 'By accident.'

'By accident? I highly doubt that.'

She whispered something under her breath. Lillian's floral crown shrivelled, blackened, and fell away.

'It was an accident, Liza,' said Lillian, sounding as assertive as she could with a blocked nose. 'Pure and simple. Love spells are abhorrent. I'd never cast one on purpose.'

Liza stalked right up to Lillian, so close their noses were almost touching. Lillian didn't flinch or draw back. She just sneezed all over Liza.

'She's got quite a bad cold,' said Esme.

One of Liza's friends, who'd been observing the catastrophe from afar, rushed over with a tissue. Liza dabbed at her face, then stepped back, fuming.

'You'll never live this down, Lillian Lovell. Just wait until …'

Liza's mouth kept moving, but no words came out. It was like someone had snipped her vocal chords in two. Her hand went to her throat, and Esme's eyes went to Vince, whose face was pinched with revulsion.

'Stop it, Vince!' she cried.

The spell broke. Liza made a strangled sound and clawed into Ricard's arm. He resisted at first, then cast Lillian one last lovelorn look as he was dragged away.

'Vince! That was brilliant,' cried Daniel.

'What else could I do? She was threatening my dearest Lillian.'

'Please, Vince,' croaked Lillian. 'Please, everyone, I'm sick, really sick, so I'm going home. Don't follow me. I don't want to infect any of you.'

The mooning musicians simply gazed at her.

'I need some time alone. So, er—off you go!'

They nodded in unison, but stayed exactly where they were. The bell rang, signalling the end of lunch. They still didn't move.

'*Please*,' she said, with an edge of panic. 'If you want what's best for *me*, then go to your next class.'

Her words finally penetrated their love-bloated skulls. Everyone drifted off, but not before trying to catch her eye or blowing her a kiss. When they were all gone, Daniel picked up one of the offerings—a muffin—and started munching on it.

'Really?' said Esme.

'Why not? It'll just go to waste otherwise.'

Lillian sunk back into her gloom. Coughing, snivelling, and spluttering, she looked so woebegone that Esme had to give her a hug. Afterward, they kneeled down and started picking up the scattered love letters.

'You're shivering,' said Daniel. 'Maybe you should burn these for warmth.'

'You can't solve every problem by setting it on fire,' Lillian grumbled.

'*My love for you is everlasting,*' Daniel read aloud. '*I know from my inflamed heart that my ardour will outshine all. I will protect you always, against any who threaten your wellbeing ... Your true paramour, Vincent Chen.*' He passed the note to Lillian. 'This is going to be awful for him when he comes to his senses. Since—you know. He liked you before the spell.'

'Don't remind me ...'

'Surely there's some kind of counter-spell,' said Esme, picking up the last few scraps.

Lillian shook her head. 'There's no counter-spell. There's nothing I can do except wait for the arrow's mark to fade.'

'And how long will that take?'

'Weeks,' Lillian said in a small voice. 'Or maybe even longer.'

Chapter Ten

With Lillian taking the next few days off school, Esme was forced to field countless questions from the victims of Cupid's Mark. What was Lillian up to? Was she all right? Was she feeling any better? Did she need anything? Anything at all? They pressed poems and letters and sweets and cough lollies into Esme's hands, begging her to pass them on. When the lunch bell rang on Friday, Esme escaped the school grounds as fast as she could and ran to catch the ferry to the Keeper's Quarter.

Soon, she stood before the imposing bronze doors of Augustine's clinic. Inside, a long entrance hall swam with moody light. Paintings, dressed up in elaborate gold frames, graced the walls. Esme paused before a portrait of Queen Sofia, one of the founders of Aeolia.

She knew Sofia's features well. Not just because the queen's face was embossed on the back of every gold merle and carved on countless busts in the city, but because she had seen Sofia in person, through her Gift. The Sofia in this portrait, however, didn't quite coalesce with the one in Esme's memory. The artist had tried their hardest, yet failed to capture a true resemblance.

When Esme scrutinised the plaque beneath the painting, she realised why.

Anna Agapios, First Keeper of Esperance.

This wasn't Sofia—it was her ill-fated first born, Anna.

Esme shivered. On the Isle of Mists she'd come face-to-face with Anna, albeit a shadowy spectre of her former self. Anna had somehow stayed alive for thousands of years, cursed by her lust for the Pearl of Esperance. While defending Ariane, Esme had been forced to end Anna's existence with a sword of light formed from the pearl itself.

No, that's not quite right, thought Esme. *No one forced me.*

The brutality of that moment was tattooed on her soul, inked into her memory banks. Her violent act may have had the imprimatur of the king, the queen, the pearl, and even Anna herself, who in the end had whispered her thanks as she faded away, but that didn't ease Esme's conscience.

The founder-queen's daughter, radiant with youth and beauty, wore a smile full of promise—a smile oblivious to the coming darkness.

Does darkness just creep up on you, bit by bit, without you even realising it?

A frosty breath wafted by. Esme froze.

'Anna?'

She spun around. Mortimer, the ghost who haunted the clinic, was hovering so close that she'd become caught up in his glacial aura. The ghastly grin on his sepulchral face vanished.

'Oh, it's only you,' he groused.

Esme disguised her relief with a scowl. 'Don't sneak up on people like that, Mortimer. You're supposed to welcome patients, not scare them off.'

'What brings you here, anyway? More leg troubles, I hope ...'

'I'm not a patient. I'm the new intern. And I'll be keeping an eye on you.'

His jaw, insubstantial as it was, dropped a foot. Esme set off down the hall.

'Pray give that treacherous keeper a message for me,' he hissed.

'Give it to him yourself.'

'I can't. I hid his divining rod the other day, and now I can't go within thirty feet of him without being repelled by a magical barrier.'

'Good,' said Esme.

She strode into the same room in which Augustine had successfully treated her only a few weeks earlier. Mortimer didn't—couldn't—follow, and drifted off, grumbling.

She closed the door behind her. Inside, the odour of dried herbs and camphor mingled with other, more indefinable smells. A fireplace crackled in one corner, beside a long wooden workbench. At the end of the room, a large window, framed by blue curtains, looked out over a canal. Augustine, who had been gazing at the view, turned to greet Esme.

He gestured to two chairs and a small, round table. 'Take a seat.'

'Your duties here won't be too difficult,' said Augustine, sitting opposite Esme. 'Sorting through the keepers' archives, greeting patients, tending to the rooftop garden, that sort of thing.'

Esme breathed a sigh of relief. Ever since the principal had told her about the internship, she'd worried Augustine had made a mistake—that she wasn't qualified enough. But this sounded like something she could handle.

'And of course, it's an eminently practical arrangement for you, with the Anais so close by. Despite how much Pierpont may talk this placement up, it's not a very taxing role. The school was planning to send me yet another enchanter—Liza Lipp, I think her name was.'

Liza?

'However, I thought it was time for a change. I've had plenty of enchanters through here. Getting in my way, mostly. Your Gift, however, is one of the most intriguing I've come across in fifty years.'

'Fifty years?' Esme repeated, dumbstruck.

He chuckled. 'I'm young by keeper standards. Eighty-two, at last count.'

'But you look younger than my father!'

He shrugged. 'We keepers age very well. You may have noticed that there are only a dozen portraits in the entrance hall. That's because there have only been thirteen of us since the foundation of Esperance. One day, I hope to compile a history of the keepers … which is why the archives are in dire need of a clean-up. There's all sorts of fascinating information buried in there. You've met the shade of Anna Agapios—she's not the only keeper with an intriguing past. I've even heard rumours that one of my predecessors had a long-lost sibling.'

A loud *bang* came from above. Esme jumped. Augustine just rolled his eyes.

'Ugh … Mortimer must be in the ceiling again. Now, let's talk about your Gift. Refresh me on what exactly goes wrong when you attempt to use it.'

'Well, first of all, I can't even "attempt to use it". It just happens. When my Gift activates, I can't control where—I mean, when—it takes me. I can't decide how long my visions last. And when they're over, I have the worst headache you could imagine.'

She dropped her gaze to the ground, despondent.

Willow tapped her on the shoulder, forcing her to look up from the worn wooden floorboards. To her surprise, Augustine's lake-like eyes were brimming with optimism.

'As the last of the royal blood, I possess a little of each Gift myself. I have mastered nearly every Gift there is to master. My version of yours is far less powerful. I can only glance back in time a few days, not centuries.'

Hope dawned in Esme. 'And you can control it?'

He nodded. 'Initially, I couldn't. Not when it activated, nor the period of time to which I went. But I never experienced headaches, and I was always able to break out of my trances without difficulty. Those complications, I fear, must be due to Mare's meddling.'

He rose, crossed to the sink, and filled a beaten copper bowl with water.

'This Gift of yours—of ours—is an unusual one. It is triggered by emotion.'

Esme thought back to all the times her Gift had activated. The first time, she'd been furious at Mavis. The most recent time, when she'd gone home to see her father, she'd been subsumed by grief and guilt. Although, something didn't quite fit with the keeper's hypothesis.

'When I dipped my feet in the Merle Fountain and went back in time to see the founders hide the pearl, I wasn't feeling—well, anything. I was totally relaxed.'

'A feeling of wellbeing is still a feeling.' The keeper placed the bowl on the table. 'A sense of complete relaxation can also trigger your Gift. In a meditative state, slipping into the past is as easy as slipping into a dream. That's how I do it, at least.'

He slid the bowl toward her.

'Dip your hand into the water and don't think about what might go wrong. Once your mind is a blank slate, urge the water to show you something. If all goes well, the magic within you will wake.'

So Esme dipped her hand into the water and tried to do just that: let her mind go blank, let all her worries fly away. She focused on her breathing, which just made her stressed; then she tried counting her breaths, which filled her head with numbers, reminding her of the maths homework waiting for her back at No 8. Telling herself to stop thinking, to stop feeling, only made her think and feel all the more. The keeper's voice wafted into her cloudy brain, urging her to open her eyes.

'Any luck?'

'No,' she murmured.

'No matter,' said Augustine. 'It's time for a tour of the clinic. And when you get home, I want you to practise your Gift, every day, whenever you can, until we meet again. Do everything you can to relax.'

Esme's brow furrowed.

Relax?

How was she supposed to relax, she asked herself on the ferry home, while her mother's life force was fading away? Relax, when someone had tried to break into Ariane's room? Relax, when her father still hadn't replied to a single one of her letters? Relaxing wasn't something one could work at. In fact, putting those words in the same sentence seemed a contradiction in terms.

Clad in a dark blue diving suit, Esme hovered, weightless, over a shipwreck off the coast of Laertes Island. Most of the ship's deck had rotted away. What remained looked positively hazardous from above, a refuse tip of rusted iron and splintered timber, stirred up by the currents into a careless brew.

All around her, fellow students swam through the clear, still waters. They were here as part of a biology excursion, ostensibly to study the aquatic flora and fauna of the Esperance lagoon. Only, nobody was doing much studying.

Mr Donnelly was relaxing up above, on Laertes Island. Daniel was up there, too, having taken out his spyglass for some drag-on-spotting. Fern was sinking in and out of the rocks below Esme. Meera and Seth were examining the derelict vessel close up, casting furtive glances at each other as they swam in synchronised circles.

Liza, on the seafloor, watched Meera and Seth with considerable envy. She tugged at Ricard's arm. Ricard, however, was in some kind of torpor, paying no more attention to Liza than he would a piece of kelp.

Probably thinking about Lillian, Esme assumed.

She stroked toward the ship's crow's nest, where she perched on a decrepit wooden plank, opened her waterproof sketchbook and began to draw the wreck.

As she lost herself in her sketch, pausing every so often to admire the shafts of light filtering through the water, she began to feel at one with the sea: completely, utterly at peace.

A great roaring filled her ears. A pulsing band of pain wound round her head. Her Gift immobilised her, and underneath her—*CRACK.*

Her timber perch gave way.

Possessed by her Gift, Esme fell like a stone, down toward the wreck's forbidding interior, toward the razor-sharp spikes of wood and metal.

✄

Esme landed on the soft, grainy bottom of the sea. Rainbow fish weaved by. Light filtered through the lagoon's crystal ceiling, patterning the sand. Her fellow students were no longer swimming above her, and the sunken ship was nowhere to be seen.

I'm in the past, she realised. *The ship hasn't sunk yet.*

The light above her dimmed. She gazed upward to see the ship's hull, moving fast—too fast—toward Laertes Island. She heard a thud, and felt a shudder, followed by a series of creaks and faint cries from the surface.

It's going to land on top of me!

Even though she knew she couldn't be harmed, her reflexes kicked in. She swam a safe distance away, then watched through her fingers as the ship sank to its grave.

She could hardly bear to look. She knew all about shipwrecks from back home. Splinter Bay had been famous for them, before the lighthouse was built. Lives lost. Bodies washed ashore, their lungs full of seawater.

She calmed the thudding of her heart.

I'm not home. I'm here … and people can't drown here.

The ship's crew swarmed around the vessel, salvaging everything they could. Esme surfaced to see crew members and passengers gathered on shore, kneeling around a prone man. His captain's hat had been placed on his chest.

'Poor fellow,' someone murmured. 'He must have had a heart condition. He fell—collapsed at the wheel.'

I fell, too, Esme remembered, panic seizing her.

What a terrible time for her Gift to take over, just as she had plummeted toward the wreck. Was she hurt or injured? Had anyone come to her aid?

As if to answer, her Gift rushed her back to the present.

'Esme! Esme, are you okay?'

Esme opened her eyes to see Daniel and Seth leaning right over her. The intense concern in their eyes turned to relief. She sat up.

'I'm fine,' she said to the class around her.

'Are you sure?' said Mr Donnelly, kneeling on the sand.

'You weren't fine five minutes ago,' said Meera. 'Seth and I saw you lose your balance, but before we could swim over, something saved you. Whatever it was, it didn't look solid. It was some kind of silver mist.'

'It was a giant turtle,' said Fern. 'Definitely a giant turtle. I was on the other side and saw you land on its shell.'

'No, it was totally formless,' Meera insisted. 'Some … shimmering substance.'

'Maybe it was an undine,' said Seth.

'That's not what I saw!' Daniel cried. 'I saw a dragon shoot out of the water, carrying Esme on its back—and, get this—it was a Pelorusian Spinner! It dropped Esme on the sand and flew off out of sight. Didn't it, Mr Donnelly?'

'I, was, er … resting my eyes,' said the teacher.

'It can't have been a Spinner,' Liza snapped, hands on her hips. 'I know nothing about dragons, and even I know that Spinners are never spotted near Esperance. You should have said it was a Scion, if you wanted us to believe you.'

'I'm not making it up, I swear!'

'Well, you can't *all* be telling the truth,' said Liza.

'Yes, they can.' Mr Donnelly's eyes twinkled. 'It must have been a shifter. It all fits. A shimmering silver substance … that's what shifters look like in between forms.'

Still dazed, Esme stood up. 'I'm sorry for making you all worry. I fell into a trance because of my Gift. I don't know how to control it yet.'

'Yeah, right,' Liza retorted. 'You did it for attention.'

Mr Donnelly scowled. 'You're smarter than that, Liza. Esme could have been seriously hurt.'

'It won't happen again,' Esme promised. 'I'm working on mastering my Gift, with the keeper.'

'How cosy,' sniped Liza.

'Oh, shut up,' said Meera. 'We all know you're just jealous. Since you wanted that internship with the keeper. Sounds like Esme's putting it to good use.'

'Actually, I've got an even better internship,' Liza boasted. 'In Celia Skye's campaign office. I'm going to make sure she wins the election.'

Ricard squeezed Esme's shoulder. 'Meera's right, Liza. Stop bullying Esme.'

Liza opened her mouth, too shocked to speak.

'Esme is Lillian's friend,' continued Ricard, 'and anyone who's lucky enough to be Lillian's friend is a friend to me. Come on, Esme. I think I saw your sketchbook down near the wreck. Let's go find it.'

On Friday, while Augustine dealt with patients upstairs, Esme spent a whole afternoon sorting through the keepers' archives. In the damp, dingy basement of Augustine's clinic, dozens of cabinets housed case files dating back hundreds of years. Esme's job was to dispose of all the documents too damaged to decipher, while reorganising the rest into some semblance of order.

She started with the drawers pertaining to Thomas Agapios. Inside, she found reams of parchment detailing Gifts gone wrong and experimental cures for all sorts of ailments. For over an hour, she organised the papers by year and alphabetical order, then stopped short.

One file, which bore the name '*Solister Greaves*', was completely empty.

There was no year on the folder, nor any other identifying information—just that name, with no hint as to what the file might once have contained.

She put it aside to deal with later.

Behind her, paper ruffled. She swung round. A stack of a hundred sheets, which she'd just painstakingly ordered, were scattered everywhere, as if they'd been swept up in a gust of wind. Out of the corner of her eye, she saw a silvered figure slip through the wall.

'Mortimer!' she shouted. 'Get back here!'

'Don't waste your breath on him.' Augustine appeared in the stairwell. He waved Willow, and the scattered papers flew back into a neat pile. 'Come upstairs and let's work on your Gift. My last patient's just left.'

A few minutes later, Esme was in the keeper's treatment room, her hand in the copper bowl of water on the table.

This time, she knew exactly what to do.

She closed her eyes and imagined herself sketching the shipwreck off Laertes Island. That sense of complete absorption in her task, the drawing coming to life in her hands, the peace that had come over her before her perch had given way …

After her vision of the sinking ship, she'd figured out what she'd been doing wrong when it came to this Gift of hers. She'd been trying too hard: trying to perform something that should be effortless. All the times she'd slipped into a reverie, it had happened without her even knowing it: dipping her feet into the Merle Fountain, travelling by gondola, staring out the window during a dull class, painting a seascape in calming blue.

That silence, that dream-state, that altered state of consciousness, returned now. She felt slightly apart from the noises around her—the lap of the canal through the open window, the creaks and sighs of the old clinic, the faint voices of passengers on passing boats.

She closed her eyes, basking in the stillness, and felt her Gift take hold of her.

Pain throbbed in her head. The ocean rushed toward her. It caught her in its wild arms …

And tried to drown her.

It didn't feel like a dream, or a vision. It felt real. Esme was being tossed about, beaten, battered, by a vast, tempestuous sea. Salt stung her tongue and burned her nostrils. She kicked and struggled as hard as she could, fighting to stay at the surface, but the ocean overpowered her.

Wave after wave swallowed her, with no break in between. Each time Esme came up for air, another wave dragged her back down. Her fear became a chokehold around her throat. She couldn't even scream for help. The world dissolved into nothingness.

Back in familiar surrounds, Esme gripped the arms of her chair and bowed forward.

Augustine closed the book he'd been reading. 'You've gone green. What happened?'

'I managed to fall into a trance, but I didn't get anywhere. I was in a stormy sea, and the waves were flinging me about like I was a dead fish.'

'That's progress,' said Augustine, looking less worried than Esme thought he should. 'You've figured out how to activate your Gift at will. We'll find our way through whatever comes next. Keep practising, and I'll see you again next week.'

/ Chapter Eleven

The first ferry of Sunday morning slipped slowly along Trader's Canal. Esme leaned over the front rail, watching the ribboned waterways pass by on either side, tributaries on their way to breathe new life into the city's ancient bones.

Autumn air bit at her nose and cheeks. The ever-present scents of salt and silt from the canal were briefly subsumed by the aroma of baked goods from a nearby square. A vision of a chocolate cake rose in her mind's eye.

Lillian had promised to bake her one this morning.

Happy birthday, the city seemed to whisper to her.

The only thing missing from today was birthday greetings from her parents. Her father *could* be here, if he wished, but he wouldn't just have to dive into a rock pool to get here. He would have to swim across a whole ocean of disbelief.

At least I can go give Mum a hug, Esme thought. *Even if she can't give me one back.*

The pale lagoon, still tinged with lilac from the dawn, came into view. A breeze creased the surface, reminding Esme of the wrinkled old turtle that had led her to the Isle of Mists. She disembarked near Pierpont Park, and within a few minutes was at the door to her PC classroom. She, Daniel, and Seth had been rostered on to watch the dragon egg, which was days overdue.

Daniel and Argent were inside, focused on the egg. The craters scattered over it had grown so large they were joining together. In addition to the usual lines of rigour on Argent's square features, the night watch had added a heavy weariness to her face.

Seth was lightly snoring on a chair. Argent roused him and he loped over to join them, rubbing his eyes.

'Now that we're all here,' Daniel said to Argent, 'how about catching up on some sleep?'

He tried to shuffle her toward the door, but the egg exerted a magnetic pull on her. 'Maybe I should stay, just in case.'

Seth gave a disgruntled sigh. He tried to wipe his unruly hair out of his eyes, but it just fell back over his face. 'What's the point of us all being here then?'

Argent's jaw jutted out. 'Fine. Daniel, I'm leaving *you* in charge. Any problems on this watch are *your* problems. Do not leave this egg alone under any circumstances.' Her eyes bored into his.

'I promise,' said Daniel. He knocked gently on the egg and let his hand rest on its blackened shell.

Seth did a double take. 'What are you doing? Why isn't your hand a smoking mess?'

Daniel held up his unharmed palm. 'I can't be burned.'

Seth blinked in disbelief. 'You what?'

'He can walk through fire,' said Argent. 'Lucky him. It's quite a rare Gift.'

She held out her own hands, turning them back to front. Large, competent hands, they were also terribly ravaged, puckered, and angry from a lifetime of working with dragons.

'I'll be over in sick bay,' she said, before stifling a yawn and leaving the classroom.

'So now we take turns watching this little fire fiend?' asked Seth.

'No need,' said Daniel. 'I'm not going anywhere.'

'Suit yourself.' Seth sidled off toward the door.

As soon as Seth was gone, Daniel went to rummage in his backpack. 'Happy birthday,' he said, handing a parcel to Esme.

'Thanks! You didn't have to ...'

The gift was trussed up with string and plastered all over with bright pink tape. Esme fumbled with it for quite a while.

'Did you wrap this in the dark?' she joked.

'My little sister insisted on wrapping it.'

Eventually, the packaging fell away to reveal a seashell: a gorgeous curve of soft pink, shot through with strands of white and blue.

'I wasn't sure what you'd like, and I didn't know, and then I thought … I thought since a shell led you to your mother …' He smiled at her uncertainly. 'I found it a while back, when I was away with my dad.'

He looked rather worried. She laughed, putting him out of his misery.

'I love it.'

She held the shell up to the light, studying its contours. When she turned it upside-down, something dropped out of its aperture.

It was another, smaller present, packaged with so much tape it was even more difficult to unwrap than the previous one. Esme smiled as she tussled with it. 'Are you sure your sister didn't want to keep this for herself?'

'Can you tell?'

Inside was a string bracelet, woven with strands of turquoise and periwinkle, and threaded with tiny shells and trinkets.

'Where I come from, everyone gets one of these on their sixteenth birthday. It's tradition.'

'This is from Thalassa? That's so nice of you.'

'Here. It's a bit tricky.' Daniel tied the bracelet round her wrist, threading the shell at one end through the loop on the other. As his fingers brushed against her skin, they infused her with a surprising warmth. She wasn't sure where to look, or what to say. She was just as tongue-tied as Daniel.

'Sorry,' he said. 'I've never gotten presents for someone from another world.'

'They're perfect. Anything from you would have been perfect.'

He sprung up, satisfied.

'Come on. Your best present's still to come. Sharing a birthday with this one.' He patted the egg. 'Come on out, little one,' he crooned. 'It's not so bad out here.'

But nothing they said or did could entice the dragon to venture out into the world. While Daniel stayed true to his word and kept guard, Esme wandered outside for a break. Seth was slouched against the wall, absently flexing and unflexing his fingers.

His gaze drifted down to Esme's bracelet. 'Nice. Is that new?'

'Daniel gave it to me.'

'That's an impressive Gift he's got. It fits perfectly with what he wants to do. His future's set.'

There was something raw in those last words. Feeling a little on edge, Esme looked out over the water. A ship in full sail was making its way across the horizon. She was about to go back inside when she heard footsteps pounding along the wooden treads.

'Sorry I'm late!' Lillian was rushing up the pier, puffing, saying five things at once. 'The ferry took forever. But I brought cake—triple chocolate! Oh, hi, Seth. Has the dragon hatched yet?'

'I wish.'

'Where's Daniel?'

'In there, brooding over his egg.'

Lillian smothered Esme in a hug. 'Happy birthday!'

Seth started, then muttered in an undertone, 'Happy birthday, Esme.'

'There's presents later,' Lillian went on. 'I thought we—you and me and Mum—could go over to the Anais later, open them up there.'

Lillian let go, then glanced at Esme's wrist with a questioning look.

'Daniel gave it to me. He said it was from Thalassa—everyone there gets one when they turn sixteen.'

Lillian lifted Esme's wrist to examine the bracelet more closely. 'Ooh, it's so pretty. Goes with your eyes.'

The door to the PC classroom swung open. 'Something's happening!' Daniel cried. 'Come quick!'

They all gathered round the egg.

'It looks the same as always,' Seth drawled. 'Like it's been left out in the sun too long.'

'I'm sure it moved an inch to the left,' Daniel insisted. 'It's definitely in a different spot. You can't tell?'

'When you stare at something long enough, it can feel like that,' said Lillian.

Daniel lifted a finger to his lips. 'Shush. Hear that?'

Everyone bent over the egg. A faint noise was coming from inside, like the clink of a spoon in a mug. The clinking went on for some time, then turned into a *tap-tap-tap*.

'It's happening!' Daniel cried.

A great crack appeared in the egg, then another, and another.

The cocoon split open, shards of steaming eggshell falling away. A baby Scion lay within, with golden wings folded tight, tiny claws, and a long, spiky head.

Daniel lifted the dragonling gently. It swivelled its head toward him. One bleary eye opened, then another. It yawned, exposing half a dozen tiny, sharp teeth, then collapsed back into Daniel's hands.

'It's smaller than a full-grown dragon's claw,' he murmured.

'I'll go get Argent,' said Seth. 'But first, let me hold it a bit.' He cupped his hands and held them out to Daniel.

'Birthday girl gets first cuddle,' said Daniel.

Seth stepped back. 'Fair enough.'

'Careful, Esme, it's still a little hot.' Daniel slipped the new-born into Esme's hands. The dragonling looked a little lost amongst all its human caretakers, but it was gradually growing more aware. Smoke curled from its flaring nostrils.

'Happy birthday, little one,' Esme whispered, gazing into its gold-flecked eyes. Its scaled body, forged of fire, thrummed with power.

As she handed the dragon to Seth, she noticed, for the first time, that his hands were covered in tiny cuts that had scarred white.

Seth stroked the crest of the dragon's head, then passed it to Lillian, who cooed all over it. The dragon stretched out a wing as thin as gossamer and let out a snort.

'Oh, it's so adorable!' Lillian held it close, her hair brushing its snout. The dragonling sneezed. 'Its first sneeze! How cute!'

'Ah, careful.' Daniel reached for the baby. 'Maybe give it back to me.'

It sneezed again. This time, sparks spurted out, catching the ends of Lillian's hair, setting it alight.

Pandemonium broke loose. Lillian let out a wild shriek and flung the dragon into Daniel's arms. Esme grabbed a nearby cloth and tried to smother the flames. Seth, however, didn't panic. He extended a hand toward Lillian.

'I've got this,' he said.

An icy mist streamed out from his fingers, just enough to extinguish the flames and leave a thin coating of frost. The acrid smell of burnt hair filled the air.

'Are you okay?' Seth asked.

'No harm done. Thanks, Seth.'

He nodded and headed out the door to fetch Argent.

'I didn't know he had an ice Gift,' said Lillian, picking shards of frost out of her hair.

'Neither did I,' Esme murmured.

She hadn't moved an inch since seeing Seth use his Gift. She stood there by the table, clutching the tattered, blackened cloth.

Except it wasn't a cloth anymore.

It was her mother, wreathed in ice, back on the Isle of Mists.

On the isle, Mare had tried to murder them both, just so he could get his hands on the Pearl of Esperance. But since he didn't have a Gift himself, he'd used a boy to carry out his dirty work. Flashes of the past kept coming: flashes of a blank-eyed, ashen-faced boy, with long, dark hair, standing in the shadows. Ice rushed from his fingers. Frost settled on Esme and her mother, turning them both blue. Mare gave a thin smile as he watched his servant crown Ariane with a tiara of deathly beauty.

'I'm so sorry.' Daniel's voice brought Esme back. He was apologising to Lillian, over and over, while she inspected her damaged hair.

He was still holding the baby dragon. It sneezed again, cinders falling from its snout, landing harmlessly on him. Then it curled up and fell asleep in his arms. He laid it back down amongst the remains of its shell.

Lillian held up a clump of charred hair. 'It's just the ends. It was overdue for a cut, anyway.'

'You're taking this much better than I thought you would,' said Daniel.

'Of course I am. The dragon didn't mean to hurt me.'

'Hey, I didn't mean it either, back when we were kids!'

'Dragons can't help themselves. You were a little pyromaniac!'

While Daniel and Lillian continued to banter, Esme struggled to let go of the threads of that terrible day on the isle. Seeing an ice Gift up close had brought everything back. Yet despite the trauma of reliving those events, something had clicked in her.

Now she knew why she had taken an instant disliking to Seth. He must have reminded her, on some unconscious level, of that boy back on the Isle of Mists.

But they weren't the same—not at all. Seth had just helped Lillian without hesitation, he'd been nothing but friendly to Esme, and clearly Meera saw something in him. From now on, Esme decided she would try to as well, despite her lingering misgivings.

'It hatched!' cried Argent, rushing in with Seth. 'At last!' She picked up the dragonling and stroked its scales. 'And it's a girl. What do you all think of the name Hestia?'

'I think it suits her perfectly.' Esme smiled. 'Let's celebrate with some cake.'

Chapter Twelve

'I have a feeling that whatever I come up with about Alexander Mann, it won't matter,' Esme complained, drumming her fingers on the cover of Rank's hardback. 'Since Rank literally wrote the book on the subject.'

'Wouldn't be the first time homework has felt like an exercise in futility,' said Lillian, eyes glazing over the notes splayed out on their reading desk.

They turned to stare out the foggy, rain-streaked windows of the Pierpont Library. Gondolas drifted like phantoms across the lagoon. More of the iconic boats, hung vertically and repurposed into shelves, lined the library's walls. These ancient gondolas were no longer seaworthy, the gilt coating on their proud figureheads worn away, but they had found a second life on land. No longer fit to carry passengers, they now carried books to the shores of readers' minds.

The beauty of Esme's surroundings, however, did little to lift her mood. She read her essay question over and over with a deepening scowl.

The long lens of history condemns the infamous otherworlder, Alexander Mann, who was responsible for some of the worst massacres of the Tyrian Wars. These atrocities may not have come to pass had Mann never set foot in Aeolia. How can we keep our world safe from barbarians like Mann in the future?

'I don't envy you, having to deal with Rank's prejudices.' Lillian, distracted from her own work, was reading over Esme's shoulder. 'Mann is probably the most hated figure in Aeolian history. His bones were buried on a deserted islet, all on their own. No one ever goes there, except to … well, to desecrate his grave. Every year, a burning effigy of him is floated through the canals as a reminder of how he almost destroyed the city.'

'Great,' Esme muttered.

She and Lillian were sitting in one of the many alcoves at the back of the library. Enchanted lights bobbed over their heads, yellow orbs that could somehow sense whenever they were needed. One floated over to Esme now, illuminating part of her question.

The long lens of history …

'Wait. If you apply the "long lens of history", doesn't that make everyone here an otherworlder—originally?'

Lillian laughed. 'Do it! Use his own words against him.'

'Somehow, I don't think it will be enough.'

'If it makes you feel better,' Lillian slid her own question under Esme's nose, 'I'm stumped too.'

> *The eyewitness accounts of ghosts comprise a large part of our historiography. Some scholars, however, have observed that ghosts are prone to exaggeration, untruth, and slips of memory. How much stock can we put in the recollections of ghosts? Discuss.*

After rereading the question aloud, Lillian moaned, 'Where do I even start?'

A soft laugh came from a few feet away. 'You could start by talking to a ghost.'

The voice had come from the vicinity of a lapis-lazuli gondola. But no one was there; only the books weighing down the shelves, a sliding ladder, and several roving orbs of light. Then, bit by bit, a figure emerged from the upright boat.

Fern joined them in their reading nook. 'If you're struggling with that question, Lillian, you should come to the ghost grim tomorrow night. You, too,' she added to Esme. 'Some of the ghosts there are centuries old. I'm sure a few of them knew Mann.'

'What's a "ghost grim"?' Esme asked.

'A gathering … of sorts. The city's ghosts throw them every month on the Palace Isle. It's like a party, if it were run by undertakers.'

'But the ghosts won't let us near their grim,' said Lillian. 'We're not of their kind.'

Fern shrugged. 'They don't mind me.'

'That's because you're practically half ghost already,' jibed Lillian.

'Don't worry,' said Fern. 'I know exactly how to get you in. Just say you've come to hear the ghosts' stories. They love telling them, over and over and over. If you're willing to listen, I'm sure they'll be prepared to overlook the fact that you're still breathing.'

At midnight the following evening, Esme and Lillian met up with Fern in the city's central plaza. It curved all the way around a shining lake, in the middle of which rose a small isle, home to the Godstone Palace and its expansive grounds. By the light of her lantern, Fern led them over an arched bridge, through the palace's manicured gardens, past the majestic Merle Fountain, all the way to the rambling parklands on the island's eastern edge.

Thick copses studded the park, looming out of the night like prowling bands of thieves. 'It's in here,' said Fern, stopping by the largest one.

'In here?' Esme said uncertainly, peering into the dark woods. There didn't seem to be a way through. Climbing figs strangled the trunks of the ancient trees, while thorns and bracken greedily consumed what was left of the space.

Fern handed her violin case to Esme and her lantern to Lillian.

Then she reached a hand into the worst tangle of creepers, straining forward, her arm twisting this way and that. With creaks and soft shrieks, the vines released their stranglehold on the trees, revealing a path through the darkness.

'Wow,' said Esme. 'How do you even know about this place?'

'The ghosts showed me once.'

Single-file, Esme and Lillian followed her down the passage. They soon arrived at the moonlit glade at the heart of the copse.

Figures glided by, silvered ghosts, dozens and dozens of them. Some moved in silent communion with the night; others restlessly flitted to and fro. A pair of sepulchral hounds galloped by, leaping around—and through—the trees. As Fern and the others came out into the open, a ghost in a long tailcoat doffed his top hat to them.

'So far, so good,' murmured Fern.

'Mortals begone!' roared a familiar voice.

Esme groaned as Mortimer, in his greyed-out waistcoat, zoomed toward them.

'Breathers,' he cried, prodding a freezing finger through Esme's chest, 'are not welcome here!'

'We're here on Fern's invitation,' Esme declared. She reached into her bag, grabbed her notebook and pen, and held them aloft. 'We've come to record your stories.'

Mortimer's mouth yawned open, stretching and stretching until it swallowed most of his face. Then it shrunk back to normal. He cast them an ingratiating smile.

'*That*, of course, is a completely different matter. I'll go first. I'll tell you every detail of exactly what that keeper did to me.'

'No, you won't,' said another spectre, swooping directly through Mortimer's middle. 'We've heard your tale a thousand times. Why don't you let someone else speak for a change?'

The same ghost pointed to a sombre-looking lady sitting half-inside a log.

'Good midnight, Fern. Why don't you and your friends go talk to Hetty?'

'Hetty, as in, Hetty the Heinous?' Lillian exhaled. 'The one who was hanged for killing her husband two hundred years ago?'

The ghost nodded. 'She insists she was framed.'

Lillian hurried over to the lady on the log, pen poised, notebook in hand. Hetty the Heinous wore a feathered hat and a fur coat. As she pleaded her case to Lillian in a thick accent—'I did nussink!'—she took great pains to point out the rope marks on her neck.

'But you can be sure,' she drawled, 'zat I took my revenge. It is difficult for us ghosts to interact with ze livink world, but with much practice, ve can touch solid things, pick up ze small objects, play … pranks, if you vill.' Hetty grinned. 'My executioner never slept a vink for ze rest of his days.'

She was abruptly moved on when another ghost, who'd decided that Hetty had spent more than enough time with the living guests, sat down right on top of her.

'How rude,' she huffed, before floating off.

The new ghost launched into a tale just as gory, as did the several others who came after him. A few of their stories were uproariously funny, but most of them had met sad, neglected, lonely ends. Many wept copiously, their ectoplasmic tears pooling on the ground. After an hour or so, Esme was wrung out from their emotional outpourings, as was Lillian. Fern, however, remained totally unmoved.

'I've heard it all before,' she said when they got a moment to themselves.

'Thanks so much for bringing us along,' said Lillian. 'I've got so much for my assignment.' She flicked through pages and pages of notes. 'Heaps of these ghosts are mentioned in the book Rank gave me.'

She had brought the thick textbook along with her. Beneath a faint, dolorous figure on the cover ran the title *The Past Made Present: The Ghosts of Esperance.*

'It's a pity no one mentioned Mann,' said Esme.

'You haven't talked to everyone yet.' Fern pointed to a blazing bonfire at the edge of the trees. 'All those soldiers around that fire—they fought in the Tyrian Wars. I'd come over there with you, but I promised I'd play a song or two.'

Fern took her violin out of its case and struck up a slow waltz. Several ghosts partnered up to dance. While the elegiac notes of Fern's song resonated through the clearing, Esme and Lillian strode over to the fire.

A dozen men in opaque uniforms sat around the blaze. Some had grimy bandages wrapped around their heads and limbs. One man's eye was hanging out of its socket and bobbed about as he spoke. Spectral swords, muskets, and pistols were scattered on the ground.

A rough-faced man rose up to greet them. 'The name's Conor. Good midnight to you, mortals.'

'Pleased to meet you,' said Esme. 'Fern tells me you fought in the Tyrian Wars.'

'Aye,' said Conor, gesturing to his comrades. 'We all did. We gave our lives for this city in the Battle of the Citadel.'

'That was the final battle, right?' Esme had skimmed enough of Rank's book to have garnered a vague understanding of the major events. 'You were fighting to take back Esperance … from Alexander Mann. I'm writing my history essay on him.'

Conor's grin revealed that he was missing half his teeth. He jabbed a bony finger to his barrel chest. 'You're looking at the man who killed the scoundrel.'

'Your memory's as foggy as you are, Conor,' groaned another soldier. 'We *all* killed Mann.'

'We did nothing,' scoffed another. 'Mann was practically dead when we found him.'

'Practically dead—and *possessed*.'

'I still don't believe he was possessed,' Conor said. 'I reckon he was putting on a show.'

Esme was lost. 'What are you talking about?'

'Sit down, lassies,' said Conor, 'and we'll tell you everything.'

Several of the soldiers shuffled along, making room for Esme and Lillian by the fire.

'Mann was wounded when we came across him, true,' said Conor. 'Lying in the mud from the rain. He was more than just wounded, though. He'd snapped. He moaned that he was sorry for all he'd done, then claimed he'd been "tricked" into his crimes.' Conor spat into the fire. 'Balderdash.'

'The mist, though,' said one of Conor's comrades. 'You skipped the part about the mist.'

'Aye,' Conor continued. 'Just before Mann started his ravings, this strange mist came from nowhere, swallowed him up, and then blew away. I reckon it was just an illusion, or a trick of the light, but I can't deny that I saw it.'

Esme jotted that detail down in her notebook. She hadn't seen any mention of a 'mist' in Rank's book, nor anything about Mann showing remorse.

'What happened next?'

'We ran our swords through him, over and over. The whole lot of us.'

'That's right,' bragged one soldier. 'We *all* dealt the final blow.'

'We were so caught up in seeking our revenge,' Conor grumbled, 'that we didn't notice the Tyrians sneaking up behind us. Not until it was too late.'

As Conor's glassy eyes gazed into the fire, Esme got the impression that he didn't want to relive the next part of the story.

'X marks the spot,' he murmured.

'Aye, X marks the spot,' echoed his comrades.

'What X?' asked Lillian.

'Mann was slumped against a stone slab when he died, and our poor widows laid out more around it, in the shape of an X to remember us by. The stones are still there today—go have a look yourself, if you want.' Conor loosed a loud groan. 'By the gods, I wish I could still drink!'

Fern's fiddle had been put away now, and only a single penny-whistle rippled through the glade. The ghosts danced alone, writhing to rhythms of their own; nebulous figures, lost in the music of the night. Esme bade Conor farewell before departing with Lillian.

Fern joined them at the edge of the glade and they sat down to watch the last dance. Under the light of Fern's lantern, Esme leafed through *The Past Made Present*, reading what historians had to say about Hetty and Conor and all the other ghosts they'd met that night.

As she turned to a passage titled 'The Silent Wanderer', another icy spectre slid between her and Lillian. They quickly made room for Maria, a bibbed and bonneted ghost who had known Esme's mother. She usually resided in Ariane's old art studio, and Esme had never heard her speak.

'Oh—hi, Maria,' said Esme.

Maria pointed to the open page.

'The silent wanderer,' Esme read aloud. 'Is this about you?'

Maria shook her head, gesturing to the book with great urgency.

'All right, all right, I'll read it.'

The Silent Wanderer

With haunted eyes and wild gestures, the silent wanderer roams the globe, crying out for help—but no sound comes from her lips.

This ghost behaves so unlike any other that she has confounded spectrologists for centuries. While most spectres linger about a certain place and rarely stray far, the silent wanderer is a nomad who has been spotted in the farthest corners of Aeolia. She never stays anywhere for long, appearing and disappearing without warning. Sometimes, she seems almost as solid as a real person; at other times, she is so translucent that she is barely visible to the eye.

Most perplexing of all is her anachronistic clothing. In each sketch, painting, and photograph of her, she wears denim jeans, and a rather modern jacket—yet, impossibly, she has featured in tales, drawings, and paintings for almost two thousand years.

For these reasons, many spectrologists believe that the silent wanderer is not a ghost at all. They argue that she is some other kind of entity, one that we cannot even begin to understand.

The next few pages were crowded with visual depictions of the silent wanderer: ancient bas reliefs giving way to paintings, and eventually to faded black-and-white photographs. The lost woman always looked utterly forlorn. Her heart-shaped face peered out at Esme—lonely, scared, bewildered, eyes edged with tears.

Those eyes … Esme knew those eyes.

She bent over the book, hardly able to believe what she was seeing.

Her hands grew clammy. Her shoulders tensed. She turned to Maria, drawing short, sharp breaths. 'Tell me, Maria. The silent wanderer … who is she?'

Maria reached forward and caressed Esme's pearl necklace. The chill went all the way through to her heart.

'She's my mother, isn't she? The Ariane who used to paint in your studio?'

Maria gave a sad smile, bobbed her head in affirmation, and drifted off to join the last of the ghosts lingering in the glade.

Chapter Thirteen

Sleep was elusive that night. Esme was too on edge to do anything but lie there, weighed down with thoughts of her mother's plight. In amongst her fears the ghosts' voices echoed, grieving for their lost lives, resigned to their half-existence. At dawn, Esme gave up any hope of rest, got dressed, and stumbled like a sleep-walker to the Anais clinic.

As Esme slipped through the city's still-slumbering corridors, she couldn't help but imagine her mother's dazed, spectral figure haunting them. *The Past Made Present: The Ghosts of Esperance* was tucked under Esme's arm, feeling as heavy as if she was carrying ten books, rather than one.

Esme caught Augustine on the steps of the Anais. He'd just finished his morning rounds. 'You're here early,' he said with surprise.

'I found something out about Mum.' She held up the book. 'It's too hard to explain. It's all in here.'

A short time later, Augustine sat by Ariane's bed, perusing the chapter on the silent wanderer. His deepening frown made Esme even more agitated. Looking over at her mother's calm expression didn't help, not now that she'd seen Ariane's lost, lonely face in the book.

When the keeper closed the volume, Esme plied him with questions.

'What's going on? What's happening to her?'

His eyes drifted to Ariane. 'I'm afraid we may have underestimated the gravity of her condition. From what I can ascertain, she's not trapped in one place. She's lost all control of her power and is being tossed to and fro by the waves of time.'

Esme's heart began to race. Her mind was running at a million miles an hour as well. 'How come people can see her? How can we? When I go back with my Gift, no one can see me, but they can sometimes sense my presence.'

'When I go back,' Augustine said, 'no one can see *or* sense me, which seems to me how things should be. The past should remain fixed, immutable.' His eyes narrowed. 'But my Gift hasn't been experimented on, like yours and your mother's.'

He reopened the book and pointed to a coloured plate.

'Have you noticed how in this painting—it's from 1463—your mother is much more … corporeal? Compared with this one, from 1530, where she's almost invisible? Then in this photograph, in 1907, she's looking more solid again.'

Esme squinted at her mother in grainy black and white. 'You're right. It's like she's more "there" in some and less "there" in others.'

The keeper mulled things over for a long while, before speaking in direr tones than ever. 'At first, it seems that there is no pattern to these variations in her appearance. But we can't assume that Ariane is experiencing time in a linear fashion. She could have been tossed from 1530 to 1463 to 1907, in that order. If this is the case, and I hope it is not, then each time Ariane is transported somewhere else, she becomes less spectral and more solid. Less attached to the present, more a part of the past.'

Esme wasn't sure she'd heard him correctly. 'She's what? Becoming … part of the past?'

The keeper nodded. Esme's hopes sank like a leaden casket being lowered into a grave.

'Nobody can be in two places at once,' he said solemnly. 'If we do not remove Ariane's Gift soon, she may well vanish from the present and be stuck permanently back in time.'

He rose to pace the room in fretful circles.

'Those who witness the past should be only silent, invisible observers. For good reason. It wouldn't take much to alter the past, even by accident, and bring about a wholly different present.'

Both sets of eyes slid to Ariane. In her sleep-deprived state, Esme could barely grasp the significance of Augustine's words. All she knew was that her mother was drifting around, rudderless, on the vast ocean of time—and without Esme's help, she might drown in those dark waters.

'I just can't figure out,' she said, clutching her head in her hands, 'what Mare wanted. Why did he experiment on Mum's Gift in the first place?'

'I suppose, once he found out what sort of Gift she had, he couldn't resist trying to meddle with it, push it past its limits.'

Every time Esme remembered that Mare and Ariane had been friends, it chilled her blood. *'You were such perfect subjects,'* he'd said, on the Isle of Mists. *'A matching set.'*

She gritted her teeth. 'I think he did it just to see if he could.'

'Very likely,' said Augustine, returning the book to Esme. 'All we can do to help your mother is proceed with the original plan, post-haste. Come and see me today, after closing time, in my clinic.'

⚹

'Try to relax,' the keeper said later that afternoon. 'Take a deep breath. Worrying about your own Gift won't help your mother with hers.'

Although Esme had been practising her Gift every day, she had made very little progress. It had gotten much easier to enter that meditative headspace from which she could activate her Gift, but whenever she managed to trigger it, she was buffeted about by towering waves. After a brief struggle to remain at the surface, she would be tossed back into her own time, like a shipwrecked sailor washing up on shore.

Willow flew over and brushed against her hands. She was surprised to see them clasped in a white-knuckled grip. One of her legs, too, was tapping out a fast rhythm. She unpeeled her hands from each other and steadied her leg.

'How's your practice been going?' Augustine asked.

'Not very well. I can activate my Gift at will now, but when I do, I feel like I'm swimming against a raging sea. Like the whole ocean's conspiring against me.'

He tapped his fingers on the clawed arms of his chair.

'Is the ocean really so monstrous a place? Perhaps all that is needed is a change in perspective. Fear can serve a useful purpose, but it can also stop us from getting where we want to go.'

'You're saying it's my own fear that's stopping me?'

'I'm just saying that whatever you're doing clearly isn't working. So let's try a different approach.'

Esme waited for the keeper to suggest something, but he merely glanced around.

'This room has a long history worth exploring. You've been reorganising the keepers' archives—I'm sure you've read about plenty of interesting cases of Gifts gone wrong. Focus on one such case and see if you can make it back there.' Hastily, as if it had just occurred to him, he added, 'Please limit your travels to the tenures of my predecessors. I wouldn't want to break confidentiality with any of my patients. Hopefully, those who died hundreds of years ago won't mind helping you master your Gift.'

He indicated an old marble basin sunk into the cabinetry along the wall.

'The clinic was partially destroyed during the wars and rebuilt under Tyrian occupation. That's why some of the inscriptions around the city are in Latin, rather than Greek. That sink, however, survived. I'd say it would make a fine conduit for your purposes.'

Despite the gnawing anxiety inside, Esme smiled.

Sinks seem to be my specialty.

After dragging a stool to the sink, she turned on the taps and filled the antique basin. Dipping a hand in, she brought an old case to mind. The eleventh keeper, Flora Agapios, had once treated a woman—a gardener—whose Gift was to make plants thrive. After the gardener's sister passed away, flowers began to wilt wherever she walked.

It wasn't long before Esme's Gift took over. The familiar roaring tore through her ears. Her head began to pound ferociously as time's ocean seized her. Mountains of water reared up before her, ready to unleash their wrath, ready to pummel her from every direction.

Terror was within. Terror was without. Fear made itself manifest before her. Like her mother, she was at the water's mercy. That thought froze her limbs, made her helpless, too.

'Try something different,' the keeper's voice echoed, far away now. 'Remember, the waters of Aeolia are different to those of your world. Here, we can breathe beneath the surface.'

Breathe beneath the surface …

Just as a great breaker was about to crash down on her, Esme dove.

Esme dove, deep down, far below the thrashing waves. As she dove, her fear subsided. The ocean's wrath diminished, too. There was no violence down here, only slow and subtle currents that wandered around her, on their way elsewhere.

Esme floated in the blue and thought about the sea.

For years, she'd been besieged with nightmares of her mother's death, visions of her mother sinking beneath the waves. But the sea had never been something she could shut out of her life. Back home, she'd lived right beside it. She'd heard its voice every day, inside and outside the lighthouse keeper's cottage. She'd watched whales migrate, and dolphins frolic, and the lighthouse trace its beam across the water each night. The sea had been there, right beside her, through the lonely years between losing her mother and finding her again. And it had brought her to Aeolia. Here, she'd swum in it, relaxed in it, revelled in it, breathed beneath it.

The sea—water itself—had always been something ancient and mysterious, something unknowable, something ruled by the moon rather than the earth. Yet it was giving Esme the chance to witness what it had witnessed, over countless millennia.

The keeper had told her he couldn't wait to see her master

her Gift. Daniel and Lillian had been so excited when it had first revealed itself. But Esme had been too scared, too scarred, to embrace her power.

Now, for the first time, she felt the same spark of elation that her friends had.

Curiosity spiked in her. The past was hers to explore: wherever—whenever—she wished. She flew along the currents like quicksilver, voyaging through liquid light. Though the waves were far above her now, she could still hear their endless roar, feel it reverberating through her. Finally, she recognised the sound for what it really was. What she'd thought was the roar of the ocean was really the roar of time set in motion.

Esme watched, invisible, as the eleventh keeper's patient wiped away a tear.

'After my mother left us, I practically raised my sister. Now she's gone, too. Since she passed, I haven't been able to find joy in anything. Not in my garden, not in my Gift.' She hiccoughed. 'But I have to be strong. For my family, for my children, for everyone else.'

The treatment room looked different, but the old marble sink was the same. Flora Agapios, a curly haired woman swathed in aquamarine robes, stood before the bench. She reached through Esme for a teapot and strained clear liquid into it, pressed from a velvety black flower. Esme recognised the blossom as a rue plant. They grew in Miranda's garden, hoarded rainwater, and 'cried' whenever they were touched.

'You're allowed to feel,' said Flora, pouring the tea into a cup.

'But I'm worried I'll never stop crying.'

'Don't worry. You'll stop eventually. You'll just see the world a little differently afterward.'

As soon as Flora's patient sipped the rue tea, tears started streaming down her face. The more she drank, the harder she cried, and soon the twin rivers down her face became waterfalls. She could have filled a bucket with her tears.

'Look,' said Flora, pointing to the pot plant the patient had brought along.

The ailing fern had lifted its fronds. All the other plants in the room were stirring, too. Esme watched, awed, as the room became a jungle of glossy leaves, tangled vines, and vivid blossoms.

The patient lifted her head and smiled, the last of her tears drying on her cheeks. That smile lingered in Esme's mind as the sea swept her away. A swift current lifted her back to the present.

'You look very pleased with yourself,' said Augustine as soon as she opened her eyes. 'Good news?'

'I made it through.' Esme gave a triumphant grin. 'The sea stopped fighting me. Or maybe I just stopped fighting the sea.'

His eyes twinkled. 'Well done. So where did you end up?'

'Exactly where I wanted to. I saw Flora Agapios treat a woman with a botanical Gift. The woman was suppressing her emotions, making all the plants around her wilt. As soon as she stopped, things started growing again. The whole room was turning into a jungle.'

'Ah, yes, I've read about that case myself. It took days for Flora to trim her plants back down. Go on, then.' He beamed at her. 'Try again, whenever you're ready.'

Spurred on by her success, Esme spent the next few hours visiting more of the keepers' old cases. She watched somebody with Fern's Gift learn to slide effortlessly through all kinds of surfaces; she saw a man with an ice Gift learn to conjure snow, rather than just hailstones. She stayed away from Augustine's era, as he had instructed, and instead met several of his predecessors, all of whom shared his royal-blue eyes. Each of them turned toward Esme when she arrived and squinted at the place where she stood, then glanced away, as if she was merely a trick of the light.

Sometimes, Esme's fears revisited her, but she managed to quell them by reminding herself that the ocean was no longer her foe.

She practised until she could practise no more. When her head-ache grew too painful to ignore and her eyes began to droop with exhaustion, the keeper sent her home, with an invitation to come back the next day.

⁂

'Do you think you're ready to visit Thomas now?' Augustine asked the following morning.

'Almost,' said Esme. 'One more practice session, then the real thing.'

She wasn't quite awake yet. For the second night in a row, she'd hardly gotten any sleep. Esme had dreamed of Mare: Mare befriending her mother, experimenting on her, hovering over her on the Isle of Mists, the faceless boy with the ice Gift at his side.

'You can give me the pearl now and save your mother, or we can extract it from her frozen digits.'

Esme submerged her hand in the sink. As the ocean bore her into the past, she tried to focus on the case she'd chosen to visit, but she couldn't stop thinking about Mare. Down she went, down into a dark whirlpool of memory.

The keeper's treatment room, looking much as it did in the present day, materialised around Esme. Sunlight glanced into the room. Augustine, busy washing his hands at the sink, called good-bye over his shoulder to a departing patient.

The years would inscribe more lines on Augustine's brow, add more gravitas to his gait, but his eyes were the same. They darted Esme's way. He stopped what he was doing, a flicker of suspicion on his face. Then he started humming a tune, shaking his hands dry.

A rap at the door interrupted him.

'I'm not quite ready yet,' he called.

The door slammed open. Two adults strode into the room, fol-lowed by a silver-haired, hollow-eyed boy. Even though he was decades younger, Esme recognised Nathan Mare right away. His parents—Esme knew them from a photograph in the *Esperance Daily*—were dressed impeccably. They also wore an unmistakable air of entitlement.

I shouldn't be here, thought Esme, with a twinge of guilt, but she was too intrigued to make any effort to leave.

'Shut that door,' Mare's father said with an imperious wave at his son.

Nathan hesitated before closing the door.

'It's called a "waiting" room for a reason.' Augustine's lip curled. 'You'll have to introduce yourselves, I'm afraid, since you haven't bothered to come through the usual channels.'

The man sniffed, looking down his nose at Augustine. 'You know very well who we are: Jules and Eleanor Mare. We've come to find out what's wrong with our son, Nathan.'

Augustine regarded the boy loitering by the doorway. 'He looks well enough to me.'

Jules's eyes flashed. 'It's his Gift. It hasn't arrived.'

'And? I can't predict when that might happen.'

'Don't you have a little of every Gift?'

'I can only glimpse an hour or so into the future, and it's quite unreliable.' He closed his eyes and opened them again. 'In an hour's time, you are no longer in this room.'

'My son is seventeen,' said Jules, carrying on as if the keeper hadn't spoken. 'His Gift should have arrived by now.'

Augustine took a long look at the skulking boy before meeting Jules's eye. 'Have you entertained the possibility that your son … might not have a Gift?'

The ghost of something violent and ugly passed over Jules's face.

'Nonsense,' said Eleanor, throwing an anxious glance at her husband. 'Jules and I come from the purest enchanter bloodlines. Nathan's Gift must be late—there's no other explanation. Jules desperately wanted to come and check. He's … impatient like that.'

Her features briefly altered, like a crack appearing for no reason on a beautifully iced cake.

Augustine cast Eleanor a curious glance. He closed his eyes and pinched the bridge of his nose, looking none too happy. 'If you wish for me to examine your son, then both of you will need to wait outside.'

'We'll stay right here,' Jules said curtly.

Augustine drew himself up, radiating his full authority as Keeper of Esperance.

'Fine,' Jules barked. 'Just … find out what's going on, will you?'

The moment Jules and Eleanor left the room, Augustine's manner altered completely. Compassion seeped from every syllable he spoke. 'Take a seat, Nathan, and Willow and I will have a look at you.'

The boy nodded and advanced, a stiffness evident in his gait. As Nathan lowered himself into his seat, Augustine let go of Willow. She circled the boy and stopped by his left shoulder. The boy flinched.

'Willow won't hurt you,' said Augustine. 'May I see?'

Nathan didn't respond at first. He'd started to sweat. Then he gave the tiniest nod of his head. Augustine moved forward and lifted the boy's sleeve.

A large, swelling bruise purpled Nathan's shoulder.

Esme didn't know where to look. She'd dropped into something unexpected—and raw. A glint appeared in the corner of Nathan's eye.

'There's more, isn't there,' said Augustine.

Nathan stood and lifted up the back of his shirt. What Augustine saw there made him swear under his breath. Esme closed her eyes, not wanting to see. When she opened them again, Nathan was back in his seat.

He sat there, pale and fragile, small and still.

'Who did this to you?' Augustine said with the kind of calm that precedes a thunderstorm.

Nathan's eyes flicked involuntarily toward the door.

'If it's your father, then your mother, surely, must know.'

The boy's voice lowered to a whisper. 'She says I'm careless. Sometimes I dream she just stands there and watches.'

A wave of sympathy washed over Esme, followed fast by a flood of revulsion. How could she feel sorry for the boy who would one day try to murder her and her mother?

'How long has this been going on?' the keeper asked.

'I can't remember when it started.' It was like a wind blew in with Nathan's words, a wind so dry and desolate it turned the room into a desert.

Augustine was having trouble keeping the disgust off his face. 'Call your father back in. I'll speak to him right now.'

'No.' With that one word, all of Nathan's pain was shuttered away. 'You're not to interfere,' he said without emotion. 'I'll deal with it.'

'How?'

'I'll tell them that you know, and if they don't stop, you'll stop them.'

'Very well,' said Augustine, leaning forward. 'But you're to come here every week from now on, so I can make sure it's not still happening. Or else I *will* take action. Now, let us proceed with the matter at hand.'

The keeper began to wave the divining rod over Nathan. Mired in the horror of what had just unfolded, Esme had forgotten the whole purpose of the Mares' visit: to find out about Nathan's Gift.

She didn't need to stay any longer. She knew what the keeper would discover. She welcomed the oncoming headache, hoping that it would wipe away what she had just witnessed.

Back in the present day, Augustine frowned at her.

'You saw something awful, didn't you? I can tell. What happened?'

Esme slumped into the chair opposite him.

'I didn't mean to go back there, I swear. I just couldn't stop thinking about Mare, and before I knew it, I saw him, the day he visited you with his parents. How *could* they?' The words tasted foul in her mouth. 'To their own son?'

He shook his head. 'Such unconscionable acts. I'm sorry you had to see that.'

'Did his father stop … doing what he was doing to him?'

'Yes, for the rest of his rather short life. Jules and Eleanor perished in a fire a few years after they brought Nathan to me. Their whole house burned to ash. Nathan didn't seem to miss them at all—and who could blame him? He poured himself into his study, topped his university course, continued their philanthropic works, carried on their legacy. And he told me to keep quiet about his father's dark side, keep his family's reputation intact. Until now, I was the only one who knew what he endured at his parents' hands.'

'It's … sickening.'

'In this room,' said Augustine, swinging a hand around him, 'I have been privy to the full spectrum of human experience. Things that have brought me the utmost joy … and things that have driven me to despair. Your Gift, unfortunately, will expose you to the same extremes.'

He retook his seat and twisted the emerald ring on his finger.

'Nathan Mare,' he said, 'is not the only child in history who has suffered at the hands of those who were meant to protect him. I've treated dozens of patients who come from similar homes. Many of them turn out to be the complete opposite of their parents. Not everybody who is abused is destined to become an abuser. Mare's childhood does not excuse him, or exonerate him. It simply sheds a little light on things.'

He gave Esme a sad smile.

'You've come so far this weekend. Accomplished so much in such a short time. Shall we stop for now?'

'No,' said Esme. 'I want to get Thomas's recipe—the whole reason I'm here.' She clenched a determined fist. 'I can't undo what Mare's parents did to him, but I can undo what he did to my mother.'

Chapter Fourteen

'Here's what remains of Thomas's recipe,' said Augustine, showing Esme a ragged sheet of parchment. She had to squint to read it; between mould spots and water damage, it was a challenge to make out any words at all.

The Elixir of Severance

1. *In a cast-iron cauldron, reduce a quart of songwater …*
2. *Add one pint of cold, fresh w … … a strand of Arteria's scourge.*
3. *Add one … … of bellachorella … … toxicity.*
4. *Set to boil. Once everything has dissolved … … seven tears of rue flower.*
5. *Take one … … bloodstone, and one fossilised … … claw. Grind them into powder and dissolve in the solution for at least seven days … … the patient against the deleterious …*
6. *Add two roots of devil's rot, and no more than one drop of pure elysium, to dull the patient's …*
7. *Taken together, the scourge and the rot should be enough to sever … … As an added precaution … … enchanted it with the following words: 'Whosoever consumes this …*
… until it had dissolved.
8. *The most crucial step: immediately prior to administering the elixir, bring again to a boil, and add one petal of auroral nightshade.*

'How did you even begin to piece this together?' Esme asked Augustine.

He sighed. 'All the ingredients that I could make out, I'd used before. For the others, we were forced to make compromises and substitutions. When Nathan and I couldn't make heads or tails of the seventh step, our patient urged us to skip it entirely. Since Thomas said it was only an 'added precaution', we hoped we could get away with ignoring it altogether.'

Willow flew into his hand, as if sensing his distress.

'But ...' he drummed his fingers against the diviner, 'it could have been anything that caused our patient's death. Some of these ingredients are highly poisonous. One is so dangerous, it's been made illegal since I last procured it.' He fixed Esme with a solemn stare. 'Knowing all this, do you still wish to proceed?'

Crushed by the gravity of what she was agreeing to, Esme forced a nod.

'Very well,' said Augustine. 'I already have songwater, bella-chorella, Arteria's scourge, devil's rot, and rue flowers in my stores.' He paused, as if unsure whether to say the next part. 'I've also got a vial of elysium, left over from last time. I'd rather you keep quiet about that being in my possession. Elysium is one of the most addictive substances known to man.'

'Is that ... the illegal ingredient?' Esme asked.

'Yes. But one drop will do your mother no harm.' He glanced down at the list again, looking grim. 'I almost threw this recipe away, after what happened last time.'

'I'm glad you didn't,' said Esme, rising to her feet. 'Time to fill in the blanks.'

Back at the sink, Esme sunk into her usual reverie. Then she dove into the depths of time, thinking only of Thomas Agapios and the tattered recipe for the Elixir of Severance. As she rode the currents, she could hardly believe that she'd overcome her fears, that the water was responding to her will instead of forcing her to bend to its own.

"I did it. I really did it,' she whispered, as the past came to life around her.

The keeper's treatment room was freshly painted, as if it had only just been rebuilt. Hunched over the fireplace in the corner, tending to a small cauldron on the coals, was Thomas Agapios. Esme knew him at once from his portrait in the clinic's entrance hall. Thick locks of golden hair ranged around his square-set face; periwinkle blue eyes shone beneath brows that spoke of a fierce intelligence and an insatiable curiosity. A young assistant stood to his side.

The patient, a raven-haired, chalk-faced boy, thirteen years old at the most, slept on a pallet by the window. He was shivering under his grey blanket.

'What's wrong with him?' asked Thomas's assistant.

'Everything. His parents are healers, but for some reason, this child doesn't just heal people; he absorbs the illnesses of everyone around him. He's so sick, he's stopped eating or drinking. The only way I can think to save him is to remove his Gift entirely.'

'Remove his Gift? Is that even possible?'

'Believe me,' Thomas grumbled, 'if I thought there was another solution, I wouldn't be doing this. Pass me that flower, please—the glowing one.'

'I've never seen anything like this,' said the assistant, picking up a flower whose petals shone with opalescent light.

'It's called "auroral nightshade". It grew under the light of the Aurora of Aeolia. These flowers never die, even after being picked. Its immortal qualities should keep our patient's Gift intact as it leaves his body. If the magic disintegrates inside him, it could prove fatal.'

The assistant handed it over. 'Nightshade … sounds poisonous.'

'Most things in this brew are poisonous, but in these proportions, they should all counteract each other. Thank you,' said Thomas, taking the bloom in his delicate fingers. Esme noticed he wore the same emerald ring that Augustine would wear centuries later.

He picked off a luminous petal, which wafted into the bubbling liquid. A prismatic glow shone out from the cauldron as the petal dissolved.

'It's done,' Thomas declared, decanting the cauldron's contents into a thin glass vial. 'Quickly, now, and let's pray to the gods that it works.'

Thomas and his assistant hurried over to the sleeping boy. Esme, however, didn't follow them. She'd just spotted a piece of parchment on the bench, scrawled all over with spidery handwriting.

The recipe.

As she crossed the room, her heart banged so hard it was like someone was playing a wild game of handball against her ribs. She stared down at the creamy parchment. There was too much information to memorise all at once—too many ingredients to manage in one trip. *I'll come back*, she thought, before willing her Gift to take her away.

She hastened to the present, repeating the missing parts of the recipe over and over in her head. When she emerged from her trance, she was still muttering to herself.

In her absence, Augustine had copied the recipe onto a new sheet of paper.

'I need a pen,' said Esme. 'Quick, or I'll forget it all.'

She leaned over the bench and started filling in the blanks.

The Elixir of Severance

1. *In a cast-iron cauldron, reduce a quart of songwater **to a teaspoon of siren's salt.***
2. *Add one pint of cold, fresh **water and a** strand of Arteria's scourge.*
3. *Add one **bud** of bellachorella, **to counteract the scourge's** toxicity.*
4. *Set to boil. Once everything has dissolved, **squeeze in** seven tears of rue flower.*
5. *Take one **draconic** bloodstone, and one fossilised **karkavore** claw …*

'I can't remember anything else,' said Esme, rubbing at her throbbing head. 'I'll go back again.'

It took two more trips for her to secure the rest of the recipe. After she'd committed it to memory, she travelled back to double check, praying that the elixir would work as well on her mother as it had on Thomas's patient. Without realising it, she overshot a day, and witnessed the boy waking up.

'I'm so thirsty,' said the raven-haired boy, sitting up in bed. 'And so hungry. I was dreaming of Mum's cooking.'

Thomas's assistant ushered the patient's family into the room. They crowded round the boy, weeping tears of joy, offering their heartfelt thanks to Thomas. He gave a modest bow. Meanwhile, Esme scrutinised the recipe, which was still on the bench.

She'd gotten everything right.

Back in the present, she handed the finished page to the keeper. 'As promised.'

5. *Take one **draconic** bloodstone, and one fossilised **karkavore** claw. Grind them into powder and dissolve in the solution for at least seven days, **to immunise** the patient against the deleterious **effects of the next two ingredients.***

6. *Add two roots of devil's rot, and no more than one drop of pure elysium, to dull the patient's **pain as their Gift is stripped away.***

7. *Taken together, the scourge and the rot should be enough to sever **the sufferer's Gift.** As an added precaution, **I obtained a sheath of crimson thrallbark, and** enchanted it with the following words: 'Whosoever consumes **this thrallbark will sacrifice their Gift.' I ground the bark to dust and boiled it in the solution** until it had dissolved.*

8. *The most crucial step: immediately prior to administering the elixir, bring again to a boil, and add one petal of auroral nightshade.*

'You did it!' exclaimed Augustine, after perusing the list. 'You really did it. Now, I suppose, I must fulfil my end of the bargain. We're missing four ingredients. I don't have any auroral nightshade left, draconic bloodstones are extremely rare, I have no idea where you'd find a karkavore fossil, and I've never even *heard* of crimson thrallbark. I'll start preparing what I have.'

'And I'll start looking for the rest,' said Esme.

'Elysium?' Daniel exclaimed. 'You're telling us we need to find some *elysium* for your mother? I don't want to end up in the Citadel!'

'No, no,' Esme reassured him. 'The keeper says he's got some elysium already, but keep quiet about it.'

She and Lillian sat opposite Daniel on the striped, squishy sofas in No 8's living room. Esme's notebook lay on the glass-topped driftwood table between them. She leaned forward and underlined the ingredients they needed in red.

'I've never heard of crimson thrallbark,' said Lillian, peering at the list, 'and auroral nightshade is the rarest flower in existence. I've got no clue where you'd find one.'

'Flowers!' hailed a voice from outside. 'Get your flowers, right here! Half a dozen tulips for five merles!'

Esme's head swung toward the glass doors that opened onto the canal. A peacock-blue gondola, laden with a multitude of flowers—roses, irises, gardenias, and sweet peas—slowed to a stop outside the living room.

Lillian groaned. 'Please, no,' she called through the open doors. 'As you can see, we've already got enough to open our own flower shop.'

It was true: one could hardly see the walls of the living room for all the bouquets everywhere, gifts from Lillian's many spellbound admirers. Miranda had refused to let Lillian throw any of them away, and now No 8 smelled like the inside of a perfume bottle.

'Well, somebody's already paid for these ones. This is 8 Nestor Street, right?' The florist nimbly alighted on the steps outside the living room, handed a bunch of pink lilies through the doors to Lillian, climbed back into the flower-festooned vessel, and departed.

'From "B"?' Lillian read off the card attached to the bouquet. 'There's no "B"s in my music class. Usually, the flowers are from Ricard. He's rich enough to afford them.'

While Esme and Lillian scoured the house for something in which to put the lilies, Daniel stayed in the living room, poring over the recipe for the elixir. When they returned, his eyes were alive with excitement.

'I know where you can find a karkavore fossil,' he said.

Esme started. 'You do?'

'We unearthed some on my last work trip with my dad, when we were helping to restore the sunken ruins of Pallas. But we had to leave them where they were, because a bunch of real live karkavores turned up.'

Esme sat down on his right. 'What *is* a karkavore?'

'They're hideous. They sort of resemble crabs.'

'They don't sound so bad,' said Lillian.

'Crabs almost the same size as us. They can scrape their claws together to produce a paralysing screech. Then, when you're all woozy, they tear you apart with their giant pincers.'

Lillian narrowed her eyes at him. 'You sound like one of those fishermen who swear their catch was'—she extended her arms—'*this* big.'

'Tell that to the person whose eye the karkavore almost took out.'

Lillian cringed.

'Where's that map you drew to find the sirens' caves, Esme?' he asked.

Esme retrieved it from her room and handed it over.

'Pallas is here.' Daniel pointed to a spot on the map. 'In the northwest of Pelorus. Not far from Rowana.'

'That's a start,' said Lillian.

'I have no clue where to begin with the others, though.' He

gestured to a painting on the wall: the original of one of Ariane's illustrations for Professor Sage's compendium. 'If we get really stuck,' he said hesitantly, 'we could always visit the Oracle's Grotto.'

'But no one knows where the grotto is, do they?' Lillian pointed out.

'I do,' Daniel confessed. 'My grandfather left a map behind. He told me to burn it; he didn't want anyone else to end up like him. But I could never bring myself to do it.'

Ariane's painting depicted a cave partly hidden by pitching waves. A faint turquoise light emanated from the entrance. Daniel's grandfather had been obsessed with finding the grotto and speaking to the oracle within, but whatever happened in there had addled his brain and he had died a few years later. A pall hung about the picture, the white lilies either side of it reminding Esme of flowers at a funeral. Daniel was looking as if he had just attended one.

'Thanks for the offer,' said Esme, 'But if the oracle's that dangerous, maybe we should only go there as a last resort.'

'Fine by me,' said Daniel, relief spreading over his face. 'I'd rather deal with a karkavore, any day.'

Esme folded up the map. 'I don't know what I'd do without the two of you.'

Daniel gave a smug smirk. 'I don't know what you'd do, either.'

Chapter Fifteen

After devoting her weekend to mastering her Gift, Esme was forced to catch up on more everyday concerns. She had no clean clothes, she hadn't written to her father in a week, and she'd fallen so behind in her schoolwork that she panicked whenever Rank glanced her way in class. She was meant to deliver a progress report on her history project by Friday and suspected that writing *'I've made no progress'* wouldn't net her a passing mark.

'But you found out *something* at the ghost grim,' Lillian reminded Esme, after a fruitless Tuesday study session in the library. 'Conor said that Mann snapped, moments before he died. Started jabbering about how he regretted everything, how he was "tricked" into it all.'

'I don't know if that's relevant to my topic.' Esme sighed. 'I don't know *what's* relevant to my topic. That's the problem.'

She eyed Lillian's fat notebook on the desk of their reading nook with envy. Lillian had almost finished her entire essay, weeks in advance—mostly because she'd spent every lunch time here in the library, hiding from her love-struck classmates.

'Still,' Lillian urged. 'What Conor gave you … that's new information, isn't it? It might be more relevant than you think. Why don't you study the Battle of the Citadel, see where that takes you?'

Inspiration crystallised in Esme's head. 'Hm … maybe I could use my Gift.'

'Huh?'

'I could go to the site where Mann died, try to look into the past. See if there's any truth to what Conor was saying.'

Lillian paled. 'Er, are you sure that's the kind of thing you want your Gift to show you? Conor said a dozen soldiers ran their swords through Mann.'

A memory flashed into Esme's mind: the water's memory, now her own, of a young Nathan Mare showing Augustine the bruise on his shoulder. Esme had decided not to share what she had witnessed with Daniel and Lillian. She felt she owed it to the teenage Mare, the Mare who hadn't yet committed any crimes, to respect his wishes and keep his confession confined to the keeper's treatment room.

'Augustine warned that my Gift would expose me to all kinds of unpleasant things.' Esme pushed back her seat and stood up. 'Might be better to prepare myself for history's dark side now, rather than get thrown into the deep end later.'

'Well, if you're sure,' said Lillian, stuffing her notebook into her bag, 'we can get a ferry there after school.' She looked out the window to the misty lagoon. 'It's been raining on and off all day, though.'

'Perfect,' said Esme.

'Why?'

'You'll see.'

✄

Ominous clouds accompanied the ferry as it crawled up the eastern side of Esperance, past the Gothic turrets of the university, all the way to the city's northernmost edge. Esme, Daniel, and Lillian disembarked amongst the ruins of the old fortress known as the Citadel: a maze of knee-high blocks of stone, swaying grass, and crumbling doorways that led to nowhere.

The only modern structure was a squat grey building by the lagoon's edge. It led down to the underground part of the Citadel, still intact, now serving as the city's prison. That was where Esme had last seen Celia Skye, who, according to a poll Esme had spotted in the *Esperance Daily* that morning, was now the front runner in the mayoral race.

'I've always admired her.' The glowing opinions of a number of Celia's supporters had been printed beside the poll results. *'She seems so genuine.' 'She's going to win in a landslide …'*

Reminded of Celia's promise to raise the city's sunken northwest, Esme looked out toward the Drowned District. The wrinkled grey water concealed it from view.

People can't drown here, Esme thought, *but places can.*

'Can't see the Drowned District today,' she said to the others.

'Half of the people locked up below us come from there,' Daniel said. 'I reckon Celia's only raising the district so she can catch them more easily.'

'Speaking of Celia …' Lillian glared at the prison's entrance. 'Here she comes.'

A trio of guards had emerged from the drab building. Between them stood a tall woman in a suit the same shade as the blustery lagoon. Despite the wind, every strand of Celia Skye's long, black hair remained perfectly in place. She and her retinue hurried over to the nearest ferry stop.

'She usually goes everywhere by private gondola,' Lillian remarked. 'I guess she hopes being seen on public transport will win her a few votes.'

A black boat with gold trim passed in front of Celia, and then she was gone.

'I don't even do history,' Daniel moaned. 'Why am I here again?'

'To help us find the spot where Mann died,' said Esme.

Lillian was checking her notes from the ghost grim. 'Conor said that X marks the spot.'

'X marks the spot?' Daniel brightened. 'I remember that game from back when we were kids.'

He grabbed a stick and started spouting nonsense words.

'Jibber-jabber, jibber-jabber, dead man now! Jibber-jabber, jibber-jabber, dead man how!' He dragged the stick through a patch of dirt, first one way, then the other. 'X marks the spot!' he barked, violently stabbing the dirt.

Esme darted back. 'What are you—'

'Stick it in his guts, stick it in his eyes,' Daniel chanted, still stabbing. 'Slice him up good, slice him up fine. When his heart falls out, stamp it to the ground.' He stamped enthusiastically. 'When his head rolls off, kick it right around.' He gave a huge kick to an imaginary head.

He threw the stick away and smiled at Esme and Lillian, who looked faintly ill.

'It's an old rhyme,' he explained. 'I've never really thought about it, but maybe it's about Mann.'

'You think?' said Lillian.

Together, they began to scour the old bones of the Citadel, searching for the place where Mann had perished. They parted the grass, peered into cracks in the walls, and scraped away muck and mould on ravaged bricks. No X appeared.

'Let's try looking from up there,' Lillian suggested.

She was pointing toward the largest structure in the ruins: a woebegone watchtower, whose curving brick walls had crumbled into a giant staircase. Taking it slow on the mossy, rain-slick bricks, they helped each other up to what remained of the tower's roof.

'I see it!' Daniel cried. 'Down there. There's your X.'

It had been too large to spot from the ground: a series of rocks laid out in a crude X formation, partially hidden by the wavering grass. Some of the stones were missing, but the general shape could still be made out.

A few minutes later, Esme sat on the stone at the juncture of the X.

'How are you even going to get back to the battle?' asked Daniel.

A gentle rain was pattering down on the ruins, pooling in the hollows of the rocks, flattening the blades of grass into bent, broken soldiers. Esme drew up her hood and held out her hand.

'I'll use the rain,' she said. 'Conor said it was raining back then, too.'

She stilled her thoughts and the waters of her Gift lapped at the edges of her mind.

Show me the day Mann died.

Her head began to pound with pain. A great wave reared before her, threatening to sweep her up in its white-capped curl. Esme ignored it and dove under. She sank down into the deep, focusing as hard as she could on Alexander Mann.

Soon, the thunderous rush of the ocean gave way to other sounds: the war-cries of soldiers, the moans of the injured, the clatter of swords. The smell of petrichor mingled with other scents now, of smoke and sweat and the iron tang of spilled blood.

When the past materialised, Esme saw, and heard, and smelled …

Death.

The Citadel lay in smoking ruins around her, its destruction complete. A leaden sky above crackled with lightning. Esme was in the midst of a battlefield filled with blood and filth, every surface caked with mud.

Soldiers were on the ground, amongst the rocks and the rubble. Some looked as if they were just sleeping; others were contorted into dreadful shapes. Esme tried not to gag at the sight. She covered her eyes, only able to watch through the gaps in her fingers.

Some of the fallen were still alive, pitifully crying out for help. A dozen blue-uniformed swordsmen picked their way amongst the wounded, silencing their cries with swift slashes of their blades.

Esme knew from Rank's textbook which side was which. The men in blue were the soldiers of Esperance, who had barely scraped out a victory in this, the final battle of the Tyrian Wars. Most of the dead and dying wore the red and black of the Tyrians.

'Will you look at that?' one blue soldier spat. 'It's Alexander Mann.'

'By the gods, that's him, isn't it?'

Esme recognised the second voice. It was Conor—Conor from the ghost grim. Now that he was corporeal, Esme could see that his hair had been bright red.

'Mann,' Conor muttered. 'At our mercy.'

A wounded man in red and black, with gold epaulettes to indicate his high rank, lay slumped against a rock to Esme's left. Beneath matted, greying hair was a battle-hardened face, desperate to get back into the fight. Mann's eyes were violent with bloodlust, the veins on his forehead popping, twisting, with the effort of trying to rise.

'You butchered my brother,' snarled Conor, approaching the dying Mann.

'You murdered my wife,' murmured Conor's comrade.

'You slew my son!' cried another man in blue.

Mann leered up at the soldiers with a madman's grin. 'And I'm not finished yet.'

The soldier who'd lost his son lunged at Mann. Conor dragged him back.

'Death's too good for him,' Conor hissed. 'You,' he instructed one of his men. 'Go fetch a healer, quick, to patch this devil up. Slow torment in this life and the next is his due for all he's done. And it still won't be enough to right his wrongs.'

Several moments later, the healer arrived. He bent over Mann and shook his head. 'He's lost too much blood. There's nothing I can do for him.'

Conor grunted. 'Then we'll send him on his way … gladly.'

Conor and his comrades raised their blades. Before they could strike, a silver mist began to issue from Mann. The Esperance troops jerked back.

'What treachery is this?' Conor barked.

The mist rose in pulsing, curling tendrils until it covered Mann completely. Then it blew away on a wind of its own making.

'Where … where am I?' Mann murmured.

His face had altered completely. The bloodlust was gone, replaced by an expression of unimaginable horror. He was staring at something no one else could see, repulsed, revolted, in a swoon of self-loathing. He pushed himself up against the rock, as if trying to retreat from some unseen terror.

'Solister,' he mumbled. 'Solister … What did you do to me?'

His voice rose to a strangled scream.

'*What have I done?*'

'He's seeing his black soul for what it is!' Conor cried. 'Sprung from the loins of Hecate herself!'

Mann started convulsing against the rock.

'What vile spell is this?' he sobbed, rocking back and forth. 'Innocent blood, spilled by my own hand! They told me that this world was free of war; they told me I'd be at peace here! Instead, I have been made an instrument of death … tricked into it!'

His agonised eyes lit on Esme.

'Gouge my eyes out, wraith!' he begged her, while she shrank back, horrified. 'I cannot bear to see!'

'Listen to him rave,' a soldier muttered. 'The spirits of those he has slain have come to take their revenge.'

Mann's strength was almost spent. He was still looking out into the unknown, but his face had changed once more. Now, he spoke with an aching tenderness.

'Belle … all I wanted was to see you once more, in the world beyond.' His glazed eyes had floated up to the firmament. 'Yet now … I am bound for the fires of hell.' He closed them with a final, tortured sigh. 'May the gods … grind me to dust for eternity … for what I have done.'

Mann slumped down, dead.

Conor and his soldiers, who had been stalled by Mann's shocking transformation, now fell on him in a rabid fury. Mad with rage, the soldiers ran their swords through Mann over and over, not noticing that a handful of red and black survivors had recovered, regrouped, and were now preparing a sneak attack.

As the Tyrians charged, Esme rushed away from the scene of devastation, through the waters of time, through the centuries.

Back in the present, she saw pools of blood in place of puddles of rainwater, Mann's form where there was now only stone, smoking ruins now grown over by grass. Gradually, the superimposed images faded away. Eventually, Esme's pulse returned to normal. Tears streamed down her face, mingling with the rain.

'I'd give you a hug,' a sodden Lillian said, 'but it'd just make you wetter.'

It wasn't until they were on the ferry home that she and Daniel began to bombard Esme with questions.

'What exactly did you see?'

'How did he die?'

'Were the ghosts there?'

'All of them,' said Esme, eyes on the rough lagoon outside the rain-streaked windows. 'Conor, and all his men. But they didn't kill Mann. He was already dying when they found him.'

She touched a finger to the foggy glass.

'He was raving, speaking to someone who wasn't there—his wife, I think. And he murmured: Solister, Solister.' She paused. 'Solister … I think it's someone's name. I'm sure I've heard it somewhere before.'

'Was it true, what Conor said?' Lillian asked. 'About him regretting everything?'

Esme nodded. 'He acted like he'd been under a spell, like he'd been forced into doing all those terrible things. But what sort of spell could do that?'

'Well, I've put my whole music class under my sway without even trying. If someone with a powerful Gift actually *wanted* to control someone's mind, manipulate them into carrying out atrocities, maybe they could.'

The mood remained sombre until they reached the Palace Lake, where Daniel started.

'Oh! Forgot to mention, I asked Argent about borrowing a dragon this weekend to go to Pallas. She agreed, on the condition that she comes with us.'

'Suits me,' said Lillian. 'I'd feel much safer riding with Argent than with you.'

'That's what she thought as well. And,' he grinned, 'I showed her the list of ingredients for the elixir, and she thinks she can help us with another one. Draconic bloodstones. They used to mine them in Mt Asha, on Rowana. I've already sent a letter to their den. It's only a few hours' ride from Pallas.'

Chapter Sixteen

Early on Saturday, Esme and Lillian caught a ferry to the dragons' den on Esperance's eastern edge. As the lagoon—and the open-roofed den—came into sight, Esme caught a whiff of acrid smoke.

Inside, the circular structure resembled an ancient coliseum—or perhaps some dark, distant chamber of the underworld. A dozen Scions lazed around an arena that stank of sulphur, its blackened floor littered with charred debris. Spirals of smoke and dust wound through the dragons' home, and the dawn sky lent a glint of red to the creatures' gold, as if the fires of Hades were licking at their scales.

'You're right on time,' said Argent, striding toward Esme and Lillian. 'Daniel's almost finished strapping on the passenger rigs.' She put her scarred hand on Esme's shoulder. 'The moment Daniel said your mother was in danger, I knew I had to help. Anyway, at his level of experience, Daniel really shouldn't be taking on passengers unsupervised.'

'*Thank you*,' groaned Lillian, stretching out her shoulders as if a great weight had just sloughed off them. 'I assume I'll be riding with you?'

'That's the plan. Esme will ride with Daniel on one of our younger dragons, Zephyr. You'll ride on Zephyr's mother, Eudora, with me and Vince.'

'Vince?' Tension drew Lillian's body as taut as a bow. '*Vince* is coming?'

At the sound of his name, Vince called out, 'Hi Lillian!'

Argent went over to help him untangle some gear. She was replaced by Daniel, who'd just finished rigging up Eudora.

'Why is Vince coming with us?' Lillian hissed. 'Did you know about this?'

'Of course.' He smiled. 'It was my idea.'

Lillian couldn't have looked more betrayed if her entire coterie of love-struck admirers had lined up to stab her in the back. 'What?'

'I already told you, karkavores stun their prey with sound. Vince thinks he might be able to disable them with his Gift. When I told him where we were going, he insisted on coming. He'd do anything for you, after all.'

'So we're just *using* him? This is so wrong. Isn't he terrified of dragons?'

'And? This'll teach him they're nothing to be afraid of. Even his mother thinks this trip's a great idea. Argent talked to her yesterday.'

Lillian glanced over at Vince. When he noticed her eyes on him, his face lit up.

'I can't ride with him,' she said desperately. 'I'll come on Zephyr with you and Esme. But no sudden dips or dives—promise?'

'I'll try my best,' said Daniel. He headed off to inform Argent of the change of plans.

Soon, eager young Zephyr and wise old Eudora rose into the blazing dawn sky. Esme's stomach soared with them; although she'd ridden on dragons before, she could never get used to the weightless sensation of taking off. She glanced back to Lillian, who'd gone green.

Once the ride smoothed out, Lillian began to regain her composure. Zephyr and Eudora rode the air currents with ease, over the islands that fringed the silver lagoon, out to the turbulent waters of the Tiamat Sea.

Esme kept a lookout for the portal to Pelorus. She soon spotted a curiously calm patch of ocean, more like the surface of a lake than somewhere in the middle of the high seas. Eudora glided down to the smooth, glassy portal, and Zephyr followed suit, skimming his right foreclaw across the water.

Inside the portal, all sound ceased except for the dragons' wingbeats. Once they were through, the sea grew wild again. Esme glanced back at the rapidly receding portal. It was hard to believe that hundreds of miles had just been cut from their journey. If it weren't for Palmina Island, the sand-fringed capital of Pelorus, rising up ahead, Esme could have sworn they'd only travelled the length of the tranquil square behind them.

Bypassing Palmina, they wheeled northwest toward the region's farthest reaches. After what seemed like hours, Esme spied a pod of whales frolicking beneath them. She craned her neck over Zephyr's flank, eager to see the creatures up close.

If I was piloting Zephyr, she thought, *I'd be down there in a flash.*

At once, Zephyr banked sharply, pointed his snout down, tucked in his wings, and plunged toward the sea. For a moment, Esme forgot that the clips of her rig were keeping her in place. She flung herself forward, flattening herself against Zephyr's spine. As the force of gravity kept her pinned there, terror gave way to pure euphoria.

Zephyr levelled out an inch from the water, so close to the whales that Esme could make out every wrinkle on their grey-black skin. The most distant whale did a half-spin in the air before splashing back down; another started flapping its tail flukes; the closest one shot out a spout of spray as Zephyr glided by.

'Why, Daniel, why?' Lillian croaked, her voice hoarse. 'You promised!'

'I swear, that was nothing to do with me,' Daniel protested. 'Zephyr dropped all on his own.'

Zephyr took to the clouds again, and the wind drowned out any further conversation.

Some time later, the dragons descended toward a circle of sandy islets: an oceanic fairy ring, holding the wider ocean at bay. Esme stared down, mesmerised, at what lay within. Running for miles beneath the water was a dream within a dream, a place of ruined stone and swaying sea grass, of fallen statues and crumbling temples.

The sunken city of Pallas.

Zephyr and Eudora alighted on one of the islets. Lillian and Vince slid onto solid ground, collapsing in dual heaps. Daniel, Argent, and Esme dismounted with a little more grace. The dragons flew off in search of food.

Vince rose shakily to his feet. 'I composed a poem for you while I was up in the air, Lillian. Would you like to hear it?'

'Maybe later,' Lillian said in a resigned voice.

Meanwhile, Esme helped Argent lay out lunch: sandwiches, fruit, chocolate, and rolled-up strips of roasted seaweed.

'Surely this spell's got to fade soon,' Lillian muttered to Esme. 'It's been weeks now. Lillian's this, Lillian's that ... I'm so sick of hearing about myself.'

Daniel reached for a sandwich. 'I am too.'

'Smooth riding on the way here, Daniel,' said Argent. 'I was impressed.'

'So was I,' Lillian conceded. 'Except for that little whale watching excursion.'

'What *was* that?' asked Vince. 'I was so worried about you.'

Argent smirked. 'That wasn't Daniel's fault. It was Esme's.'

Esme almost dropped her sandwich. '*My* fault?'

'Zephyr was a bit bored,' Argent explained, 'and he knew you wanted a closer look, so he checked in with me. I told him to go ahead.'

'What—how?'

'Telepathy.'

Esme's jaw went slack with astonishment. 'Is that a kind of Gift?'

'No,' Argent replied. 'I don't have a Gift, but the Scions chose me to become their dragonmaster. I maintain a constant mental connection with all the dragons in the Esperance den. Anyone can become a dragonmaster. Even Daniel could, one day, if the Scions take a liking to him.'

She paused to watch the water wash gently over the ruins.

'This place is spectacular. I can see why the Pelorusian

government wants to preserve it. Your dad's doing some useful work here, Daniel. The karkavores must have complicated things.'

Daniel nodded. 'We uncovered karkavore fossils on our last trip here, while we were excavating an old temple. Didn't occur to us that there'd still be living karkavores nearby—not until one of our crew was attacked. I wasn't there that day; my dad told me about it afterward.' He squinted into the rippling water. 'Turns out there's a whole colony of them living under the temple, right where we found the fossils.'

He started ferreting around in his bag. 'Here, I brought a set of earplugs along for everyone. They're enchanted to block out all sound—and I mean *all* sound. Just make sure they stay in.'

Vince's eyes were aglitter. 'Don't worry, Lillian. I'll silence those karkavores before they can get anywhere near you.'

'Us,' Daniel reminded him. 'Before they get anywhere near *us*.'

'Oh, yeah … you guys too.'

'Also, it's pitch black inside the temple. Take some ashlight.' Daniel passed round a bag of powder, and everyone took turns coating their fingertips with the glowing ash of wood burned by dragon fire. Soon their hands were five-fingered beacons of green light.

'One last thing,' he added. 'Strap your diver's knives on. They might come in handy. And don't forget, this place is an archaeological site. Let's try not to damage anything too much. Including the karkavores.'

Soon, all five of them were gliding over the sunken ruins, Zephyr and Eudora patrolling overhead. Pallas was a jumble of fallen arches, grand buildings, and the remnants of more modest dwellings. Fish flitted in and out of gaping holes that had once served as doorways and windows. Stone carvings of deities lay in eternal repose on the seafloor.

On the outskirts of the city, Daniel pointed down to a trail of fish skeletons. He and the others followed the path to a half-buried temple in the Corinthian order. Esme helped Daniel and Argent heave at the stone Medusa mounted on its roof. The gorgon, its serpentine locks green with algae, creaked aside, revealing a hole into the blackness below.

Inside the temple, the light of day was a distant memory. Unremitting darkness swallowed all, and the ashlight did little to relieve the tomb-like gloom of the place. Ice threaded Esme's veins. Shut off from light and sound, she sunk down with the others into the temple's inner sanctum, where broken pots and urns encircled an altar dedicated to Poseidon.

Daniel swayed by a large stone slab on the floor. It took all their strength to push it aside, revealing a tunnel that led beneath the temple.

Esme slipped in first. As she swam through the long passage, she felt certain that its walls were narrowing, but they weren't—it was only her own fear, closing in on her. It didn't help that it was freezing down here. She couldn't stop thinking of the secret chamber in the Merle Fountain, the chamber full of cannibalistic stygians, whose ice-cold waters she had braved in search of the pearl.

A shadow crept up the curving wall, and Esme frantically searched for its source. It was only Argent, right behind her. Soon they emerged in a large chamber. Several more tunnels led off into blackness, any one of which might lead to a karkavore's lair.

Daniel swam ahead to the chamber's far corner. When the others reached him, he pointed downward.

Beneath them lay the abandoned remains of an archaeological dig.

Chisels, trowels, and other tools were scattered about the site, as well as the mineralised exoskeletons of a number of karkavores. Some were still embedded into the rock.

Esme dropped faster than a seagull diving for scraps. Daniel and Lillian followed, keeping watch while Esme sifted through the loose fossils. None of the exoskeletons were complete, and the bones were jumbled about at random. Still, Esme could piece together in her mind just how enormous—and terrifying—these creatures were. Daniel hadn't been exaggerating.

The silence around her was deafening. Her instincts, however, howled louder than ever. This place was full of dead things, and things that wanted her dead.

She quickly found three pincers, each as long as her forearm. She stored one in her pack and gave the spares to Daniel and Lillian. They rose back up to Argent and Vince.

One down, three to—

That triumphant thought was cut short by a piercing screech: a high-pitched, strident sound that bore directly into her skull. Her earplugs were doing nothing to drown it out. She twisted round, searching for its source.

The karkavore remained hidden.

Vince was right beside her, his face screwed up in concentration. If he was trying to use his Gift, it wasn't working. He cast Esme a desperate look, then mouthed something unintelligible.

Her thoughts and movements began to grow sluggish. She was trying to kick back toward the exit, but it somehow seemed even further away than before. Meanwhile, the noise was growing louder—closer. It was different now, more discordant.

There's more than one of them.

The karkavores were probably scuttling through the tunnels as fast as they could, making for this chamber and the five-course meal within.

Everything in Esme bent toward escape, but she wasn't swimming so much as sinking. She reached for her diver's knife, ready to chop off the karkavores' every limb.

Her hand wasn't working.

Her brain, reduced to sludge, couldn't figure out how to move her fingers.

So much for Vince's Gift, she thought vaguely.

Something bumped against her. Vince. With great effort, he pinched his thumbs and forefingers together, and held his hands like goggles before his eyes. Then, in what seemed even more nonsensical an action, he started waving his ashlit hands toward the tunnels, as if trying to invite the karkavores in.

Esme knew she must be missing something, but her thoughts were as slow and thick as honey dripping off a spoon.

Finally, it clicked.

He has to see the karkavores for his Gift to work.

With a huge effort, she threw light toward the tunnels. Monstrous shapes lurked at the entrances, waiting for their prey to be subdued, waiting for the right moment to strike. The karkavores' screeching grew to its height: interminable, unbearable, unstoppable.

Then it stopped.

The fog in Esme's brain finally lifted.

Vince's Gift—it's working!

Her senses returned; not in full, but enough to comprehend what was going on. Argent and Daniel were hovering nearby. Lillian, however, was nowhere in sight.

Esme frantically stroked back toward the dig, tailed by the others. Lillian floated amongst the fossils, sprawled out, face up, eyes wide open. Her earplugs must have fallen out—so they *had* been making a difference. Argent and Daniel heaved Lillian up and headed for the exit, while Vince continued to silence the creatures.

As soon as the karkavores realised their prey was escaping, they began to move.

Like cockroaches emerging from cracks in a kitchen, the temple's inhabitants scuttled out into the open. There were five of them, their armoured abdomens two feet across, their muscled legs six feet long. Five pairs of black, beady, glistening eyes were fixed on the intruders. The subterranean creatures were as colossal as the fossils had promised, their claws raised in front of them like boxers' fists.

Instinct took over. Esme grabbed Vince's arm and gestured to the ceiling. If they stayed high enough, the karkavores might not be able to follow—they didn't look like they could swim. He rose with her, eyes still on the karkavores, still working his Gift—

Something clamped around her calf, stopping her mid-stroke.

The closest karkavore had her leg in a vice. The pain was excruciating. Its pincer ripped through her diving suit as if it were made of paper, pulling her back down. Vince yanked her one way, the crab the other, and it felt like her leg was going to part from her body. She squirmed and struggled, kicking at the creature's eyestalks, until finally the claw loosened its hold.

Free at last, she and Vince sailed along, above the grasping claws, then powered through the tunnel to the temple. Soon, Argent's strong arms were dragging them upward and out of the hole at the end.

The moment Vince was safe, Daniel and Argent slammed down the stone slab. No one looked back as they shot up through the temple with Olympian speed, past the altar to Poseidon, past the statue of Medusa, all the way to the water's surface.

Daniel and Argent broke through, Lillian slung over their shoulders.

'Will she be okay?' Esme asked, panicked at her friend's limp, lifeless state.

'It's only temporary,' said Daniel. 'Give her a few hours and she'll be back to normal. What about your leg?'

Blood trailed from the wound, clouding the water around them. Leaning on Vince, Esme only just made it back to the islet. As soon as she set foot on land, the ground came up too fast. The world dissolved. She keeled over and hit the sand with a thud.

She woke to find her leg propped up against a tree. Argent had retrieved some bandages and made a tourniquet—the way Daniel once had with his shirt when a stygian had swiped at the very same leg. This wound was deeper, an endless tide of crimson, but at least the karkavore's claw hadn't been tipped with venom.

'You should feel better once the bleeding stops,' said Argent. 'I'll stitch you up properly when we get to Rowana.'

Daniel had unrolled a long stretcher, and with Vince's help was securing Lillian in place under Eudora.

'We've only got one stretcher,' Argent said as she finished bandaging the wound. 'Can you ride on Zephyr if I give you something for the pain?'

Esme nodded.

Argent offered her a small pastille, and Esme slipped it under her tongue. As the pain diminished, Esme felt slightly removed from the world around her, which suited her fine. The wind was up and it would be a turbulent trip.

The dragons lifted off, the stretcher containing Lillian hanging under Eudora like a kangaroo's pouch. As worried as Esme was about her friend, she couldn't suppress a bemused smile as Daniel spurred Zephyr into top speed.

If there was any time that Lillian might *want* to be unconscious, it was right now, during the bumpy ride to Asha, capital of Rowana.

Chapter Seventeen

By the time Zephyr and Eudora reached Asha, the volcano that gave the island its name and conical shape had vanished under the velvet cover of night. The dragons' den was isolated from the main township and harbour, and a bonfire beside it spun sparks into the air. A ranger waited by the blaze. Upon sighting the Scions overhead, she swung a lantern, waving Zephyr and Eudora into the immense stone barn behind her.

The dragons landed on a floor as black as the cinder sand outside. Amongst the striking orange-scaled Rows, the Scions stood out like two gold coins in a hoard of shining copper. Rhys, the seventeen-year-old son of the Rowanan dragonmaster, hurried over. His long red hair had slipped out of its usual ponytail and hid some of the scars on the left side of his face. He wore a welcoming smile.

'Daniel,' he said as they slid off Zephyr's back. 'Esme. Dad and I were wondering when you'd get here. Where's Lillian?'

A slurred voice issued out from Eudora's stretcher. 'Hurro, Rhysh.'

Rhys bent over Lillian. 'What happened to you?'

'Nothing to worry about,' said Daniel, helping Rhys unclip Lillian's stretcher. 'The karkavores—those creatures I mentioned in my letter—they can stun their victims with a paralysing shriek. Lillian got a full blast of it, but she should be fine by morning.'

Lillian rose to her feet. 'M'awl righhh, really,' she insisted, wobbling a little before falling into Vince's waiting arms.

'I'll protect you, my love,' he declared, oblivious to the sniggers of the Rowanan rangers who had gathered round them.

Rhys raised an eyebrow. 'What's going on there?'

'Lillian cast a songspell on him,' Esme explained. 'Not on purpose, of course.'

'She had a cold,' said Daniel, 'and was singing a little flat. Accidentally cast a spell called "Cupid's Mark". Now her whole music class is in love with her.'

Lillian's efforts to struggle out of Vince's arms ended with her on the floor.

Rhys took the news in his stride. 'So you're a songstress now!' he cried, helping Lillian back up, while Vince, like an overzealous valet, dusted ash off her shoulders. 'Congratulations. It must feel incredible.'

'I'll take her to Tristan's,' said Argent, sweeping Lillian up in her arms. Lillian promptly fell asleep, her head lolling on Argent's shoulder. Vince trailed behind them, exhorting Argent to be careful.

Rhys eyed Esme's leg. 'Maybe you should rest up as well.'

'I'm feeling fine. At least, for now. Argent gave me something for the pain.'

'One of the karkavores nearly got her,' explained Daniel.

'Yikes.'

Their conversation was cut short by the approach of Tango, one of the dragons who had helped Esme save her mother. Her scales glowed scarlet and smoke emanated from her slit-like nostrils. She bent her long neck down in welcome.

'Hi, Tango,' said Esme, lost in her fiery eyes once more.

Argus, slow and regal, padded over to the group. He was the dragon on whose scarred and weather-beaten back Daniel had learned to fly. Argus's scales were the colour of beaten copper and his still-sharp eyes were sunk deep into his wrinkled flesh.

'I'm afraid Argus won't be here for much longer,' said Rhys. 'He's close to his leaving.'

Esme knew, from Argent's class, what that meant. One day soon, Argus would depart the company of the den and find an isolated place in which to spend the rest of his days.

After taking the rigs off Zephyr and Eudora, Daniel, Esme, and Rhys left the den. The dragonmaster's house, with its smoking chimney and steep-pitched roof, awaited them beyond a stretch of black sand. Daniel slung an arm around Esme, and she leaned into him as she limped up the beach.

'You're not complaining much,' he murmured in her ear.

'I will be when Argent gets the needle and thread out.'

'I must warn you, Daniel,' said Rhys. 'Dad's against our whole plan.'

'What exactly is our plan?' asked Esme, who hadn't been privy to Daniel and Rhys's communications over the past week.

'The only place you can find a draconic bloodstone,' Rhys said, 'is in the mines of Mt Asha. But the entrance has been blocked for years—a landslide saw to that. Although some think it might have been caused by Kendra. The miners could have disturbed her slumber, or perhaps she simply got sick of them plundering the mountain's resources.'

Esme had heard of Kendra before: the ancient, venerable dragon who was said to live inside Mt Asha. Her existence was usually confined to folklore and legend.

'Since we can't enter the mines the regular way,' Daniel said, 'I'm going to fly into the mouth of the volcano and access them from within.'

Esme stopped walking, aghast. 'You're *what?*'

'I'm heatproof, remember?'

'I can see why Tristan is opposed,' Esme said in disbelief. 'How do you even know it's possible to get into the mines via the summit?'

'Because I've done it myself,' said Rhys. 'When I was younger … too young to have any sense.' His fingers travelled lightly over the puckered skin on his face. 'I wanted to see if Kendra really existed. I wore one of the rangers' fire suits—it was too big for me, of course—and got Argus to fly me down into the vent. We got all the way through to the mines, but I was woozy from the fumes. Then my mask fell off, and a jet of fire scorched my face.'

Esme clapped a hand to her mouth. 'Do you think it was Kendra?'

'I'm sure it was,' said Rhys. 'But I didn't get to see her. Argus had the good sense to fly me straight home. I was hanging half off him, unconscious, my face a mess. I haven't been up to the summit since … and neither has Dad.'

Dinner was served in a dining hall that took up the entire first floor of Tristan's home. Lit by the red glow of an enormous hearth were several wooden tables, crowded with rangers. Bursts of raucous laughter punctuated loud conversations that seemed always to revolve around dragons, conversations lubricated by ample goblets of Rowanan wine. This house, with its high ceilings, moth-eaten tapestries, and countless spare bedrooms, served as a home not just to Rhys and Tristan, but to half the rangers on Rowana.

'After my wife—Rhys's mother—passed,' Tristan said after dinner, 'the house felt so empty I couldn't bear it. So this bunch decided to move in and keep me company.' He eyed the other tables. 'I plied them with enough food and wine to make sure they stayed.'

The Rowanan dragonmaster was an older, stocky, grizzled version of his son, and sat at the head of the table closest to the fire. He, along with everybody except Lillian—who was asleep upstairs—had just polished off a meal of roasted sea bream and crispy potatoes.

'I'm so sorry,' murmured Esme. 'What was your wife's name?'

'Gwynne,' Rhys answered for his father. 'She's been gone about four years, now.'

Esme put her hand to the pearl pendant on her chest. A skein of sadness wound its way around her heart. The tragedy, she thought, must have split everything into before and after for this family—the way Ariane's disappearance had for hers.

Watching Esme tuck her necklace away produced a curious look on Tristan's face. He excused himself, left the dining room, and returned with a pendant of his own. After tenderly touching the pink gem set in it, he passed it to Esme.

'This isn't a draconic bloodstone,' he said, 'but it's from Mt Asha. I gave it to Gwynne the day Rhys was born. The jewel in it was mined over a century ago.'

After admiring the necklace, Esme glanced at the wall where a tapestry depicted a coiled-up Kendra swathed in smoke. Daniel, Rhys, and Esme had spent the whole dinner trying to convince Tristan to go ahead with the plan, but he'd refused to budge. Now, the sight of the winged beast, spun in vermillion thread, inspired Esme to broach the topic once more.

'Don't you want to see if Kendra's really down there?' she ventured, passing back the necklace.

'Don't start this again,' Tristan groaned.

Argent, who had said very little throughout dinner, cast a knowing look at Tristan.

'I remember that awful year, when you lost Gwynne. You were at your lowest point when Rhys went inside the volcano.' She paused. 'But Rhys was struggling with Gwynne's death, just like you were. You numbed yourself with wine, while he—he acted his age. What were you, Rhys—thirteen, at the time?'

Rhys nodded. Tristan, meanwhile, finished the rest of his wine in one long draught.

'I couldn't bear the thought of losing both of them,' Tristan said, setting down his goblet. 'I was so afraid ...'

'And now you're letting that same fear blind you.'

While Tristan threw her a mulish look, Argent pressed on.

'This situation is totally different. Daniel's older, and a better rider than Rhys was back then. He can't be burned ... and Esme's mother *needs* a bloodstone.'

'That's right, Dad,' added Rhys. 'We didn't help save Ariane to abandon her now.'

The dining hall had almost emptied. Rhys's plea hung in the air, over the crackling fire. Tristan folded his arms, chewing his bottom lip.

Esme waited, on edge, for the dragonmaster's response. Argent casually reached over Tristan's empty plate to pour herself another glass of wine.

'Tristan,' she said, 'I seem to recall you doing a few stupid things in your youth, too. You might have conveniently forgotten, but I haven't. I could tell a story or two.'

'Don't,' Tristan rumbled.

'Fine, I won't.' Her eyes twinkled with secrets. 'All I'll say is that if you had Daniel's Gift, you'd be down in that volcano in a flash.'

Tristan's scowl became a barely concealed smirk, then an involuntary chuckle, then a hearty guffaw. Argent joined in, and their laughter echoed round the empty dining hall.

'Fine,' he conceded at last. 'Fine. We'll go up there at first light … on Argus and Tango. If Kendra is really down there,' he said, rising up to clear the dishes, 'then she won't want any Scions stinking up her lair.'

At dawn the next day, Tango and Argus landed in Asha's crater: a wide, grey, shallow depression on the mountain's summit, strewn with rocks and pebbles. The view from the crater's edge was spectacular, stretching for miles and miles across the waking sea. Where the rising sun met the water, it looked as though the ocean was kissing the sky, sending the first delicate blush of rose into the cheeks of the new day.

Without a word, Argent, Tristan, and Rhys dismounted Argus, while Daniel helped Esme off Tango's back. Lillian and Vince had opted to stay behind. The former was still a little woozy from the karkavores, and the latter had declared it his sacred duty to serve his true love tea and hot chicken soup.

The volcano's vent, stretching a hundred feet across the crater's base, drew everyone with hypnotic fascination toward it. Together, they stood awestruck at its edge, peering down into the mountain's molten heart. Asha's depths were aglow with orange light.

Even though they were a mile above the magma chamber, the mountain's breath, rising up its rocky throat, still generated plenty of heat. It also stank. The sulphurous smell of a dragons' den was nothing next to the fumes emanating from here.

'Do you ever worry about Asha erupting?' Esme asked Tristan, trying to avoid thinking about Daniel's descent.

'Of course. But we've got plenty of warning systems in place, and we run evacuation drills every year. Meanwhile, our farmers get to enjoy the finest, most fertile soil in Aeolia.'

'Incredible wine in exchange for imminent incineration.' Argent chuckled. 'Seems a fair enough trade-off to me.'

The longer Esme gazed into the mountain's innards, the worse her own gut churned. Behind them, the usually placid Argus paced about irritably. He looked about as happy with the plan as Tristan had been the previous night.

'He must be remembering what happened last time,' said Tristan.

The two dragonmasters steadied Argus while Daniel clambered on the old stalwart's back. Ashlight coated Daniel's fingers, and he wore a mask over his mouth and nose to protect him from any fumes.

'Calm down, Argus,' Tristan said, patting the dragon's flank. 'Daniel knows what he's doing … or so I've been told.'

Argus snorted, flapping his wings.

'Don't go down too far,' Rhys called out as Argus rose. 'The entrance to the mines is only a little way down.'

Daniel nodded. 'See you soon!'

High above the crater, Daniel banked sharply, before plunging headlong into the fiery pit.

'Show-off,' grumbled Tristan.

'Come on,' said Argent, her hand on his shoulder. 'I'll distract you with a story or two.'

The two of them strode off, pacing back and forth along the rocks. Argent did all the talking while Tristan cast oblique glances back at his son. Rhys and Esme, meanwhile, stayed by the crater's edge.

'I don't know why I ever went down there,' said Rhys.

'It's hard to believe you did.'

'For some reason … I thought that if I did find Kendra, she wouldn't attack me. But she probably didn't even notice me on Argus's back. That breath of fire—if it was her—was probably just a warning shot.'

His green eyes drifted over to Tango, who'd flown to the opposite side of the crater. Her long neck was slung over the edge, eyes closed as she luxuriated in the heat.

'I've thought long and hard about why I did what I did,' said Rhys. 'I was curious, yes, but I also didn't know how to deal with Mum's death. It was like an empty hole inside me.'

'So you found a literal hole to throw yourself into?'

Rhys sniggered. 'Dumb, huh?'

A rumble came up from below. They shot to their feet.

'I just sensed Argus!' Tristan cried out. 'Daniel's on his way up.' His eyes widened. 'And someone's right behind them. Quick—take cover!'

Esme and Rhys scrambled behind a nearby boulder.

'Watch out!' yelled Daniel.

The old dragon emerged, Daniel crouched low on his back. On Argus's tail was another creature—an enraged, razor-scaled beast, powering up into the daylight.

'Kendra,' Rhys breathed.

Asha's protector erupted from the belly of the mountain, her translucent wings spread in full magnificence. She paused and swivelled round, mid-flight, to examine the humans at the edge of her domain. Her once-brilliant scales had turned russet with age. Her eyes were half-blind from living in the gloom so long.

Her breath, however, still burned just as hot.

Kendra opened her jagged maw and unleashed a surge of flame, charring the crater in a spectacular, lethal display. The back of the boulder behind which Esme and Rhys hid heated up like a frying pan. After spraying the ground once more, Kendra twisted away and chased Argus up into the low-lying clouds.

As soon as she was gone, Esme and Rhys came out from cover. Tristan and Argent ran over to them, and all four watched in open-mouthed fear as Kendra and Argus began to duel. Whenever the dragons passed behind a cloud, it glowed red, lit up from the inside like a giant paper lantern.

As Kendra attacked Argus again and again, Esme could barely breathe. Her heart swung with each dive, each feint, each barrel roll that Daniel executed on Argus's back.

'I'll try to talk Kendra down,' said Tristan. 'She lived in the Rowanan den once, long ago. If she listened to the dragonmasters of the past, she might listen to me.'

He stared up at the clouds, his brow furrowed in fierce concentration.

Gradually, the flashes slowed. Argus swept down first, landing close by. The faithful Row was singed and smoking, but still in one piece. Daniel bowled off him, a tattered bundle of blackened clothing.

'Sorry, Esme.' He ripped off what remained of his scarf. 'I don't have any bloodstones. I couldn't get past'—he pointed skyward—'her.'

Kendra descended from the clouds, coming to a stop at the edge of the vent. She balanced there, one wingbeat away from retreating back into her lair.

Panicked that Kendra would disappear, Esme limped off over the grey gravelled landscape, ignoring the protests of the others. Inch by inch, she advanced across the stones. Sheer determination pushed her forward; sheer terror tried to haul her back. She'd seen what Kendra had done to Rhys. Was she next?

Six feet away from Kendra, she halted, a small figure stranded on the barren lunar landscape, beside a yawning maw and a mighty dragon.

Kendra's mind seared into Esme's in a blaze that almost threw her backward. It took all Esme's strength to stay steady on her feet.

Why did you disturb my slumber?

'I need one of your draconic bloodstones,' Esme said as calmly as she could. 'For my mother. She's trapped in a trance. I'm brewing an elixir to wake her up … and it won't work without a stone.'

A twist of smoke curled from Kendra's nostrils.

You want something from the mountain. Like everyone else.

Kendra hadn't blinked once. Her pearlised eyes bored into Esme's. Then they narrowed, and the dragon bared her yellow teeth.

Why should I help you? How are you any different from the miners who cut out Asha's heart?

Esme didn't let her fear show. 'I'm a protector, like you. So is my mother. We're guardians of the Pearl of Esperance.'

The force of Kendra's wordless inquisition returned, searching Esme's mind. Memories came to the fore, memories of the pearl on the Isle of Mists, the pearl in her mother's hand, the pearl in her own. Memories of its return to Esperance, its rightful home. She was on Tango's back, with Daniel, gliding through the uncharted tunnels under the Esperance lagoon. Keeping the pearl covered from Daniel's eyes, Esme passed it to the only living being who could ensure its safety: the wise, ancient dragon, patron to Esperance as Kendra was to Asha, named Amaris.

Amaris. I know of Amaris. Amaris … let you into her lair?

Hope rose in Esme. She gave a nod. 'Please,' she said. 'Without the bloodstone, my mother will perish.'

Esme's hope was dashed as seven words, seven devastating words, imprinted themselves on her mind.

All perish in the end … even dragons.

Kendra spread her wings, took off, and circled above Esme and the great bowl of Mt Asha. After one last glimpse of the world outside, she slipped back into the volcano's depths.

Esme crumpled to the charred ground, bereft. Moments later, a pair of strong arms wrapped around her, lifting her back up.

'I can't believe you walked right up to her like that,' said Daniel.

Esme buried her head in his shoulder. 'It made no difference. She's not going to give us a bloodstone.'

'I wouldn't be so sure about that,' said Tristan, coming up beside them, along with Argent and Rhys. 'Listen!'

Wings beat up through the vent once more, followed by a tawny blur.

High above Esme and the others, Kendra unfurled her wings. She raised her long neck and let out a great breath of fire, scorching the other side of the crater.

Look amongst the ashes, Kendra's voice echoed in Esme's mind.

With a thundering heart, Esme broke away from Daniel. She stumbled around the vent, all the way across the crater. The others, not quite sure what was happening, followed after her. When they arrived at the black mark Kendra's breath had left behind, they gasped.

Glowing in the smouldering embers were a dozen small red stones flecked with green, like rubies veined with emerald, like tongues of real fire intermingled with enchanted flame.

While Daniel retrieved the stones—they were still too hot for anyone else to touch—Esme swung round to thank Kendra. She was no longer hovering in mid-air. She was over by Argus. They were standing side by side, shoulder to shoulder, both so motionless that they could have been carved from the mountain.

'Seems like they've struck a truce,' said Rhys.

'It's more than that that,' said Tristan. His corrugated features were cut with grief. 'This is his leaving. He's finally decided where to spend the rest of his days. He wants to help Kendra protect Mt Asha from plunder.'

Esme blinked. 'He's going back down there with her?'

Slowly, the group strode over to Argus. With tears in his eyes, Tristan put his ravaged hand to where the dragon's scar met scale. He stayed there a long while, before Argus's forehead met his in a final farewell.

Esme wished she had her sketchbook with her to capture the memory, but the image was already seared into her, as was Kendra's gesture of goodwill.

'Goodbye, old friend,' murmured Tristan.

Kendra and Argus slipped away, into the deep recesses of Mt Asha, to slumber their remaining days away.

Without a dragon to ride back on, Daniel and Rhys decided to walk. Esme would have gone with them if not for her leg. The mood was sombre as she, Tristan, and Argent departed on Tango. The dragon soared down Asha's rough slopes, past the caved-in entrance to the mines, past the grapevines that clung to the rich loam, before landing on the black quartz beach.

As Esme approached Tristan's house, she could hear Lillian singing. It wasn't a songspell, just an ordinary song, but it nonetheless possessed a kind of magic. There was a song in Esme's heart, too: a song of gratitude, happiness, and hope. As she felt for the bloodstones in her pocket, she was glad, very glad, that it had been Argus, and not Daniel, who had stayed behind in Asha's molten depths.

Chapter Eighteen

Drained by a weekend of riding dragons, battling karkavores and watching Daniel plumb the depths of a volcano, Esme practically sleepwalked to school on Monday. By lunchtime, sitting with Daniel, Lillian, and Vince at the end of Pier Two, she was struggling to stay awake. The insistent throb of her injured leg was the only thing keeping her from dozing off.

'No, Vince, I'm fine,' Lillian was insisting. 'I don't need a massage. I should never have mentioned my sore muscles.'

'But my love, you've been through such an ordeal. You should be at home resting right now.'

'How about you give it a rest, Vince?' Daniel groused.

Through half-closed lids, Esme watched a pair of Scions dip in and out of the lagoon. Then her gaze drifted over to Vince, and she idly wondered when—and if—his fascination with Lillian would ever end. He'd been under her spell for about a month now. How much longer could it last?

Then something peculiar happened.

Vince's face twitched, as if he'd been bitten by an ant. The glassy expression he'd worn for weeks began to slip away. He yawned like he'd just woken from a long sleep.

Esme nudged Lillian. 'Look at Vince. Something's happening.'

Lillian shot upright. 'Vince?' she asked, her eyes agleam with hope. 'Is everything okay?'

'I—I don't know. I'm feeling fuzzy. Like I've just had a really weird dream. It's all so … hazy. You were in it, though. A lot.'

'You're back!' Daniel cried.

'Of course I'm back.' Vince looked baffled. 'We all just got back from Rowana, didn't we? But I feel so strange. Did I knock my head or something?'

'No,' said Lillian, 'Nothing like that. But you haven't been yourself for a while, at least not while you've been around me. I'm really, really sorry, Vince. You've been under a love spell.'

Vince blinked. 'A what?'

Lillian drew a tremulous breath. 'I cast it by accident. It was a few weeks back, in music class. We were mucking about, practising songspells, and mine came out all wrong. I had a cold that day and it twisted the spell.' She winced. 'You, and everyone else in the class, have had a crush on me ever since.'

Vince gaped at her. 'You're joking, right?'

'Unfortunately not,' said Daniel. 'We can show you all the flowers you sent her, if you'd like. She didn't keep the love poems, though.'

Vince flung his arms out in a cease-and-desist motion. 'Stop, stop. I get it. I can't hear any more. Why did this go on for so long, Lillian? Why didn't you make it stop?'

'I wish I could have!' she cried, looking just as mortified as him. 'It had to fade on its own. We've been waiting and waiting for it to disappear.' She wrung her hands together. 'Please don't hate me …'

Vince shifted his wounded gaze away from Lillian, toward the Scions, who had taken to the clouds. As he watched them, the cloud on his own brow lifted a little.

'Is that Zephyr and Eudora out there?' he asked.

'I think so,' said Daniel.

'I can't believe I rode a dragon all the way to Rowana and back. And—I stopped those karkavores, didn't I?'

'You sure did,' said Daniel.

'We can't thank you enough,' added Esme. 'Your Gift saved us all.'

The struggle on Vince's face was apparent. 'You're saying the whole class was under the spell? Not just me?'

'All of them,' confirmed Daniel.

Vince rose up and paced the boardwalk. 'Well, the whole school must have had a good laugh behind our backs. I suppose we'll be able to laugh about it ourselves, one day. But right now, it's not funny at all.'

The bell rang. The contrite Lillian stayed put. After one last, long, reproachful look at her, Vince hitched up his backpack.

'I don't hate you, Lillian. I never could. And I guess—it hasn't been all bad. I used to be terrified of dragons; now I can see exactly what you see in them, Daniel. And I hated my Gift, but I don't any-more.' He turned away. 'I'll see you in music, I guess.'

'See you there.' Lillian gave a wan smile.

'Well, that went better than expected,' Daniel said to Esme after both Lillian and Vince were gone. 'But he liked her before the spell. That probably smoothed things over a bit.'

'Can't say the same for Ricard,' said Esme, fearing for her friend. 'Or Liza. She wasn't even under the spell … but she'll be fuming.'

Over the next few days, the fallout from the love spell was swift and brutal. Lillian went around apologising to anyone who would listen. Few did. Anti-tributes flowed onto her desk: dead roses, half-eaten chocolates, scornful limericks instead of starry-eyed sonnets. Most people, however, just cast stony glances her way or muttered insults behind her back. Lillian tried to put on a brave face, but Esme and Daniel saw the true one when they were with her. All they could do was remind her that the worst was over.

'You didn't cast it deliberately,' said Esme. 'Remember that.'

'And there's only a certain amount of grovelling you can do,' said Daniel. 'Accidents happen. Everyone does something embar-rassing at school.'

Esme nodded. 'Everybody who's going to forgive you has already. Just ignore the rest. They'll get over it someday.'

In the one free period they all shared, they were sitting outside the hole-in-the-wall canteen at the end of Pier Four, next to the seniors' study area. Campaign posters for Celia Skye were plastered all over the walls. In one, she was kissing a baby; another showed her beside a model of the Drowned District; in the largest, she was standing on the Palace Bridge, teeth gleaming in a wide, unnatural smile. They looked enchanted, even brighter than the Godstone Palace in the background.

'Why are these posters even here, anyway?' Esme wondered aloud. 'We're not old enough to vote.'

'A lot of the seniors are,' said Lillian. 'I bet Liza put these up.'

Lillian glanced around to make sure nobody was watching, scrabbled in her bag for a marker, strode up to the poster, and blacked out some of Celia's teeth. She added several wrinkles, too, for good measure. As she stood back to admire her handiwork, the thick black lines began to wriggle. They peeled themselves off the poster and flew straight at her, landing on her face.

'Oh, no!' Daniel cried.

Esme hastened to help Lillian wipe off the ink. They were partway through when Liza's clique came sauntering around the corner.

'My spell worked,' said Ricard, looking pleased with himself.

'Of course it did.' Liza glared at Lillian. 'But after all she's done to you, you really haven't gone far enough.'

Liza glanced to her left and right, then flicked her wrist toward the poster. It came alive. The poster sprang at Lillian and curled around her head, covering her nose and mouth. Lillian tried to tear it away, but it stayed there, smothering her, clinging to her face like plastic wrap. She let out a muffled scream.

'Liza!' Esme shouted. 'Stop!'

While Liza's admirers observed without a word, Esme and Daniel tried to rip the malevolent poster away. It was no use—it continued to throttle Lillian. She fell to her knees.

'She can't breathe!' Esme cried, turning back to Liza. 'Stop it!'

'I'm not sure if I can,' Liza said smoothly, a strange thrill on her face. 'It's like Cupid's Mark … it has to run its course.'

Ricard took hold of Liza's wrist and twisted hard. 'Undo it, Liza! Now!'

Liza shook him off and hissed something under her breath. With another casual flick, the paper flew back onto the wall and smoothed itself out. She turned on her heel and marched off with her retinue.

Ricard, however, stayed behind.

Esme and Daniel were on their knees too, comforting Lillian. She was heaving in great gasps of air, punctuated with sobs.

'I'm so sorry,' said Ricard, helping Lillian to her feet. 'The first enchantment—the anti-graffiti spell—that was me. But I had nothing to do with that second spell, I swear. Liza's been going on about wanting to teach you a lesson. I kept telling her you've been through enough. She just … doesn't know when to stop. And it's only getting worse.'

As he stared after Liza, a mixture of pity and anger distorted his classical features.

'I'm done with her,' he muttered.

When Esme arrived at the keeper's clinic the following afternoon, Augustine's treatment room was in a state of chaos. Drawers and cabinets were flung open, their contents in total disarray. Augustine was crouching down, his head stuck inside one of the cupboards under his workbench. He emerged empty-handed, looking grave.

'I'm afraid I've got some bad news.'

Esme froze, fearing the worst. 'What?'

'One of the ingredients for the elixir has gone missing.'

'Which one?' Esme cried. 'Not the bloodstone, or the fossil, right?'

'No.' Augustine waved an arm toward the fireplace in the corner, where a small cauldron simmered over the embers. 'They've been steeping for days. It's the elysium that's gone.'

'How can it just be "gone"?'

'I've no clue. The clinic was locked, and there's no signs of a break-in.'

'Can we get any more?'

'I'm not sure,' said Augustine. 'Let's keep looking here, first. Maybe one of my assistants misplaced it.'

Still fretting over the loss of the elysium, Esme retreated to the rooftop, taking the stairs slowly—her leg was still healing. Up there, she busied herself pulling weeds. Over the past few weeks, tending to the rooftop garden had become one of her favourite duties, on par with sorting through the archives. Both gave her a break from the clamour of the often-busy clinic, and a chance to be alone with her thoughts.

Today, however, she wasn't alone.

Mortimer was hovering over a herb plot at the rooftop's edge, blasting the fragile fronds and stems with his icy aura.

'Stop that! I just planted those last week.' Esme hobbled over to him. 'Shouldn't you be downstairs, bothering patients?'

'Shouldn't you be looking for some elysium?'

She eyed him suspiciously. 'How do you know the elysium's gone missing?'

Mortimer gave a grating, tinny laugh. There was a feverish excitement about him he couldn't quite suppress.

'*You* took it, didn't you?'

'So what if I did? He shouldn't have it, anyway.'

Mortimer glided over to another garden bed, one recently laid with fresh soil.

'Why would you do a thing like that?' Esme cried, stalking after him. 'Why do you even hang around here?' He ignored her, lying prone on the soil like a sunbather. 'Why do you hate Augustine so much?'

Mortimer's expression turned sour.

'Why should your mother be saved,' he hissed, 'when *I* wasn't?'

'What are you talking about?'

'You really don't know much about this place, do you? Why do you think Augustine lets me stay here—why he never banishes me? I'll tell you why: guilt. Pure, unadulterated guilt. I'm his greatest shame … his failed experiment.'

Pouring out of him was a wounded aggression. As it seeped toward Esme, his words from the ghost grim echoed in her ears.

'I'll tell you every detail of exactly what that keeper did to me …'

'You're the one he tried to save, aren't you?' she said softly. 'He brewed the Elixir of Severance … for you.'

The old ghoul gave a bitter nod. 'Decades ago, I went to Augustine and begged him to take my Gift away. It was out of control—I set almost everything I touched alight. Augustine offered to help me master my Gift, but I didn't *want* to. I was terrified. I wanted it gone, before it killed me. So he found the recipe for the elixir, and … you know the rest.'

'I'm sorry about what happened,' murmured Esme, kneeling by the plot. 'But things aren't the same this time. We've got the full recipe and I'm gathering the exact ingredients.'

'Good luck,' he said without an ounce of emotion.

He sank into the freshly turned soil as if it were a grave.

'Augustine's a hack,' he muttered with a mouth full of dirt. 'With his beetles, and his bedside manner, and his pompous ways. He *destroyed* me with his second-rate elixir. Do you really think your mother will fare any better?'

'Not without the elysium.' Esme stood up. 'So hand it over.'

Cackling madly, Mortimer dug into the dirt and retrieved a tiny, pale blue bottle. He glided over Esme to the edge of the roof. She ran after him, as fast as her leg would allow, hand outstretched.

'No!' she shouted.

Mortimer loosed his loudest laugh yet. He uncorked the bottle and tilted it toward the water, two storeys below.

'Please, Mortimer! *Stop!*'

Mortimer stopped.

Or rather, he froze, six feet above Esme, his ghastly grin fixed in place. Only his eyes could move. They darted toward the steps leading up to the roof, where Augustine stood, wielding Willow like a weapon.

'I could hear him cackling from my window,' said the keeper.

Augustine raised Willow, and the precious elysium floated from Mortimer's fingers into the keeper's free hand.

'I'll undo this freezing spell after I've put up a barrier around my treatment room,' he told Mortimer with a scowl. 'You're not getting anywhere near my stores until the elixir's done and Esme's mother is safe.'

Chapter Nineteen

Over prawn and chilli pasta later that week, the conversation turned to Esme's injured leg. Esme and Lillian, unwilling to volunteer the whole truth, managed to convince Miranda that Esme had merely brushed against some unusually sharp coral.

'Still, I wish you'd be more careful, Esme. What you're going through … it can't be easy on your own.'

'She's got me,' Lillian pointed out. 'And Daniel.'

'Yes, but—isn't there anything *I* can do to help?'

Esme swallowed. 'Actually …'

She'd spent a whole week researching the remaining ingredients, scouring the Pierpont Library, the Temple Library, and the keepers' archives, to no avail. She'd even used her Gift, several times, to try to learn where Thomas Agapios had sourced them. All she'd come back with was a headache, worse than ever. At least she knew what auroral nightshade was, but all the recipe revealed about crimson thrallbark was that it had something to do with enchantment. Ricard had never heard of it, and Esme wasn't about to ask Liza.

Miranda, however, worked in the same building as the most powerful, knowledgeable enchantress in the city.

'The next thing we need for my mum … it's something called "crimson thrallbark". If you get the chance, could you ask Celia if she knows where to find some?'

'I'll try,' said Miranda. 'She's hard to catch these days. She spends every spare moment on campaign business. Her intern is always skulking around, though. What's her name, again? Libby? Lisa?'

'Liza,' Esme offered.

Lillian made a retching sound.

'To be honest, I think Celia's avoiding me.' Miranda broke off a chunk of garlic bread. 'It's a bit awkward talking to her, when she knows I support Bernice. But not to worry—she won't be able to avoid me next weekend.'

'The mayoral debate's on then, right?' asked Esme.

Miranda nodded. 'And the Winter Festival. The parade and the debate have been scheduled for the same night. I don't know how I'm going to manage.'

'You always do, Mum,' said Lillian.

'Not without help ...'

Lillian, a prawn speared on the end of her raised fork, eyed her mother with suspicion. 'What do you need?'

'The frost queen for the parade hasn't been feeling well. We might need a last-minute replacement on the day, and her costume would fit you perfectly.'

The fork, prawn and all, clattered down. 'You want me to be in a parade? I've just had people fawning over me for weeks! All those eyes on me—that's the last thing I want! I couldn't think of anything worse. I absolutely won't do it.'

'I'll give you twenty merles,' Miranda said flatly.

'Done,' said Lillian.

After dinner, with a face flushed by chilli, Esme sat on the sofa and flipped through Professor Sage's compendium. She'd lost count of how many times she'd read the whole thing. This time, however, she was scanning it for a mention of auroral nightshade.

She found nothing.

Across the room, above the other sofa, Ariane's painting of the Oracle's Grotto drew Esme's eye. Therein lay the only avenue she hadn't yet explored. In thrall to temptation, she flicked to the relevant entry in the compendium.

The Oracle's Grotto

Of all the Gifts the gods have granted us, the ability to see the future is one of the rarest of all. Those with such a power, known as 'scryers', are afforded only mere glimpses of what is to come. Their predictions are notoriously unreliable, their visions vague and infrequent.

The mythical Oracle of Abyssia is an entirely different sort of seer. Allegedly, she possesses absolute knowledge of past, present, and future, and is bound to answer truthfully any question that is posed to her.

The oracle is said to live in an undersea grotto, somewhere in the vast, empty ocean west of Thalassa: the Abyssian Sea. However, according to those who claim to have encountered her, she rarely grants an audience. Apparently, using her powers takes such a toll that she requires years—even decades—of rest to recover afterward.

No one knows where the oracle came from, or when she was born. Some theorise that she predates the foundation of Aeolia. Others believe that she is a goddess who journeyed to Aeolia from the other world. Others, still, claim that she is the ghost of a scryer who served as adviser to Mikhail and Sofia Agapios. After sending courtiers mad with her knowledge, this scryer was driven out of Esperance, never to return.

Those who seek an audience with the Oracle of Abyssia do so at their own peril.

Esme shut the book, feeling queasy inside. She left the tome on the driftwood table and approached the painting on the wall. The turquoise light emanating from the oracle's home had a kind of beauty to it—the sinister beauty of forbidden knowledge, sequestered beneath the waves.

Early the next morning, Esme took the scenic route to see her mother: down the curving, lagoon-side path at the edge of the Keeper's Quarter, then through the tree-lined garden that led to the Anais clinic's back entrance. As she approached the old building, she saw several of the staff, including Augustine, crowded around outside Ariane's window.

She broke into a run, slip-sliding through the dew-slick grass toward the group.

'What happened? Did someone try to break in again?'

Augustine nodded. 'Through the window. Just like last time.'

Esme, breathless, looked through the glass. Her mother lay there, eyes closed, utterly oblivious to the people outside fretting about her safety.

'Fortunately, my magical protections held. Whoever it was didn't even leave a scratch on the glass. We only know it happened because a nurse heard a commotion outside. Someone battered at the window, then there was a scuffle and a shout.'

'Could it have been Mortimer?'

'No. He was whingeing in my clinic all last night.'

'Augustine!' called a nurse, hurrying over. 'We just found this.'

Clutched between the nurse's gloved fingers was a speckled feather, matted with dried blood.

'That's from the sea eagle,' said Esme, aghast. 'I'm sure of it. Maybe it tried to defend my mother.'

The nurse nodded. 'I thought I recognised this colouring. That bird comes to visit your mother as often as you do.'

'It's not just a regular bird. It's got some kind of connection to my family. Every time I write a letter to my dad, it lands on my balcony, ready to deliver it.'

'Such a loyal companion,' said the nurse. 'I really hope it's all right.'

Shaken, Esme went inside and sat by her mother. Every time the breeze rattled the window, she jumped. Whoever had tried to break in wasn't just a regular thief; there was nothing in this room to steal, apart from her mother's life.

Someone was coming for Ariane … someone determined to do her harm.

❧

Over the next few days, Esme visited the Anais every afternoon. Each trip was more torturous than the last. Her mother looked more and more delicate, more like a fragile piece of porcelain, with each passing day. The keeper's enchantments had, blessedly, kept the window from shattering, but they could do nothing to fortify Ariane, who appeared as though she might fracture beneath the slightest touch.

In art class on Thursday, they studied portraiture. Meera and Seth painted each other in profile, and Esme was surprised to see Seth using a varied palette for the first time ever. Across from them, she painted Ariane from memory, an Ariane so grey and sombre that Miss Merrow asked if Seth and Esme had swapped bodies.

After school, Esme couldn't bring herself to visit her mother yet again. Instead she travelled, by ferry and then by foot, to Conte Canal in the city's southwest.

Last time she'd come here, the place had been deserted, due to the damage wrought by the quakes. It was still just as derelict, the canal's murky waters blocked by the remnants of ruined houses. When Esme reached No 136, she slipped round back into the overgrown garden.

Beyond the snarl of greenery beckoned an old studio with a gabled roof. This was where Ariane had painted the illustrations for the compendium. Inside, on an old wicker sofa under a skylight, a tawny heap of tabby cat purred in sleep.

'Hello there, Hunter,' said Esme.

The haughty feline lifted his head, peered at her, and buried his face in his forelegs once more. The misery of missing Reuben sliced into Esme like a claw.

In the corner of the studio wafted frosty Maria, painting a landscape of rolling green hills. Esme could feel the ghost's curious eyes follow her over to the sink. Paint—old and new—caked the basin, splattering the base and running down the sides.

Esme filled the sink, dipped a hand in, closed her eyes, and plunged into the past.

Soon, the studio was transformed. Warm, diffused shafts of late afternoon sun filtered through the skylight. Hunter—a much younger Hunter—capered round the room, playing with scraps of torn paper. Maria was there, too, looking exactly as she did in the present.

Esme's gaze, however, was fixed only on her mother.

Ariane stood in her corner, painting, bathed in the golden hour's ambient glow; no longer pale and wretched, no longer asleep, no longer separated from everyone she knew and loved. Embracing life, not teetering on the brink of death.

A stream of emotions eddied and swirled inside Esme, a bittersweet draught that intoxicated her.

She drew a long breath and approached her mother, shaky on her feet, eyes brimming. Ariane's long glossy hair framed a curious face. She was peering, with a puzzled frown, at the painting before her: a depiction of the Pearl of Esperance atop a pedestal.

She sighed, turned her head, and looked directly at her daughter. 'Do you think it's finished? I can't decide. But if I don't stop now, it might not dry in time for the exhibition.'

Esme's knees almost gave way. *Can she see me?*

Ariane, however, had been looking right through Esme, at Maria. The ghost and the cat were both on their way over: the latter with his ears pricked, and his tail waving warily; the former with her lips pursed, shaking her head slightly.

'Mum!' Esme called out, trying to bridge the gap. 'Mum. It's Esme. I'm here!'

Ariane shivered. 'The strangest thing just happened, Maria. I thought I could feel my daughter's presence, right beside me.'

She put a hand to her pearl pendant and glanced at the ghost.

'After this exhibition, I'm going home for good. At least until Esme's older. I'll bring her over then … She'll love this place.'

The warmth in her eyes, the warmth in her smile, the sheer vitality of her stirred up that bittersweet brew in Esme once more.

'You can use my paints while I'm gone, Maria. I'd hate for them to just sit here.'

Esme longed for her mother to see her, acknowledge her, speak to her—but just imbibing her presence was more than enough. She stayed in the past longer than ever before, until Ariane packed up and left the studio.

Esme's usual headache started up, but rather than returning to her own time, she found herself mired in a murky sea. She couldn't hear any waves above, just the indistinct gurgles and creaks of the deep. She kicked upward, trying to reach the light, but it was like swimming through mud. Something kept dragging her back down, as if the past was as reluctant to let her go as she had been to leave her mother.

When her Gift finally returned her to the present, Maria's face was inches from hers.

On the spectre's features was written a stern rebuke. Placing an icy hand on Esme's shoulder, the agitated ghost guided her to a table crowded with canvases. She pointed to a painting depicting the ancient hero Orpheus and his departed wife Eurydice.

Esme knew the tale well. Hades, moved by the music of Orpheus's lyre, had allowed the hero to lead his wife out of the underworld, on one condition. Orpheus was not allowed to turn back and glimpse Eurydice during the journey to the surface.

In the painting, the hero's head was turned back, dooming Eurydice with his forbidden glance. Her arm was drawn helplessly toward him, her face an agonised mask of sorrow as she was dragged back into the land of the shades.

Maria took up a pencil from the table, drew something on a scrap of paper, and handed it to Esme.

On it was written three words, in a delicate script.

Don't look back.

Chapter Twenty

When Esme arrived in the palace grounds on Saturday, the Winter Festival was in full swing. The gardens' topiaries were silvered with enchanted frost, streamers hung between sky-high pines, and the Godstone Palace glistening above the treetops looked like it had been sculpted out of ice. Nearby, children swarmed over a magical skating rink, whose crystal surface smoothed itself out after each cut of the skates.

A chill on Esme's shoulder spurred her gaze skyward. There were no clouds, and yet it was snowing. A row of Gifted volunteers, atop the palace roof, were sending flurries of flakes down over the crowds.

As the crystals melted on her skin, she wondered if her mother had ever been to a Winter Festival before. She was almost tempted to use her Gift to check—

Don't look back.

Maria's words were burned into her mind.

In the studio, she'd almost gotten trapped, just like her mother. And her headache had been more severe than ever. Something similar had happened during one of her recent trips to see Thomas Agapios, one in which she'd followed him around for ages. She hadn't found herself trapped in a sea, but the currents had been slower than usual to take her away. It seemed that the longer she lingered in the past, the harder it was to get back. If she wasn't careful, Augustine would have to brew two batches of the Elixir of Severance.

'Esme!' Daniel strode up to her. 'You look like you're a million miles away. Are you here on your own? Where's Lillian?'

'You'll see her soon—in the parade. She's the frost queen.'

He laughed. 'How appropriate.'

Together, they wandered through the palace grounds, drinking spicy hot chocolates and eating light, pillowy fritters dusted with cinnamon. After passing by the frozen Merle Fountain—icicles hung from Poseidon's nose—they stopped before an open-air stage. An illusionist stood on stage right, casting spells on volunteers from the audience.

'Come on up!' With a grand flourish, he summoned a wall of purple flames. 'Who has the courage to walk through fire?'

Daniel smirked. 'Not me.'

A giggling young couple climbed the stairs. As soon as they stepped into the fire, they became nothing but skeletons. The crowd cried out in shock and wonder; the lovers, however, burst into laughter. Spurred on by jeers and whistles, they leaned in for a kiss.

'What's it like?' Esme asked Daniel.

'What—kissing?'

Daniel's dark eyes shone violet with the fire's reflection. He leaned toward Esme and brushed a snowflake off her hair. She flushed.

'Er—I meant—what's it like to walk through fire?'

'Oh. Right. It feels … incredible. A bit scary at first, but once the flames are all around me, it's like I'm slipping through quicksilver.'

The fire up on stage was a different colour now. Green flirted with red: the colour of a draconic bloodstone.

'Hi, Esme!' someone called.

Esme swung round to see Meera and Seth, side by side. Meera, swathed in a shimmering blue sari, radiated joy as she ran up to Esme. Seth trailed back with his shoulders slouched and his hands in his pockets. He was in one of those sour moods that Esme knew so well from art class.

'Enjoying yourself, Seth?' asked Daniel.

Seth's gaze was like a pick striking into ice. 'What's it to you?'

'Oh, shush.' Meera clapped Seth on the arm. 'I'm having fun, at least. Lillian's mum did a great job.' She pointed to the stage, now occupied by another couple. 'If you don't manage a smile, Seth, I'm dragging you up there.'

Seth gave Meera an incredibly fake smile.

'We're going to practise portalling later,' said Meera. 'I'm getting so much better.' She snaked an arm around Seth's to lead him off. 'Enjoy the rest of your night, you two!'

'I don't envy Meera,' Esme muttered once the couple were out of earshot. 'How does she put up with his moods?'

Daniel shrugged. 'Some girls like angst.'

She and Daniel walked on, closer to the lake's edge. The snowfall had ceased and the sky was taking on a dusky hue, awash with mauves, pinks, and violets.

'Look!' cried Daniel, pointing up. 'The parade's starting.'

High above the crowd soared a menagerie of paper creatures, lit from within. Streaming octopi, open-beaked pelicans, ethereal jellyfish, and giant turtles swam through the air, bobbing along without aid of string or motor. Trailing them were stranger creatures, drawn from the abyssal depths, like vampire squids and spider crabs. One crab dipped down close enough that Esme could have touched one of its long, spindly legs, if she wanted to.

After her run-in with the karkavores, she wasn't tempted at all.

A Scion swooped down on broad wings and roared. A huge jet of flame flared across the water, razing it red. It was Eudora, with Argent on her back. The crowd whooped and cheered as Eudora took off into the skies and floats began to sail across the lake.

Figures clothed in blue and white rimmed the first float's perimeter, using their Gifts to create a spectacular interplay of fire and ice. Dancers spun between the plumes and spouts with practised ease. Coming up next were three see-through gondolas, each vying for the lead. Banners billowed out behind them: 'Esperance Glassblowers' Guild'.

So many floats followed that Esme lost count. One of the most impressive was an enormous kraken, made of coral, kelp, and seashells. Its tentacles stretched from the edge of the plaza to the isle. The biggest cheers of all, however, were reserved for the final float: a miniature recreation of the Godstone Palace, shimmering with a thousand diamond drops of frost.

Lillian wasn't recognisable at first. She'd been swallowed by an elaborate blue dress, and a silver crown half her height shadowed her features. She sat on a throne beneath the palace's tallest tower, waving at the crowd. Catching sight of the awestruck Esme and Daniel, she cast a sly wink their way, before trailing the rest of the floats out of sight.

After crossing the Palace Bridge, Esme and Daniel lined up outside the town hall for the mayoral debate. The ice sculptures closest to the hall were rather ominous, compared to the rest of the festival decorations. Six-headed Scylla reared up on Esme's right; the fanged maw of Charybdis yawned to her left.

'Politics,' grumbled someone in the crowd. 'Always a choice between the lesser of two evils.'

'Except in this case, there's three,' remarked someone else.

Daniel chuckled. He and Esme edged forward, into the shadow of a skeletal stallion with empty eyes and draconic wings: Pegasus, if he'd died, decayed, and been resurrected by Hades.

'What does the dead horse represent?' Daniel muttered to Esme.

'Trevelli's career!' shouted someone behind them.

From the outside, the town hall resembled an Ancient Greek temple, long and narrow and fronted with fluted Corinthian columns. Blue banners bedecked the building's arched entrance.

The hall's interior was just as opulent, with detailed frescoes and bas reliefs adorning the walls. The place was packed. Amongst the crowd, Esme and Daniel spotted some familiar faces: Vince, Fern, and Meera, sans Seth.

Up on stage, the candidates had already been introduced. They each stood behind a wooden lectern, shuffling papers and smiling out at the crowd.

Beneath his thatch of silver-grey hair, Everett Trevelli's brown forehead shone with sweat. Beside him, Celia Skye, in an indigo suit, looked as cool as ever. Liza fixed an oversized brooch to the chief enchantress's lapel, wished her luck, and darted offstage.

Bernice Chen, in a dark green pantsuit, was instantly recognisable to Esme. She had the same round face, kind eyes, and cropped black hair as her son. The moderator, however—journalist Basil Roth, whose columns Esme followed in the *Aeolian Eye*—looked nothing like Esme had imagined. While she'd expected an owl-eyed, crusty old newshound, the real Basil Roth was youthful and nimble, with a shock of ginger hair and a sharp, decisive air. His first question was directed toward Bernice.

'Ms Chen. You've built your platform around a promise to support Esperance's disadvantaged and downtrodden—particularly those with less practical Gifts, or with no Gifts at all. How exactly do you intend to achieve this?'

'Well, for one thing, Basil, I don't think any Gift is less "practical" than another. However, there are certainly Gifts that are less …' Bernice's eyes flicked Celia's way, 'monetisable.'

Celia's hand, with its nails like black opals, fiddled with her lapel. Her brooch, a silver trident studded with emeralds, resembled the enchanted one with which she pried the truth from prisoners in the Citadel.

'I intend,' said Bernice, 'to enact stricter laws preventing enchanters from monopolising the city's industries. I also believe we should increase taxes on Esperance's top earners, almost all of whom are enchanters.'

Loud boos—and cheers—rippled through the crowd.

'Enchanters pay a pittance compared to what they make,' Bernice insisted. 'If they contributed their fair share, the council would have enough money to raise the Drowned District without the Skye Foundation—'

'Bernice,' Celia interrupted, 'with all due respect …'

'Ms Skye,' said Basil, 'I caution you against speaking out of turn.'

Celia brushed her brooch and glared at Basil. He fell silent.

'With all due respect, Bernice,' she carried on, 'we enchanters, just like the Giftless, don't have a choice in what we are. By disadvantaging us, aren't you just tipping the scales the other way?'

Murmurs of accord echoed through the hall. Esme was surprised to find herself nodding, too. She didn't actually agree with Celia—in fact, she'd thought it rather rude, the way Celia had cut in—but for some reason, everything Celia said sounded ten times more convincing than it should. Daniel, Fern, Meera, and even Vince were nodding too.

'I'm not disadvantaging enchanters,' said Bernice. 'I'm making things fairer for everyone.'

'Mr Trevelli,' said Basil, turning to the final candidate. 'Do you have anything to say on this topic?'

When Trevelli smiled, his affable, courteous persona radiated forth, reminding Esme and the crowd why he had managed to hold onto the mayorship for so long. 'I'm sure we can find a middle ground between helping the less privileged Gift-wise, and keeping enchanters happy,' he said. 'Without raising taxes.'

The debate continued in this vein for almost an hour: Bernice passionately standing her ground, Celia interrupting at every turn, Trevelli always suggesting something 'in between' but offering few practical solutions for anything. Despite agreeing with everything Bernice said, Esme found herself applauding every time Celia spoke.

When Basil had finished quizzing the candidates, he opened questions up to the crowd.

'Ms Skye,' said an elderly lady waving a cane. 'Seven years ago, an earthquake struck the Citadel and countless prisoners escaped under your watch. Including killers like Nathan Mare—'

'Nathan Mare did nothing wrong!' someone shouted.

The old lady pointed her cane at Celia. 'How can you have let these criminals run free for so long?'

Celia, unfazed, flicked a speck of dust off her blazer. 'Any questions about the quakes,' she replied, with a pointed glance at Trevelli, 'would be better directed toward my colleague, the current lord mayor. They occurred under his tenure, after all.'

The candidates were barraged with question after question about the earthquakes, about the Drowned District, about elysium abuse, and most frequently of all, about taxes.

'Ms Chen,' complained one bewhiskered man, 'I can't afford to pay more than I do already!'

'I'm not proposing higher taxes for *everyone*. Ask one of my aides for a pamphlet after the—'

'And don't forget to pick up one of mine,' Celia cut in, 'if you want to see all the flaws with Ber—*gurk*—'

Mid-sentence, Celia went mute.

'Celia,' Bernice said calmly. 'That's the twentieth time you've talked over me tonight.'

Celia was still trying to talk, but no sound came from her lips. No one in the audience could figure out why she'd been struck silent—nobody except Esme and the other Pierpont students, who had witnessed the Chen family Gift before.

'Ms Chen!' Basil barked, finally realising what was going on. 'We established that no Gifts were to be used during the debate!'

'What do you call what she's doing, then?' Bernice pointed at Celia's lapel. 'That brooch of hers—it's enchanted! She's using it to sway the audience! Even I want to vote for her when she shines it my way!'

The audience, already in a fervour, erupted into a frenzy. Half of them were infuriated that they might have been subject to an enchantment; the other half seemed outraged by Bernice's accusation, and chanted Celia's name.

'*Celia! Celia! Celia!*'

'What,' croaked Celia, her voice returning, 'a baseless allegation!'

A woman screamed at the back of the hall.

Esme swung round to see a ghostly apparition flying through

the open doors: a spectral creature that gleamed in the moonlight. Desiccated wings, like those of a dragon, carried it toward the stage. Those in its path cried out and ducked for cover. As its jagged frame passed in a glacial rush over Esme's head, she realised it wasn't a ghost.

It was the ice sculpture from outside—the undead Pegasus, come to life.

Trevelli hid behind his lectern. Bernice shouted in shock. Celia just stood there, speechless, as the horse soared directly toward her.

With a menacing thud, it landed on the stage.

Celia screamed, turned on her heel, and tried to run, but it was too late.

The horse folded her in its wings, lifted her high above the stage, and dropped her back down in a pitiful heap.

While Liza, Basil, and the other candidates ran to assist her, the creature took flight again. As it passed overhead, on its way out, Esme saw something glitter in its mouth—something that then fell to the ground, to be lost amongst the frantic audience.

'Quiet down, everyone!' Basil shouted over the chaos. 'Quiet down! There's no need to panic. We'll evacuate the hall, row by row, starting with those at the front …'

When Basil instructed Esme's row to leave, she didn't depart right away. She dropped to her knees and hunted, beneath the chairs, for the glittering object dropped by the Pegasus. She suspected it was Celia's brooch, but it was nowhere to be found.

Outside, the Esperance police were trying to make sense of what had happened. The Pegasus, immobile once more, was being torched with a fire Gift, lest it come alive again and attack someone else.

'Esme!'

Esme twisted back toward the town hall. Fern had come out of nowhere. Celia's brooch shone in her palm.

'You found it! I was looking for it, too!'

'Lillian's mum works on Bernice's campaign, right? You should give it to her. They can have it looked at by an enchanter, see what kind of spell's inside it.'

'Er …' Esme gestured to the uniformed officials nearby. 'Shouldn't we give it to the police?'

'Why would you?' said Daniel. 'The police all answer to Celia.'

Fern pressed the brooch into Esme's hand. 'I can't believe she'd resort to such a dirty trick. I might pay her office a visit sometime … after hours.' She glared at the palace across the water. 'See if there's anything else she's hiding.'

As soon as Fern vanished, Lillian turned up, wearing normal clothes but still in her dramatic frost queen make-up.

'Did you two see what happened?' she cried. 'Mum and I only caught the last few minutes. We got here just as the Pegasus swooped in and—where is Mum, anyway? Is she okay?'

'She's over there,' said Daniel, pointing into the distance. 'With her suitor.'

'With her what?'

Miranda sat on a bench beneath the plaza's enormous wind harp. Beside her, arm around her shoulder, was one Basil Roth.

Daniel smirked. 'Looks like those flowers from "B" weren't for you after all.'

Lillian sprinted toward her mother, Esme and Daniel trailing along behind her.

'Lillian!' Miranda cried, reddening as she extricated herself from Basil's embrace. 'Er, this is Basil.'

'I know who he is, Mum!'

'I was going to tell you sooner, but—'

Lillian wrapped her arms around her mother. 'I don't care. I'm happy for you.'

They broke apart, Miranda looking very relieved. She glanced over at the police, still milling around the town hall's entrance.

'That Pegasus gave me such a shock,' she said. 'Who would ruin the festival by doing a thing like that?'

'The festival wasn't ruined,' said Esme. 'You did an incredible job. Is Celia okay?'

'She's fine. Bernice's chances were ruined, though,' Miranda moaned, sitting back down beside Basil. 'Nobody's going to care about whether Celia was manipulating the debate now. They'll just feel sorry for her.'

'I imagine they'll accuse Bernice of orchestrating the attack,' said Basil.

'Such a cynic,' said Miranda, a little fondly.

'You'd become a cynic too, in my line of work.'

Esme, meanwhile, produced Celia's brooch. Basil stopped defending his journalistic ethos to gawk at it along with Miranda.

'How did you get a hold of this?' Miranda breathed.

'The Pegasus dropped it.'

Miranda secreted the brooch in her pocket. 'I'll pass it on to Bernice. Better in her hands than with the police. Oh! I almost forgot. I've got something for you, too.'

'You do?'

'I finally got the chance to ask Celia about crimson thrallbark.'

'And what did she say?'

'She reacted very oddly. Didn't seem to want to talk about it. But I needled her until she gave in. She said there was only one place she'd heard of where a crimson thrallbark tree grew: in the garden inside the lost villa of the enchanter, Solister Greaves.'

'However, no one's been able to find the villa since Solister's time. And he lived almost three centuries ago. I'd never heard of him before.'

Esme had. She was sure that Alexander Mann had mumbled the name 'Solister' in his final moments. She'd seen it even earlier than that, she finally remembered, on a suspiciously empty folder in the keepers' archives. While Miranda looked apologetic, Esme was ecstatic to have a lead once more—even one as thin as a long-dead enchanter and a lost villa.

'That's more than enough to go on,' said Esme. 'Thanks, Miranda.'

Chapter Twenty-One

At dawn the next day, Esme woke to the sound of Daniel's voice, calling her name from the balcony. Startled, she crossed to the shutters, opened them, and darted back in fright.

'Strap yourself in,' said Daniel. 'We're going to see the oracle.'

He sat astride the thorny back of Zephyr, whose golden scales were muted in the grey light.

'The oracle?' Esme went out onto the balcony. 'We said we'd only go to her as a last resort!'

'Seems like last resort time to me.' Daniel rose and fell a foot with each massive wingbeat. 'You need two more ingredients, we've only got a lead on one of them, and somebody's tried to attack your mother—twice.'

'I'm sure there's another way.' Cold wind bit at Esme's cheeks. 'I know the grotto's the last place you want to go, after what happened to your grandfather.'

'I can handle it. In fact, I kind of want to ask the oracle something myself. So hurry up—I'm not supposed to bring dragons this low over the city. Zephyr's already knocked off a couple of roof tiles.'

'Does Argent even know you've taken him?'

He grinned. 'I told her about the trip we took under the city, on Argus, to hide the—' Esme shushed him. 'Well, I didn't say *why* we went, but I told her how narrow and twisty those tunnels were. After that, and the volcano, I've got a free pass to take Zephyr out whenever I want.'

'Fine,' Esme relented. 'Exactly how far away is the Oracle's Grotto?'

'Halfway round the globe.'

'Uh … what about school tomorrow?'

'I know all the right portals to take. We'll be back by day's end. You might want to wear your diving suit—you're going to get wet.'

Tucked into the corner of Esme's wardrobe was a backpack full of ranger's gear that Argent had lent her. It contained a number of ropes and clips, some ashlight, a compass, a sea-silk blanket, and a diver's knife. Esme got changed and slung the backpack over her shoulder. After leaving a note for Lillian, she hurried back outside, where Daniel was trying to stop Zephyr from lashing his tail against the next door neighbour's chimney.

Strapping herself into Zephyr's passenger rig was second nature now, and it wasn't long before he was carrying them over the rooftops, out toward the lagoon.

Beyond the lagoon's placid waters, the Tiamat Sea was flexing its muscles. Zephyr headed west, skimming low over the wild waves.

After an hour or so, a portal came into sight. The waves smoothed out, and Zephyr soared over the patch of quiet water. They emerged into a foggy rainstorm. When the mist briefly shifted to reveal another portal, Zephyr floated right past it.

'We're not going that way?' asked Esme, wiping wet hair out of her eyes.

Daniel shook his head. 'If we took that portal, we'd end up near Thalassa. Where I grew up.'

'I'd like to go there one day.'

'I'll take you sometime. Once your mother's woken up.'

After half an hour's cruising, Daniel leaned over Zephyr's side. A long, silver rope glimmered just below the surface, twisting in and out of view.

'What *is* that?'

'That's the next portal, one that will take us even further than the regular kind. Hold on tight,' he said with a grin. 'To use it, we've got to go under.'

Esme took a deep breath, purely out of habit, just before Zephyr dove beneath the surface. Daniel reached for the silver rope, now trailing alongside them. It wrapped itself around his fist, then pulled them forward so fast that Esme's surroundings became a blur.

Several minutes later, they were on the other side of the world.

'We're here,' said Daniel. 'The Abyssian Sea.'

Under a soft purple sky raged a fierce black sea, the kind of sea that could swallow whole ships without compunction, leaving not a single splintered mast or shred of sail behind. After another hour of flying, Daniel every so often consulting his map, Zephyr approached a scattering of barren basalt rocks, huddled together like they were trying to stave off marauders.

'Sailors used to think this place marked the end of the world.'

The rare note of fear in Daniel's voice made Esme, for a moment, feel like the sailors' tales were true. She hunched over on Zephyr's saddle, shivering.

As the dragon touched down on a wide stone pillar, Daniel pointed into the surging waters. Twenty feet away, waves washed over a rock shaped rather like a bald man's head. Beneath a craggy nose was a gap-toothed smile. Water rushed in and out of the entrance. A faint turquoise light emanated from within, just as it did in Ariane's painting.

'It's not too late to turn back,' said Esme, as she and Daniel dismounted Zephyr.

Daniel shook his head. 'I want to do this. I want to speak to her. It's just … this place was in so many of my nightmares. Too many.'

Together, they stood on the edge, staring at the water pulsing a dozen feet below.

'If it helps,' Esme squeezed Daniel's hand, 'I'm just as scared as you are.'

'I know. You're squeezing so hard, I don't think I'll ever be able to use my hand again.'

Embarrassed, Esme let go, but he drew her hand back into his. There they stood for a long while, drawing courage from each other, before finally taking the plunge.

Instead of fighting the waves, Esme and Daniel let the current carry them toward the bald man's head, through his crooked smile. Inside the grotto, a system of tunnels awaited them. They didn't need ashlight to find their way. All they had to do was follow the pulsing turquoise light. Together, they swam through endless undersea corridors, choosing whichever path glowed brighter. The further they went, the more beguiling the light became—and the warier Esme grew.

The depths shallowed and they clambered out into a sea-worn chamber. The light was so strong here they could hardly bear to look at it. It concentrated into an orb, which hung before them in the centre of the cave.

A disembodied female voice resounded in Esme's head.

Here you will find the answers you seek.

The mesmerising orb flickered with each word, and Esme realised that the light that had led them here was the oracle herself. She shone with a terrible beauty, a beauty that inspired both awe and avarice. Esme hadn't felt such a hunger for knowledge—for power—since she had first laid eyes on the Pearl of Esperance. As she stared up at this being who transcended time, she understood why the ancients had brought gifts and made sacrifices to their gods.

My power wears thin. Three questions … no more. Then, I sleep.

'I can hear her in my mind,' Esme said to Daniel.

'I h-h-hear her too,' he stammered, looking sickly in the oracle's light.

She stepped forward. 'I'm looking for a flower called "auroral nightshade". Where can I find it?'

The oracle transmuted into water, a shimmering, quivering, perfect sphere. Light still pulsed beneath her rippling skin, marbling the walls blue.

The boy named Seth, the oracle whispered, like a river murmuring over pebbles. *He will lead you to the nightshade.*

Esme faltered. That wasn't the answer she'd expected.

Why would Seth know anything about auroral nightshade?

The vague suspicions she'd harboured about him all term rose to the forefront of her mind. She remembered the day that Seth had used his Gift on Lillian … the same Gift the pale-faced boy on the Isle of Mists had used on her mother. Her violent dislike for him, that inexplicable aversion she felt whenever he was in her presence, stirred again in her now.

'Who *is* Seth?' Esme blurted out without thinking.

'Esme, no!' Daniel cried. He turned to the oracle, and pleaded, 'Can we take that one back? I don't think she meant to ask it—'

It was too late. Like a fierce wind, the oracle's truth rushed into Esme's mind.

Seth is the son of Nathan Mare and Celia Skye.

Esme's jaw dropped. She stumbled backward. Daniel caught her and guided her to a corner of the chamber.

'Just a moment, please!' he called to the oracle. 'We need to figure out what we're going to ask next …'

I am well accustomed to waiting, human.

As soon as they reached the wall, Esme slumped back against it. The damp rock was ice-cold—exactly what she needed right now. Unable to think straight, she drew panicked breaths, while Daniel's firm grasp kept her from collapsing altogether.

It was Seth. Seth was the boy with Mare on the Isle of Mists.

'What are we going to ask her now?' Daniel jabbered. 'I came here with one question, but now I've got a boatload—and—and they're all about Seth! Is he in league with his father? Is that why he's in all your classes? What about Celia—is she working with Mare, too? And you still need to ask about the crimson thrallbark …'

Esme glanced up at the waiting oracle.

'I don't want to waste our last question on Seth,' she said. 'Or the thrallbark. We can find those answers elsewhere. Ask your question, the one you came here for.'

'But—your mother—'

'I asked my questions,' Esme insisted. 'It's your turn.'

Daniel nodded. He went up to the oracle.

'My grandfather, Leo, came to you many years ago. Afterward … he was never the same. Can you tell me what happened in here that day?'

The oracle transformed from water to fire. Esme shrank back from the sparks shooting out of the flaming orb. Daniel stayed right where he was, the whole cavern glowing red around him.

Leopold Swift asked me to reveal to him the day that he would die.

Daniel drew a sharp breath.

'That … knowing that would drive anyone mad.' He clenched a fist. 'And you just told him, knowing what it would do to him?'

Many minds have been shattered by my knowledge, intoned the oracle. *Your grandfather is far from the only human to have asked me such a foolish question. When I answer … they call me evil. They call me cursed. But I am not cruel. The truth is cruel, and I am bound to tell it.*

'But you *are* cruel!' Daniel cried. 'Don't you feel a thing for the people you've made suffer? Empathy? Remorse? *Anything?*'

Three questions, the oracle replied. *Now, I rest.*

Then there was only the tang of salt and the sound of the sea hammering the rocks.

Esme and Daniel were back on the rock pillar, unharmed, twenty feet from the entrance to the grotto. She wrapped her arms around her distraught friend. When they broke apart, Zephyr landed clumsily beside them, sending part of the pillar crumbling into the ocean.

'Yeah …' Esme stroked the dragon's warm neck. 'I don't know how we got out of there either.'

Esme couldn't focus in art class on Monday. She was still reeling from the oracle's revelations about the boy standing just a few feet

away. Every so often, Miss Merrow would come round, frown at the blank page before Esme, and offer a few words of inspiration. Thus far, she'd failed to inspire Esme to even pick up her pencil.

Esme could only stare at Seth, who was gluing shards of broken mirror to a black canvas, creating a shattered skull.

How did I never notice how much he looks like Mare?

The bell rang, and the classroom emptied out for lunch. Seth lingered, packing away his paints. When he was done, he cast a fur-tive glance at Esme and opened his mouth, as if to say something to her. Her features remained immobile. He shrugged, tucked his bag under his arm, and made to leave.

'Seth,' she plucked up the courage to say. 'Wait a minute. I need to talk to you.'

He dropped his bag back down. 'About what?'

'I …' Her gaze fell to the blank page. 'I don't even know where to begin.'

'Well,' he said, closing the distance between them, 'I know where we can start.'

Disconcerted, she looked up. His face was uncomfortably close to hers.

'What are you doing?'

He leaned even closer. 'Nothing you don't want.'

All at once, like the flaming skeletons on stage at the Winter Festival, he kissed her. She froze, shocked beyond belief, barely registering the feel of his lips on hers, as if all the blood had drained from them, robbing them of the sensation of touch. Then every-thing exploded inside. A towering inferno of rage, containing not one single spark of attraction, blazed through her.

She slapped him hard across the face. He jolted back.

'Ouch!' he rubbed at his cheek. 'I thought—'

'You thought *what?*'

He sounded genuinely confused. 'You were staring at me the whole class, and then you said you wanted me to stay back! I thought we'd finally—'

'*Finally?* How could you be so blind? Meera's the one who likes you, not me!'

'Meera and I are just friends!'

A tiny choking sound came from the door to the pier.

Esme swung round. Meera was there, in the doorway, dark eyes shining with tears. She must have been there the whole time, waiting for Seth to leave with her. She took one grief-stricken look at him, then sprinted out of sight, her blue-and-gold shawl trailing in the wind. Esme wanted to chase after her, but she had to deal with *him* first.

'I wanted to talk to you because … I found out who you really are.'

Seth went very still.

'You're the son of Nathan Mare and Celia Skye. You were there, with Mare, on the Isle of Mists. You tried to kill me and my mother. Those scars on your hands, the bruise on your face when we met. They're from that day.'

He didn't deny it. He didn't say anything, in fact. He just froze, the way she had during the kiss. The accusation hung there, turning slowly in the air.

His gaunt cheek twitched.

'I never tried to get rid of you and your mother.'

'So you're saying that wasn't you on the Isle of Mists?'

'I—I was compelled. My father made me. It's all a blur; I can hardly remember that day.' He was flailing, clearly coming up with excuses on the spot. 'How did you even find out about my parents? I haven't told anybody. Not Meera. Not even the principal knows.'

'I went to see the Oracle of Abyssia.'

'The oracle? I thought she was a myth.'

Esme was tired of his talking around the point. 'Why did you enrol here, anyway? Just to stalk me? Is Mare keeping tabs on me through you? Trying to find out where the—'

She stopped herself from mentioning the pearl. Meanwhile, Seth was starting to get as fired up as she was.

'I shouldn't have to explain myself to you. My personal life is none of your business.'

'You *made* it my business,' Esme shouted, 'when you tried to kill me, then tried to *kiss me!*'

In a flash, she recalled the puddle outside her mother's window, after the first break-in. There had been no rain the night before, no way to explain that water on the pavestones—apart from, maybe, an ice Gift.

'Did you try to attack my mother at the Anais clinic?'

'I'm nothing like my parents,' Seth hissed. 'I hate them, both of them. What happened at the debate—that should be enough to show you how I feel about them.'

'What do you mean, at the debate?'

'The Pegasus,' he snarled, as if she'd been stupid not to figure it out. 'That was me. I used my Gift to control it and attack my mother, to tear that enchanted brooch off her. She can't be in charge of Esperance. She has enough power already.'

'You used … your Gift?'

What Seth had just described seemed way beyond the limits of a regular ice Gift. He wasn't just conjuring icicles and hailstones and frost. He'd brought a statue to life, possessed it, bent it to his will.

A horrifying thought occurred to her.

'Did your father experiment on your Gift … the way he experimented on mine?'

There was a glimmer of something like shock in Seth's eyes, replaced in an instant by the anger of earlier.

He turned his back on her, strode off, and slammed the door on the way out. Esme was left alone in the studio, in amongst the paint and dust, staring at her wild-eyed reflections in Seth's shattered skull.

Chapter Twenty-Two

'I still can't believe he kissed you,' Lillian said, shaking her head as she and Esme descended the stairs at No 8. It was Tuesday morning, and they were about to leave for school. 'Did you at least get him to tell you where to find the nightshade?'

On the landing, Esme paused before her mother's painting of the house, viewed from the bridge over the canal outside. Seeing that painting, the day she first arrived here, had been enough to convince Esme that Aeolia wasn't a dream. Seth's kiss, however, still felt like a protracted nightmare.

'I didn't get a chance to ask.' Esme marched down the next set of stairs. 'He just got angry and stormed out. I don't know how I'm going to bring it up again.'

'Well, you can't avoid him forever,' said Lillian, fixing her hair in the hall mirror.

'I know.' Esme opened the front door. 'I'll talk to him when I've calmed down.'

If I ever do.

But Seth wasn't at school that day—or the next, or the day after that. So Esme turned her attention to the other ingredient: the crimson thrallbark. She asked the school librarians, Augustine, and even Professor Sage if they knew anything about Solister Greaves, but none of them could help her.

Alexander Mann, however, had mentioned the enchanter in his final moments.

'Solister … Solister … What did you do to me …'

The deadline for her history essay was coming up fast, and

Mann and Solister clearly shared a connection. Maybe if Esme tried to finish the essay, she would stumble upon the very information she needed. After school, she scoured the Pierpont Library for books on the Tyrian Wars, carried them to a reading desk, and dumped them down with such force that several floating lights darted away in fright.

The books before her were mostly thick hardbacks, a few of which bore the name 'Dr Percival Rank'. She saved those for last and leafed through the rest. One tome, titled *A Brief Overview of the Tyrian Wars*, was anything but brief. After wading through it for an hour, she finally found an entry that mentioned the elusive Solister.

Many historians neglect to include the powerful enchanter, Solister Greaves, in their accounts of the Tyrian Wars. Whether this is due to a dearth of proof as to his influence, a lack of academic rigour, or a fear of him attacking from beyond the grave, one cannot say. There is certainly enough evidence to indicate that Solister was a real person who lived during the wars. Yet nobody has been able to determine when he was born, when he died, or where he lived.

Eyewitness accounts abound, however, of a great villa hidden in the northernmost mountains of Tyria. The villa's courtyard is said to house a garden in which Solister cultivated rare magical flora, including a crimson thrallbark tree. Sources indicate that Solister may have used the thrallbark's mind-altering properties to influence the outcome of the Tyrian Wars. His possible motivations, however, remain a mystery.

Esme read the passage three times over before flipping to the next page, where she saw a painting of a gloomy mansion atop a cliff. It was hewn of black stone, and its steep Gothic roof was covered in snow.

The only known depiction of Solister's villa—unknown artist, 1702

Scrutinising the illustration, Esme didn't notice that somebody had come up behind her until their shadow fell across the page.

'Hi, Esme,' said Meera.

Esme froze.

Meera had been avoiding Esme since the day of Seth's kiss. Even now, Meera's gaze dropped to the floor, unable to hold Esme's for long.

'I wanted to talk to you about … you know,' Meera mumbled. 'What happened.'

'Sure,' said Esme, choosing her next words carefully, lowering her voice so the library's other patrons couldn't hear. 'Meera … I didn't want Seth to kiss me. Not then, not ever. You have to believe me.'

To her surprise, Meera gave a slight nod.

'I believe you. After he did—what he did—I stayed outside the art block and heard your whole conversation through the wall. I'm sorry I didn't come and talk to you sooner. It just … took me a few days to get over it. To realise just how much he'd kept from me.'

She slumped down next to Esme.

'He never told me any of that stuff he told you. Anything about his mother and father, or his life outside school. You think he would have mentioned being related to Celia Skye, seeing as she's one of the most famous people in the city right now, but every time I asked about his parents, he clammed up.'

'No wonder,' said Esme. 'If it got out that Celia had a secret son with Nathan Mare, it could destroy her campaign. I'd love to leak it to Basil Roth.'

'Why don't you?'

'Seth's got something I need. Information that could save my mother.'

Meera nodded. 'I couldn't care less about Seth kissing you,' she insisted, although the strain in her voice told Esme otherwise. 'All I want to know is … did he really try to hurt your mother?'

Esme sighed. 'He was definitely there on the Isle of Mists, where

I found her. But I don't know whether to believe what he said, about … not being in control, about everything being a blur. For all I know, maybe he was under the influence of crimson thrall-bark, or something.'

Meera looked baffled. 'Crimson what?'

'Crimson thrallbark,' Esme repeated, pointing to the relevant part of the text.

Meera, backed by a trio of floating lights, examined it over Esme's shoulder.

'I need some for the elixir, and the only lead I have is that this enchanter, Solister Greaves, grew it in his villa.' She turned the page to show Meera the illustration. 'His mythical villa in the middle of nowhere. I guess I'll have to go to the Temple Library tomorrow and find out more.'

'Or you could leave it to me.'

'What do you mean?'

'If that painting is an accurate enough representation, then I might be able to portal you there. I've gotten so much better at it. I can activate my portals at will and hold them open much longer.'

She reached for the open book. Esme shielded it from view. 'You don't have to—'

'I want to,' she said with such purpose that Esme felt compelled to hand the book over. 'Anything to take my mind off Seth.'

Chapter Twenty-Three

On Saturday morning, Esme, Daniel, and Lillian met up with Meera in Burner Lane. A new piece of street art dominated the alleyway: a square-metre recreation of Solister's villa, looking three-dimensional thanks to Meera's magic. The portal's filmy surface rippled as if that part of the wall were made of water.

'You must have stayed up all night to finish this,' said Esme. 'I can't thank you enough.'

'Oh, it only took a couple of hours. Anyway, I hope you've all put on enough layers. It's freezing on the other side. I popped through before, to test it.'

Everyone was wearing warm jackets except for Meera. 'You're not coming with us?' Esme asked.

'If I do, the portal will close in an hour or so. I need to stay here to hold it open … and make sure no one else goes through.'

With a last glance of gratitude, Esme stepped into the painting, followed by Daniel and Lillian.

Compared to the last time she'd travelled through one of Meera's portals, the journey to Tyria was incredibly smooth. Esme's eyes had barely adjusted to that in-between space of blind darkness before another world, a realm of pure white, spun into existence.

The three friends stood at the base of a steep hill, at the top of which Solister's villa perched like a carrion crow. Snow fell hard and fast; wind whipped at their faces. Esme shielded her face and dug her shins into the snow, trying her hardest not to slide back down the slope.

After a vertiginous climb, they reached the house. Solister's villa was hewn of huge stone slabs, with few windows. Stark branches clawed at the walls, leafless stems that curved in tortured, twisted shapes. Square, black, and grim, the house was as unforgiving and unyielding as the storm that raged around it.

Esme climbed the front steps and stood before the double doors. She touched one of the knockers—and jerked back in fright.

Desolate faces bulged out of the wood, eyes wide, mouths yawning. In voices low and high, in pitiful moans and screeches, they warned:

'*Stay away! Stay away!*'

Esme drew a deep breath and twisted the door handle. A glacial gust threw her to the side, threatening to sweep her off the porch. She held on tight while Daniel wrapped his arms around her waist, and Lillian clung to both of them. The wind abated, and the shrieking doors swung open.

Gasping, Esme, Daniel, and Lillian fell into a drawing room. The double doors slammed shut behind them.

The air inside was sweet and nauseous, a cloying smell, as if someone was trying to cover up more unpleasant odours. In the dim light streaming through the grimy windows, Esme could see the outlines of old armchairs and tables covered with dust cloths.

A floorboard creaked so loudly she jumped.

'All right.' Daniel lifted his foot. 'Floor's not very stable. Watch your step.'

A narrow corridor led off from the drawing room. Partway down it, the sickly sweet smell faded and the underlying odour broke through. It wafted around Esme, seeping into her mouth and nose, coating her throat, sliding into her lungs. It was the stench of things best left buried.

Esme looked down—and screamed.

A second ago, the floor had been covered with mouldy old carpet. Now it was a graveyard of human bones. She was standing on a leg: a leg stripped dry of flesh.

Lillian shrieked. 'Daniel!'

Daniel had sunk, waist-deep, into the skeletal remains. He gave Esme one last fearful glance before going under.

'Daniel!' Lillian cried. 'Daniel, come baaaa—'

Lillian didn't finish. She was gone, too.

The bones gave way under Esme, and everything went black.

Esme was ensconced in darkness, swathed in shadows so thick it was like being smothered in velvet. She couldn't see; she could only hear soft, poisonous whispers, whispers that curled around her like smoke from a funeral pyre.

You should never have come here.

'Let me go!' Esme pleaded.

You'll never see your mother again.

The voice's poison spread through Esme's veins, tainting her with doubt. 'I will,' she mumbled. 'I'll wake her up—'

It's too late. It's too late …

She squeezed her eyes shut. The darkness behind her own eyelids was preferable to that of this prison.

'Esme?' a petrified voice cried. 'Esme!'

'Lillian!' Esme shouted back.

'Th-th-there's a voice,' Lillian stammered. 'It's telling me—that I should never sing again. That my songspells will only cause chaos and destruction.'

'Don't listen to it!' called Daniel, somewhere far away. 'The same voice is telling me that this is the day I'll die. It says it can see the future, and this is the day. Can't you see, it's playing on our fears. The oldest trick in the book!'

His tone turned to one of mockery.

'Go see the Oracle of Abyssia! She'll teach you a thing or two about scaring people. Now bunk off and leave us alone.'

The shadows dispersed so quickly, it was as if they had never been there at all.

Esme was back in the corridor, on the mouldy carpet, no bones in sight. Lillian and Daniel were only a few feet to her left.

'Come on,' said Daniel, unfazed by what they'd just been through. 'Let's get going.'

They hurried along the hallway until they reached a rectangular room, housing an oval table and a dozen chairs. Axes and claymores hung on walls plastered with maps, charts, and portraits of Tyrian generals.

Esme's eyes were drawn to the largest map. Countless rusty pins were stuck into the parchment. The pins were joined together by lengths of crimson thread, revealing a web of conquest all across Aeolia.

'I recognise all these places,' she said. 'They're all … Alexander Mann's battles in the Tyrian Wars. Look, there's the Citadel, but with a black X instead of a pin.'

'Because Mann lost,' murmured Lillian.

'I found Solister,' said Daniel, over by one of the portraits.

Esme crossed to the painting and stood beside Daniel, stumped by the figure in the golden frame. She'd seen that friendly face, those royal-blue eyes before.

'That's not Solister. That's Thomas Agapios. What's his portrait doing here?'

'It *is* Solister. Look. It says it on the plaque.'

Daniel was right. Esme sat on one of the dusty chairs, at a loss.

'That's *definitely* Thomas. I've seen pictures of him, and I've seen him through my Gift.'

'Does it really matter?' said Lillian. 'Let's just find the thrallbark and get out of here.'

'It matters,' Esme said in a small voice, 'because Thomas Agapios is the one who created the Elixir of Severance.'

Lillian paled. 'Oh.'

Esme glanced at the far wall. She hadn't noticed the tall, wide windows at the room's end. They looked out into a snowy courtyard, filled with flowers that resembled throwing stars, berry bushes with withered limbs, thorned brambles, stinging nettles, and, in the centre of the garden …

A leafless tree with bark the colour of blood. Even through the glass, it radiated malevolence.

With great trepidation, Esme crossed the room, Daniel and Lillian in tow. One of the windows, latticed with ebony, was in fact a glass door. The catch on the door was rusted, but she managed to force it open.

Ankle-deep snow blanketed the garden. The blizzard had abated, but the atmosphere outside was just as menacing as it had been inside. Carefully, Esme, Daniel, and Lillian trudged toward the thrallbark tree, wary of more traps. The tree's trunk was scored with scratches from where the bark had been hacked away.

'Wait. I—I'm not so sure about this,' said Esme. 'What if Thomas isn't who we thought he was? What if he was like Mare—experimenting on his patients, poisoning them under the guise of helping them?'

'Use your Gift,' suggested Daniel. 'See if you can find out whether Thomas can be trusted.'

'Okay.' Esme swallowed. 'But I'll have to be careful.'

'Why?'

'I've noticed lately that the longer I stay in the past, the harder it is to get back.'

Lillian blanched. 'You're not going to get stuck, are you? Like your mother?'

'Not if I'm quick.' She scooped up some snow and let it melt in her hand. 'And I will be. There's no way I'm going to hang around here any longer than I need to.'

When time's currents slowed, Esme was back in the garden, under the crimson thrallbark tree. A tall, slim man stood in the tree's shadow. He wore a long robe with fur cuffs. He turned his square face, set with blue eyes, toward Esme.

'Thomas?' she blurted out. 'Thomas Agapios?'

The man's eyes narrowed. 'Is someone there?' he barked.

'Just me, Solister, Your Grace,' called a voice from inside the house. 'Your faithful servant.'

The latticed door to the garden creaked open. A man in Tyrian military attire emerged. He was dragging a prisoner, bound in chains. The captive, bowed over with grief, looked more husk than human.

'I present to you … Alexander Mann.'

Mann glanced forlornly up at his surroundings, before the Tyrian soldier yanked on his chains, heaved him up the last few feet, and dumped him on the ground.

'Where am I?' Mann moaned.

Solister paced back and forth, his eyes fixated on Mann.

'Tell me … where did you find this one?'

'Half dead on a battlefield, surrounded by his fallen comrades. The only survivor of an ambush. I nursed him back to health, and he told me his wife and child were butchered by the enemy. After I healed him, he said he wished I'd let him die … But there's no use putting this one to waste. He's a top-ranking officer, a cunning tactician … a perfect weapon.'

Solister's thin lips twisted into a smile. 'Very good. Just as I instructed. A strategist, full of sorrow, anger, and above all … talent.'

He glanced down at Mann.

'You otherworlders … it's incredible, the way you wage war, without the aid of Gifts. I look forward to seeing you in battle.'

'No,' Mann gasped as realisation slowly dawned. 'No, I'm not fighting for you. I've seen enough. I'm done with war—'

'I'm afraid you have no choice in the matter.'

Solister drew a knife from his cloak and began to scour the thrallbark tree.

'The thrallbark's effects are more potent when it has something to work with,' said Solister, hacking away at the trunk. 'Grief, sorrow, rage, trauma … all can be transmuted into vengeance, into bloodlust. With the right combination of ingredients, I may be able to make the thrallbark's influence last this man's entire life. If all goes well, he could even lead the Tyrian army to victory.'

His eyes shone with desire.

'I'll use him to eradicate the royal family … including my brother.'

'Your brother?' repeated the baffled Tyrian soldier.

'Thomas Agapios,' Solister growled. 'He was born four minutes before me … so he was named as keeper. But I, too, possess a part of every Gift. I, too, possess a divining rod. The gods meant for both of us to be keeper … yet I was banished from Esperance, all because Thomas didn't approve of my *methods*.'

He waved a hand around his poisonous garden.

'Mann will be the instrument of my revenge.'

Esme had seen enough. She closed her eyes, willing the vision to fade. Back in the present, she slumped down in the snow, head in her hands.

'Are you all right?' asked Daniel.

'Twins,' she breathed. 'Thomas and Solister were twins—and Mann was innocent. Solister was orchestrating the whole war behind the scenes. He was pure evil.'

Daniel whistled. 'At least he left something useful behind.'

He gestured toward the thrallbark tree.

Lillian shivered. 'Let's take some and go. I can't wait to get out of this horrible place.'

Daniel, who'd worn his diver's knife, reached down to unstrap it. 'Want me to do the honours?'

Esme shook her head. 'I saw how Solister cut the bark in my vision.'

Knife in hand, she approached the tree. Blood-red branches speared out, as if to ward her away. Swallowing her fear, she stood before the trunk and made the first cut, deep and wide.

Her left shoulder seared with pain, worse than when the karkavore had clenched her in its claw.

She peered under her top. What she saw made her pale. Her shoulder had split open like a sliced melon. The gash was the same length as the one she'd just inflicted on the tree.

She pressed her hand to her mouth to stop herself from screaming.

'What is it?' called Lillian.

'Nothing.' Esme kept going. As she scoured the tree, using shallower cuts now, she felt each and every incision. By the time she'd twisted off a sheath of bark, she could barely stand. Shaking, she staggered toward Daniel and Lillian, holding her hard-won prize. Spotting the blood trail staining the snow, they ran up to her.

'*Esme!*'

'Solister cut the tree just fine …' Her eyes glazed over. 'He must have enchanted it … to stop people like me from …'

Dropping the bark, she fell face-first in the snow, world turning white—then black.

Chapter Twenty-Four

Esme woke to the sight of royal-blue eyes staring into hers. An image of blood-specked snow flashed before her. She gave an involuntary shudder.

'You're safe, Esme,' Augustine said in a soothing voice. 'You're in my clinic. Your friends brought you here and stayed while I treated your wounds. They wouldn't leave until I told them a dozen times you'd be all right.'

She glanced at her injured shoulder, wincing. It was swathed in bandages. 'The tree—it cut me back—'

'I know. Daniel and Lillian explained everything while I stitched you up. They did the right thing, stopping the bleeding before you got here. If they hadn't …'

He didn't finish. Instead, he fetched her a glass of water and helped her off his treatment table into a chair.

'How bad is it?' asked Esme. 'Can I see?'

He lifted the bandages, allowing her a glimpse of her stitched-up shoulder. The first—worst—cut ran along the top. A series of shorter, shallower cuts beneath ran beneath, where she'd scoured the bark more tentatively. An ugly graze blemished the area just below her collarbone.

She pointed to it. 'That must be from when I tore off the bark.' She bit her lip. 'I just wanted to get it over with.'

'Your friends also told me what you unearthed with your Gift,' Augustine said. 'Astonishing … absolutely astonishing. So the rumours about a secret sibling were true. All record of Solister must have been expunged from the archives. What a despicable man to inflict such agony on you, even from beyond the grave.'

'At least he's long gone now,' said Esme.

She was surprised by how calm she sounded—and felt. The keeper must have given her something to dull her senses. She watched, feeling vaguely dislocated, as he crossed to his bench to grind the thrallbark with a mortar and pestle. She was glad to see it being crushed to dust.

'You've made some monumental discoveries with this Gift of yours,' he mused as he worked. 'First, stygians in the Merle Fountain. And now, you've exonerated Alexander Mann. I'm sure there are many more to come ...'

Esme bowed her head. 'I'm not so sure. There's ... something wrong with my Gift, Augustine. I found out that if I stay too long in the past, it's hard to get back to the present. *Really* hard. And when I return, my headache is worse than ever.'

The pestle paused. 'That's disturbing. How long is "too long"?'

'I don't know. Longer than an hour, maybe.'

'*Mare*,' he growled. 'This has to be due to his influence. I've never had any problems leaving the past; the currents always carry me back smoothly. When did this happen?'

'About a week ago. I went to Mum's old art studio and used my Gift to watch her paint. I lost track of the time. When I tried to leave, I got swept back into the ocean and I was stuck there for ages. The water was as thick as tar.'

'Yet ... when you looked into Solister's past, today, you had no difficulty returning?'

'No, but I wasn't there for long. It was easy not to linger. Solister was so awful, I couldn't wait to leave him behind. But when it comes to Mum, I—I ...'

She choked up, tears stinging her eyes. The keeper laid down his pestle, its tip coated in a film of red dust. He took the seat opposite, compassion softening his features.

'In my vision, Mum was talking to Maria, the ghost who hangs around the studio. Mum was smiling, full of life, so different from the way she is now. Her eyes were sparkling … the way I remember them. But when I finally returned to the present, Maria warned me not to "look back". She sniffled. 'I suppose ghosts know, more than anyone, what it's like to live in the past.'

Augustine's tone grew pensive. 'It is not easy to sit beside a loved one, who may be on the verge of death, and think about their feelings rather than your own. Maria is right: the best thing you can do for your mother is be here, with her, in the present.'

Esme held those words close to heart when she visited the Anais the next day. Maria was there, too, floating beside Ariane's bed. In the subdued light of sunset, there seemed little difference between the living woman and the dead one. They were both as grey and insubstantial as each other.

'Just hold on a little longer,' Esme whispered, clasping her mother's hand. 'We're almost there.'

Esme had long given up trying to couch her letters to her father in words that wouldn't send him running for another glass of whiskey. They read more like diary entries now, detailing everything she went through, no matter how unbelievable it might sound. Her father probably wasn't even reading them anyway. It just helped to pretend that one of her parents knew what was going on, and putting everything down on paper made it easier to deal with.

Dear Dad,

Things over here are getting really hard. I'm worried Celia's going to win the election, become lord mayor, and I don't know what she's planning. Probably something awful. I'm weeks behind on my schoolwork as well. Because I'm doing everything I can to save Mum, and it still doesn't feel like enough.

I saw her tonight, and she was like a ghost. I'd know. I've met ghosts, and she seems closer to the next world than any of them.

I only need one more ingredient for the elixir—a petal of auroral nightshade—but to get it, I have to talk to Seth (that boy I told you about—turns out he's Celia and Mare's son.) I don't know what he's going to tell me, but I haven't got a good feeling about it.

I know it's futile to try to convince you to come here, but I'll try anyway. Believe me: if this was a world I'd made up in my head, things wouldn't be so dire. Picton almost seems like a paradise, compared to what's going on here. Please, come over. This might be your last chance to see Mum.

Love, Esme

Esme drew the Spindrift rock pool at the bottom of the letter and folded it into an envelope. She waited a long time for the sea eagle to show up, but it never came. She hadn't seen the messenger bird, she realised, since one of its bloodied feathers had been found outside the Anais.

She left the letter out on the balcony, hoping the bird would pick it up overnight.

It was still there the next morning.

'Seth!' Esme cried, sprinting up Pier Two on Monday morning.

He was leaning—more like loitering—against the wall outside the art room. As Esme approached, he glowered at her. 'I thought you never wanted to talk to me again.'

She doubled over, clutching her shoulder, then lifted her head and braved his eye.

'The elixir for my mum. It's almost complete. But there's one last thing I need. A petal of auroral nightshade.'

If she'd had any doubts about the veracity of the oracle's prophecy, the expression on Seth's face right then would have wiped them all away. His narrowed eyes grew wide with shock, then contracted again with disgust.

'So … you're just here to use me.'

'You know where I can find it,' Esme pressed. 'Don't you?'

He folded his arms. 'Who told you I could help you?'

'The same person who told me who your parents are.'

'Oh, right.' His words, thick and acrid, dripped out of him like bitter resin. 'The all-knowing oracle.'

He put his hands in his pockets, turned around, and started walking away.

'Seth!' Esme cried, so loud he stopped short. 'Without the nightshade, my mother will never wake up. This is important!'

Seth swung round. 'What's important,' he hissed, his eyes edged with tears, 'is that I never go back to my father's laboratory, ever again.'

Esme blinked. 'Your father's laboratory?'

'That's where the nightshade is.'

Students up and down the pier were staring, ears pricked by the loud altercation. Seth glared at them, then ushered Esme into the empty art room.

'I've always been a stain on my family,' he said bitterly. 'I've always been my parents' darkest secret. My mother's parents—they were patriarch and matriarch of one of Esperance's oldest, most powerful enchanter families. They would never have approved of their daughter marrying Mare. Not only is he not an enchanter … he doesn't have a Gift at all.'

He sat down on Miss Merrow's desk.

'So … I was born out of wedlock. Tutored at home, kept hidden, while my parents rose to some of the highest positions in society. Celia Skye, chief enchantress; Nathan Mare, renowned scientist, fellow of the University of Esperance. Then, when I was eight years old, my father went to prison. That's when everything went wrong.'

Esme scowled. 'Your father killed people. He ruined lives. You're talking to one of the subjects of his experiments. He was imprisoned for good reason.'

'I wish he'd *stayed* in prison! I wish he hadn't broken out during that earthquake. Because the night he escaped, he went to see my mother, convinced her to let me leave Esperance with him. He told her it would ruin her reputation if people found out about me. He told her he'd take good care of me. And she believed him.'

A shadow passed over his face.

'He built himself a laboratory, far, far away from Esperance. And then he resumed his experiments. I was his lab assistant, but not by choice. I had nowhere else to go. When I turned thirteen, my Gift came in, and I became his weapon, too. I helped him … acquire new subjects, and … subdue them. I helped him coax information out of people. I … attacked you and your mother on the Isle of Mists.'

Esme clenched a fist. 'So you admit it.'

'I told you, I can't remember it very well. I felt woozy the whole time. I could have been under some sort of spell. Everything's … fuzzy.'

He rubbed at his temples, as if struck by a fierce headache.

'After you stopped my father from getting the pearl, he became obsessed with you. When he found out you were going to study here at Pierpont, he bleached my hair and enrolled me, too. He told me to befriend you, to keep tabs on your mother.'

Esme was reeling. 'Why are you telling me all this?'

A muscle on his neck twitched.

'Because the past few months here at school, with you and Meera and everyone else, they've made me realise what a normal life is, how much I've missed out on. So I swore I'd never see my father again.'

Esme's heart sank. Not just for herself, and her mother, but for him. She had no idea how much of what he'd just told her was true, but it was impossible to fake the level of anguish in his eyes.

Seth slid off the table and strode toward the door. He shoved it open. The salt of the lagoon cut the air.

'Just … tell me how to get to the lab myself, then,' she pleaded. 'You don't need to come with me. I'll go there on my own.'

'If you do, you'll get caught.'

He was standing in the doorway, half in shadow, half in sunlight.

'I told myself I'd never leave this city again, that I'd never go back to that hellhole of a laboratory.' He sighed. 'But if going back means I can atone for what my father and I have done to you, then …'

He gave a minuscule nod.

'Really?'

He gritted his teeth. 'We'll go tomorrow, if your mother really can't wait. Don't bother coming to school. Meet me on Laertes Island, first thing in the morning.'

'Why Laertes?'

'It's out of the way. We can portal from there.' Seth's nostrils flared. 'Meera still hates me, but if I tell her it's for you, I'm sure she'll agree to help.'

Chapter Twenty-Five

The next morning, *Talia* crossed the blustery lagoon, and the thick foliage of Laertes Island rose into sight. Esme, Daniel, and Lillian disembarked and started trudging up the sand.

'My parents think I'm taking a day off school to help Argent in the den,' Daniel said. 'She's covering for me. That's the only way I could explain taking *Talia* out so early. What did you two tell Miranda?'

'That we had to go find an ingredient for the elixir,' Esme said.

Lillian shrugged. 'Technically, it's the truth.'

At the far end of the beach yawned a rocky overhang. Esme glimpsed Meera inside, painting on the wall. Seth stood beside her.

She entered the cave with trepidation, expecting the air to thicken with tension between Meera and Seth. Meera, however, was immersed in her work and seemed totally comfortable with Seth's presence.

'Add a little more grey there,' Seth suggested, and Meera nodded, daubing the corner of the painting with her brush. 'Okay, that's enough.'

From Seth's description and a sketch he'd provided, Meera had painted a narrow, utilitarian room, with a single bunkbed and a chest of drawers. A silver circle signified a porthole on one wall.

Seth turned to greet Esme and scowled at the sight of Daniel and Lillian. 'What are you two doing here? Shouldn't you be at school?'

'We're coming, too,' said Lillian.

'No, you're not! This is a stealth visit—in and out, as quick as we can. The more of us come, the more likely we'll get caught.'

Daniel eyed the painting. 'Looks like you're already planning to portal Esme straight into a prison cell.'

Seth glowered at him. 'That's my childhood bedroom. It's underwater. The lab is hidden inside a shipwreck on a deep sea reef.'

Meera waved her paintbrush. 'I can't focus with everyone talking. The painting needs to be as precise as possible to become a portal. Give Seth and me a few minutes.'

Esme, Daniel, and Lillian retreated to the beach, beyond which windblown trees hid the south side of the island. Through that thicket lay the rock pool leading to Spindrift … and home. Right now, that portal seemed much more appealing to Esme than the one being created in the cave.

'Maybe Seth's right,' she said. 'Maybe I *should* go on my own. It'll be quicker—and safer—for everyone.'

'Safe?' Daniel scoffed. 'Mare still wants the Pearl of Esperance. If he catches you …'

'There's no way we're letting you go on your own,' Lillian said.

Meera's footsteps sounded up the gritty sand. 'I did it! The painting's now a portal.'

'Thanks so much, Meera.' She lowered her voice. 'It must have been an awkward few hours for you, on your own with Seth.'

'It was, to start with. But then he told me everything … about his childhood, about how Mare treated him, about how terrified he was of going back home. I couldn't help feeling sorry for him. He apologised, too … for what it's worth.'

Back inside the cave, the three-dimensional painting beckoned. Seth climbed in and vanished.

'I'll be here when you get back,' called Meera. 'Take care!'

The last thing Esme saw before crossing over was Meera's soft eyes. Then blackness swallowed her, transporting her to the depths of an ocean unknown. Once more, she was in free-fall, the same way she'd been weeks ago, when she'd plummeted toward another shipwreck. Sick with terror, her fears running riot, Esme couldn't shake the conviction that Seth was delivering them straight into Mare's arms.

Seth's bedroom was dark, cramped, and stuffy. The only noises came from below: grunts and groans that raised every hair on the back of Esme's neck.

'What's making those sounds?' Lillian hissed.

'Quigley's chimeras,' Seth whispered. 'He was a scientist who used to work with my father, and he died a few months ago. My father hasn't been able to keep Quigley's creatures under control, so he's caged them all down in the brig.'

Esme shuddered. She'd met Quigley and his chimeras before.

Seth stepped forward and lit a gas lamp by his bed. In the flare of orange light, Esme saw drawings plastered to the walls, as if this room were a dark mirror of Ariane's at the Anais. These were simple sketches, in a child's hand, depictions of the monsters the younger Seth might have imagined lurked under his bed.

Except there really were monsters, one floor below.

He had drawn the fanged stingrays that had stalked Esme last summer. He'd drawn scorpions with eight eyes and bristling legs, that looked like they'd been crossbred with giant spiders. He'd drawn turtles with tentacles instead of heads, flippers, and tails. The largest sketch showed an eel with the head of a goblin shark, a flat snout and needle teeth affixed to a winding body.

Lillian sat on the bed and looked out the dark porthole. 'Is it night or day here?'

'It's around two in the morning. With any luck, my father and his assistants should all be asleep. When we get outside this room, I don't want to even hear you breathe. Keep your eyes on me. We're going up to the ship's top level, to the main laboratory.'

He advanced noiselessly toward the door. The atmosphere felt changed, charged with static. Seth's persona had altered. He was more indifferent, more dispassionate. Like he'd slid back into the skin he'd worn to survive living here.

No one else was as adept at emotional camouflage. Lillian's knuckles were clenched so hard by her sides, they'd gone white. Daniel was looking grimmer than ever. Fear coiled in Esme like a hangman's noose.

Outside Seth's room, red night lights illuminated a corridor. Steel doors ran down both sides, each a blank replica of the one beside it. Seth put a finger to his lips, then pressed his palms together and held them to his cheek. It wasn't hard to translate.

People are sleeping nearby.

He ignored the first set of stairs they passed, stopping instead at a spiral staircase further along. He grasped the handrail and gestured for everyone to follow him up.

'Skip the third one,' he whispered. 'It creaks.'

The steps led into a storage room stacked high with boxes. Everything was in order, nothing out of place.

Except us, thought Esme.

'The stairs to the top floor are down that corridor.' Seth motioned to his right. 'But if we go that way, we'll have to sneak right past my father's room. I'd rather not risk it.'

He opened a waist-high door in the corner, revealing a tiny goods lift, barely large enough to fit a person.

'Who wants to go first?'

'Uh, I don't think that lift is designed for humans,' said Daniel.

Seth shrugged.

After a moment's hesitation, Daniel squeezed himself onto the rusty grate inside the chute. A series of ropes and pulleys hung on the wall outside.

'Yank the cord when you get up there,' Seth said, 'so I know to bring the lift back.'

He wound a crank until Daniel disappeared out of view.

When the empty lift came down, it was Esme's turn. She

contorted herself into the tight space, her knees up against her chin, her head tucked into her chest. All she could see, to her left, were Seth and Lillian's legs.

Then they were gone. The trolley rose in jerky movements.

Inside the claustrophobic contraption, Esme's brave front collapsed. Her heart pummelled frantically against her ribs. When the lift creaked to a stop, she couldn't escape fast enough. She extricated herself and pulled on the cord. The grate slid back down.

Mare's laboratory, lit with the same sinister lights as the corridors below, was a spartan space, scrupulously clean. A strong antiseptic smell invaded Esme's nose and throat.

Trays full of gleaming, sharp instruments, along with microscopes, beakers, and jars, covered several workbenches inset with sinks. Three of the walls were lined with wooden shelves, housing hundreds of thin glass vials filled with some kind of vapour.

The fourth wall was floor-to-ceiling glass. The lab's low lights illuminated the depths outside. Viscous, orbed jellyfish with long, swaying filaments pulsed through the red-tinted sea. Bioluminescent lures dangled from invisible predators. A small fish, caught by a mucous-ridden monstrosity, jerked in its death throes. Slivers of flesh trailed along beside it.

'Seth's coming up the stairs instead,' said Lillian, crawling out of the lift chute. 'Since there was no one to hoist him up. He said he'd be able to get past his father without waking him, but he didn't trust us to.'

She scanned the lab, her nose wrinkling. 'What's in all those vials?'

'I don't want to know,' said Esme. 'Let's just find what we need and get out of here.'

Just as they started to search, Seth entered via a door on the other side of the lab.

'This way,' he said, leading Esme to a small adjoining storeroom. Daniel and Lillian waited by the door while Esme and Seth rifled through boxes and drawers. It wasn't long before Seth handed her a twist of paper that glowed from within.

'Here.'

Esme unwound the paper, holding her breath. Inside were half a dozen delicate flowers: thread-thin stems with shining, tapering petals, radiant with all the colours of the Aurora of Aeolia.

Auroral nightshade.

Esme wrapped up a single flower, secreted it in her pocket, and nodded her thanks to Seth. When she turned to leave, he grasped her arm, pulling her toward him.

'What are you doing? That hurts.'

A commotion came from outside. Lillian screamed. Daniel shouted. A struggle ensued, swiftly silenced. Then a bright light illuminated the storeroom, momentarily blinding Esme.

A figure appeared in the doorway: a tall, thin, foreboding silhouette.

Esme turned to Seth. On his face was an expression of infinite sorrow.

'I'm sorry, Esme.'

Outside, she heard a smooth, silky voice, a voice that made her whole body recoil in fear and revulsion.

'Thank you, my son,' said Dr Nathan Mare. 'I knew you wouldn't fail me.'

Chapter Twenty-Six

'Traitor!' Esme shouted, lunging at Seth.

Mare yanked her back, pinching her shoulder in a vice-like grip, so brutal she thought his fingers and thumb might meet in the middle. He dragged her out of the storeroom and into the lab. Her friends were being restrained by two of Mare's accomplices. Half a dozen more surrounded them.

'That one's a songstress.' Mare pointed at Lillian. 'Cover her mouth before she sings her way out of here.'

'How dare you!' Lillian writhed in her captor's grip, her eyes blazing, as Seth muffled her with a length of cloth.

A spiky lump rose in Esme's throat. There was only one way Mare could have known about Lillian's Gift—if Seth had told him.

Seth must have told him *everything*.

An arctic wind blew through her at the breadth of his betrayal.

'Leave her alone!' Esme cried.

She tried to wrench out of Mare's grip. He increased the pressure on her shoulder until her eyes rolled skyward, stars flashing before them. Pain ricocheted through her; she was sure one of her stitches had burst. She dragged in a long breath to stop herself from fainting.

With a roar, Daniel broke free and flew at Mare. He was halted, mid-flight, by another of Mare's accomplices—the only woman amongst the brawny men. She stretched out a finger and touched Daniel on the shoulder.

Like a bird shot in the wing, he fell to the ground.

Esme saw it frame by frame, like a slow-motion film. His face sagged. His eyes fluttered shut. His body crumpled, and then he was a motionless heap on the sterilised floor.

'What have you done to him?'

'My Gifted assistant has merely put your friend to sleep.' Mare turned to his son. 'Throw those two in the brig with Quigley's lot. I'll keep Ariane's daughter here with me.'

One of Mare's assistants slung Daniel over his shoulder. Another jostled Lillian toward the exit. Lillian managed to kick Seth hard in the shins on the way, then twisted back to give Esme one last panic-stricken look.

'Let *go* of me!' Esme roared.

It was no use. Mare was dragging her across the room, fingers digging into her wound as if he knew exactly where it was. Her nerves were on fire. He shoved her into a seat by the window and tied her hands behind her back.

He bore no trace of the artifice, the allure, that he had worn on the Isle of Mists to obscure his true motives. Instead he sported the satisfied smile of a hunter who has just subdued his prize catch.

A fish clear as glass drifted through the sea outside, its internal organs on display. It bumped into the window before sliding back into the gloom.

'That happens a dozen times a day,' Mare said casually. 'Everything down here is used to living in the shadows. The light … confuses them.'

His steely eyes bored into her petrified ones. His face was like an undead version of Seth's, pale skin stretched taut over bone.

'Tell me. Where is the pearl?'

'Even if I knew, I'd never tell you,' Esme spat.

'You know. And you'll tell me. Or I'll get my son to use his Gift on you again.'

'He wouldn't,' she said without thinking.

Or would he? How much of what he told me was a lie?

Mare smiled. 'Are you really still under the illusion that my son is on your side? I've spent years training him to do my bidding.

I told him to befriend you, to get close to you, to lead me to the pearl … and he did even better. He brought you to me.'

Esme turned her face away, swallowing back tears. She stared out to sea, desperately seeking inspiration, wishing she had a Gift like Fern's or Lillian's—one that might actually be of use right now.

Luminous spheres trailed along in the dark: the lures of angler fish, developed to fool prey into swimming straight down their throats.

The pearl's my lure, Esme realised. *It's the only thing I have over him. If I can just keep him talking while I figure out what to do …*

'Why do you want the pearl so badly?'

'Because it will complete my life's work.'

Esme knew that he was masking the true fervour of his desire. The pearl itself corrupted people, drove them mad with a desire to possess it. She'd been under its sway herself not so long ago, and had come dangerously close to giving into temptation.

'Your "life's work"?' she hissed. 'My mother's dying because you tampered with her Gift. And you've ruined mine, too. What *were* you trying to do to her? To us?'

'Extend your powers, of course. Imagine if you could not just witness the past … but interact with it. Remake it. If your mother hadn't turned against me, I might have succeeded in creating the world's first time traveller. I could have used her to change history.'

He leaned in close.

'I'll ask you one last time,' he growled. 'Where … did you hide … the pearl?'

She couldn't answer that question. No matter what Mare threatened her with. No matter what he did to Daniel and Lillian, down in the brig with Quigley's chimeras.

Think, Esme, think. There has to be a way out.

She glanced out the window, and the answer came to her.

'Water,' she croaked. 'I need some water.'

Mare hesitated, then crossed to a sink and filled a glass.

He held it to her lips.

She butted her chin forward, and half the water spilled onto her bare neck.

Get me out of here, she willed her Gift.

Esme didn't feel Mare shake her, slap her, scream at her to come back. She was no longer present. She was plunging down, deep down, into the past, knowing that Mare couldn't prise anything from her, no matter how hard he tried; knowing that he would never possess the pearl, the power he sought.

Knowing, too, that she might never come up for air.

When Esme materialised in the past, she was still in the lab, standing by the wall of glass. The universe outside was pricked with stars, predators moving to and fro in search of prey.

She heard a *crunch* from a workbench and turned around. Someone who looked like Seth—a slightly younger Seth—was grinding something with a pestle. He scraped the contents of his mortar into another bowl, then stared morosely out to sea.

This Seth's hair wasn't blond. It was dark, like his mother's, the way it had been on the Isle of Mists. His face was the thundercloud that had so often rained on Esme's art class.

'Got that powder ready for me?' Mare asked, striding into the room.

Seth shoved the bowl at his father. 'Here.'

Mare scowled. 'Your foul mood infects the whole ship. Learn to control it.'

'But I *hate* it here. I want to go home.'

'One day, you will … But not yet.'

When Mare was gone, Seth stared up at the shelves populated with the vials Esme had spotted earlier. He took one down, examined it, then slotted it back into its stand.

Esme's curiosity got the better of her. She went up next to Seth and studied the thin tubes, swirling with a mysterious, cloudy substance.

'*F Trask*' read the label on one vial.

'Is someone there?' Seth asked.

He'd gone very still, his eyes on the spot where Esme stood.

She backed away.

Seth didn't pursue her. Instead, he began to play around with his Gift. Ice streamed from his fingertips, taking the form of a tiny, sleeping dragon. He brought it to life, the way he'd animated the Pegasus at the Winter Festival.

'Go on,' he said, prodding the beast. 'Fly away. The way I can't.'

He watched the ice dragon flutter around the room, before catching it and flinging it into a sink, where it shattered into innumerable shards.

He wasn't finished. Bullets of ice shot from his hands. He funnelled them into a circle, faster and faster, until they were a blur. Then he flung out his right hand.

The bullets struck the glass wall with such force that the whole room shook.

'Are you deliberately trying to destroy the lab?'

Mare had been watching from the doorway. Seth's hands fell to his sides. After a tense silence, Mare wandered off.

The moment Mare was gone, Seth fashioned a pair of gleaming swords, which duelled each other until they were a pile of frosty fragments on the floor. As they melted, he wandered over to Esme.

'I can't see you, but I know you're still here. You're not a ghost, are you? You're something else. Something odd.'

His searching hand passed straight through her chest.

'I wouldn't hang around here if I were you. My dad likes to collect odd things.'

Esme, seized with dread, took Seth's advice. She fled back into the ocean between past and present, and hid amongst the curves and folds of the deep.

The rippling sea rocked her like a cradle, soothing her to sleep. But she couldn't sleep—sleep might doom her. She struggled to fight off the water's sedative effects, but she was so tired …

Some time later, she woke with a bump. She'd drifted a long way down. Around her floated the grit and sediment of the ocean floor. Esme had no idea how much time had passed. She had to leave, but if she did, where would she end up?

Back in that chair in Mare's lab?

Then, through the strange echoes and far-off reverberations of this liminal world, she heard a faint sound.

A siren's song.

Lillian was singing the first songspell she had ever cast: the summoning song, the spell that reached into one's soul and pulled them inexorably toward the singer.

Esme kicked upward, but it was like swimming through concrete. No matter how hard she tried, she got nowhere. Entombed on the ocean floor, she listened to Lillian calling through the chambers of the deep: a life buoy thrown again and again and again.

Esme forgot about Mare, forgot about everything except her friend.

Lillian, Lillian, Lillian.

At long last, the water began to swirl around her, catching her in its arms. No longer resistant, it lifted her toward freedom. Esme was released from the abyss, thrust into whatever darkness awaited her in the present.

Chapter Twenty-Seven

Esme woke, fearing the worst, fearing she was still tied up on the chair. A fetid smell assured her that she wasn't. The red lights on the roof were so dim, it was difficult to make out her surroundings. Her hands were no longer bound. Her shoulder screamed in pain, but the stitches were still in place. As her eyes adjusted, she made out a row of metal bars to her side. She thought she could see more criss-crossing over her head.

She was in some kind of cage, down in the brig.

Lillian was still singing, over ominous hisses and growls.

Esme manoeuvred herself into a kneeling position and squinted into the gloom. Her cage was one of many in a huge, low-ceilinged room. At the room's far end, at least a hundred feet away, light fell on a steel staircase.

There were more than just cages down here. Glass tanks lined the walls as well. In one, the slender outlines of stingrays cut through the water.

Not stingrays—monsters.

Quigley's chimeras.

'Lillian,' Esme whispered. 'I'm awake.'

Lillian stopped singing. A trembling hand reached through the bars. Lillian was in the cage right next to hers.

'You were out for ages. I was frantic with worry.' She squeezed Esme's fingers tight. 'I'm so glad you're awake.'

'Your songspell woke me, too,' Daniel said groggily from a cage close to Esme's.

'How did I get here?' Esme asked, rubbing her head. It was

throbbing like it had just been put in a vice.

'Seth dragged you in. He didn't say a word to me. Just tossed you in that cage and left. And then you wouldn't wake up …' Lillian sniffled. She sounded like she'd been crying. 'That woman—the one who put Daniel to sleep. Did she get to you, too?'

'No. I did it to myself. Mare kept asking me where the pearl was, and the only way I could escape was by using my Gift.' She ground her teeth as pain pounded through her head. 'Where do we go from here? Do you have any ashlight, Daniel?'

'Oh, I do!'

After coating his fingers with ashlight, he threw the bag to the others. When Esme's fingers were glowing green too, she heard a *caw* behind her.

She turned around, casting ashlight toward the source of the sound. Within her cell was a smaller cage: a mesh one, tucked into the corner. Squished inside, ruffling its feathers, was the sea eagle—the loyal messenger bird, white with speckled grey wings, that Esme had known half her life.

Then it was gone.

In its place was a shimmering vapour, which churned in its confines like an angry cloud. It resolidified as a mouse, which tried and failed to squeeze through the gaps in the wire. Seconds later, it reassumed the form with which Esme was familiar.

She blinked.

It's a shapeshifter.

'Daniel, Lillian, look!'

They pressed up against the bars of their cages, gawking at the sea eagle. It began to transform again, sprouting fur and claws.

'That—a second ago, th-that was a sea eagle,' Lillian stammered. '*The* sea eagle. Now it's a cat—oh! But there's feathers, and a beak— it's a bird again!'

A duck, a quoll, a rabbit, and a pangolin appeared in quick succession. Then the shifter became a python, its glistening length slithering around the cage. It cycled through the forms of a meerkat, a fox, and a monkey, before growing the chestnut coat and bushy tail of a squirrel. The agitated animal shook the bars of its cage with two tiny fists, before becoming an eagle once more.

'You saved me that day, didn't you?' Esme murmured. 'When I was sinking toward the shipwreck … you caught me.'

Its yellow eyes bored into her own. She shuffled closer in wonderment.

'And you tried to protect my mother, at the Anais. But Seth—or someone—caught you and took you here. That's why I haven't seen you around lately.'

She glanced down at the padlock on its cage. Something had glinted in the ashlight.

A tiny, silver key.

'There's a key here. In the lock.'

'Open it!' Lillian urged. 'Set it free.'

'Wait,' Daniel warned. 'You know what Mr Donnelly taught us about shifters. When they've been wronged, they go on wild rampages. It can take a whole team of rangers to subdue them.'

Esme hesitated, weighing her options. Mare was still upstairs. He might turn up at any moment, drag her back to the lab, start interrogating her again. That trick with the water, using her Gift to escape Mare's clutches … she doubted he would fall for that again.

The eagle shrieked and shook the cage, desperate for release.

'This might be our only way out,' said Esme. She twisted the key in the lock and scurried back.

The shifter burst forth, misting over once more. It billowed out into a giant cloud, one so thunderous and furious it would have moved Poseidon. Through the haze, Esme saw curved claws spring into being, and white fur envelop a muscular frame.

When the shifter grew solid, it adopted the guise of a polar bear.

Boxed in by the low roof of Esme's cage, it was forced to crouch on all fours. When it tried to straighten up, its sinewy back decimated the bars above. Rising from the broken metal, it thumped its chest and roared with incalculable rage.

'Esme,' Lillian cried. 'Be careful!'

Ten feet tall, the bear towered over Esme, baring a fearsome set of teeth designed to eviscerate prey. Esme, heart in her mouth, stood up and met the creature's black eyes. In them she saw a store of bestial rage, built up from weeks in captivity, but also the same intelligence that shone in the eyes of the sea eagle.

'It's not going to hurt us,' she said to the others. 'I'm sure of it.'

Mare, however, might not be so lucky.

The snowy bear lifted a clawed paw. Instead of swiping at Esme, it warped the bars around her. Both Esme and the shifter climbed out of the wreckage, and the beast set to work on Lillian's cage. Lillian screamed as the bear tore through the bars as if they were made of straw. Then she cowered, trembling, in the debris.

'Are you all right?' Esme asked, hauling Lillian to her feet.

Lillian's lip quivered as the bear advanced toward Daniel.

'Nice shapeshifter,' Daniel muttered, holding out his palms. 'Good shapeshifter … We're not going to hurt you.'

He cringed as it sprung at the bars that held him hostage.

Once freed, Daniel sprinted over to Esme and Lillian. The bear bolted off in the other direction, determined to free every captive creature in the room.

CRASH—BANG—THUD—

Cages were torn apart and knocked aside. The nets atop the tanks were ripped to shreds. A ray leaped out of its enclosure and thrashed about on the floor. Esme, Daniel, and Lillian stayed flattened against the wall, breathlessly watching the chaos unfold.

The chimeras—creeping, crawling, slithering out of their confines—finally tasted freedom.

Even half-concealed by shadows, Quigley's experiments were stomach-churning. Slimy atrocities with eyes in all the wrong places—clawed, scaled *things* with dislocated jaws—tangles of mangled flesh that Esme couldn't even begin to make sense of.

She flinched as the giant scorpion from Seth's drawing approached. It passed straight by, scuttling toward the staircase.

Its eight spider's eyes shone emerald in the ashlight. In the farthest corner, what looked like an alligator snapped its jaws. Most dreadful of all was the electric eel, with its snarling goblin shark's head. The water around it lit up as it thrashed about in its tank, trying to jump out the top the way the ray had.

'We have to get out of here,' said Daniel, staring at the writhing ray. 'The shifter might not want to harm us, but these chimeras won't see a difference between us and Mare.'

Lillian was fixated on the shifter, shrouded once more in mist. 'What's it turning into now?'

Within the shifter's violent storm, Esme saw an eye spin into being: a bulging blood-orange eye with a slit for a pupil.

Beneath the eye, a maw manifested itself, lined with scimitar teeth. Long limbs swelled from the cyclopic head: a dozen muscular tentacles, growing thicker by the minute, covered in suckers.

'It's a kraken!' Daniel cried.

The mist dissipated, but the kraken didn't stop growing. Its tentacles curled under the roof and pressed against the walls, which began to groan and buckle. Jets of seawater shot in through the corners. The baying chimeras egged the beast on, implored it to turn its rage on the ship itself.

So it did.

It tore the metal covers off each porthole, then used the panels to smash in the glass. Freezing water poured through the windows, surging up to Esme's knees. The flopping ray caught a wave, then disappeared under the surface.

With one fierce lash, the kraken sliced a wall clean in two.

CREAK—

The ground shifted beneath their feet.

The water was up to their waists already. They started wading toward the stairs. Something washed by Esme, brushing her hip. A turtle, but it had no head. Instead of limbs, mottled feelers protruded from its shell.

The monsters from under Seth's bed had come to life.

The ray leaped out of the water, rearing its cobra's head. Hissing, it hurtled toward Esme, but the kraken batted it away just in time. It was sucked out through the crack in the wall, along with the tentacled turtle.

The shifter was still growing—the room still flooding—Esme's friends still struggling along beside her. She tried not to think about what the black water concealed. Her ears were assailed by the chimeras' cries, the kraken's cacophony. From high above came the shouts of Mare's men.

'What's happening down there?'

'The chimeras! They're loose!'

'*Seth!*' Mare roared. '*Where are you? What's going on?*'

Esme heard no more. A wave swept her under. Beneath the surface, broken bits of metal speared up toward her. Monstrous shadows swam about in a bouillabaisse of horrors. The eel-shark lunged at her, jaws wide. Just in time she was wrenched up by Daniel.

'Hold my hand!' he cried.

Clinging to each other, dodging tails, teeth, tentacles, and claws, the trio reached the staircase. As they splashed up the steps, each tread was swallowed by the greedy tide. At the top, they found themselves in the corridor lined with identical doors.

'Stop them!' Mare bellowed.

Esme swung round. Two figures were silhouetted at the corridor's end: Mare, and the woman who had put Daniel to sleep. They sprinted toward Esme. She tried to outrun them, but they swiftly caught up.

'You won't get away!' Mare was right behind her. 'Not again.'

The woman's outstretched fingers reached for Esme …

And through the porthole to her left, Esme saw the kraken's eye rise into view.

Two tentacles punctured the wall. Spurts of seawater soaked the ship's interior. The suckered appendages wound, like boa constrictors, around Mare and his accomplice. White horror flooded their faces as they were pulled outside, into the abyss.

The kraken, now far too big for the brig, had escaped the ship. Still swelling in size, it was wrapping its length around the vessel, strangling it. Bangs, creaks, and cries echoed above. Dents and bulges riddled the walls and roof. Everywhere Esme looked, ice-cold water gushed in.

CREAK—

Esme's gut lurched.

The ship rocked forward, throwing her flat on her stomach. More water surged up the stairs from the sunken brig, then swept through the corridor. She, Daniel, and Lillian flew down the tilted passage, not sliding so much as falling.

'That's Seth's room,' Daniel yelled. 'Quick! Grab the handle.'

Lillian flung out her arm, catching at the door. It swung open, allowing the three of them—and several gallons of water—to enter.

CREAK—

The ship pitched the other way, and the water surged back to the brig.

Esme staggered to her feet. Seth's drawings had come off the wall. They floated past her, out the door. His blankets were in disarray. All the drawers had slid out of his dresser. As Esme took one last look at the sad cell in which Seth had spent his childhood, comprehension dawned.

Did Seth just save us? Did he leave the key in the shifter's cage because he knew it would help us escape?

Daniel was tugging on Esme's arm, trying to pull her toward the portal.

Maybe Seth's still on our side.

The ship went vertical.

The door slammed open again, admitting another torrent of brine.

The water poured into the portal, taking Esme with it. Powerless to fight the current, she, Daniel, and Lillian crash-landed on Laertes Island's sodden shore.

Chapter Twenty-Eight

Surfing a white wave, Esme, Daniel, and Lillian were swept through the cave and washed out onto Laertes beach. Meera stood beside the portal, eyes wide, taken aback by the flood of seawater rushing forth.

'Meera, close the portal,' Daniel yelled.

'But where's Seth?'

'He's not coming. We'll explain in a minute. Just close it, quick!'

A tentacle was now thrashing about inside what was left of Seth's room. Meera cast one panicked look back, then touched the cave wall. The tentacle vanished as the portal became a motionless painting once more.

'What *happened* in there?' Meera sprinted out into the open. 'You guys were gone for hours! Did you get the nightshade? Where's Seth?'

In a fit of panic, Esme dug into her pocket. To her relief, the nightshade was still there.

'Here,' she said, showing the flower to Meera. 'Seth found it for me.'

'And then he betrayed us.' Lillian dragged herself to her feet. 'His plan was to lure us to his father all along.'

Meera's lower lip trembled. Her eyes shone with tears. 'No!'

'I'm not so sure,' Esme said. 'I think Seth might still be on our side.'

'How can you even say that, after he locked us down there with those creatures?' Lillian snapped.

'I think he left behind the key to the shifter's cage on purpose. He must have known we'd escape.'

'Maybe he left it there by accident. Or *maybe* he wanted that shifter to kill us. And it might have, if we'd stayed there a moment longer.' Lillian put her hands on her hips. 'You can believe whatever you want. *I'm* never making the mistake of trusting Seth again.'

But unlike Esme, Lillian hadn't seen the younger Seth spray bullets of ice on the glass wall. 'He hated that lab just as much as we did.'

'Don't try to make me feel sorry for that creep!'

'I guess if he's innocent, we'll never know,' Daniel murmured.

He bent down to pack up Meera's paints, since she was too distraught to move.

'I don't know how much innocence he has left, after living in that awful place for so long,' Esme said.

She didn't get a chance to say more. Something brushed against her shins, then mewed at her: a wet black cat with streaks of grey. Its piercing green eyes glared into hers: two glowing slits of utter reproach.

'Reuben!' Esme scooped him up in her arms. 'What—how?'

If you're here, then …

She let the cat down and sprinted toward the trees, Reuben racing alongside her.

'Esme?' Meera called with a sniffle. 'Where are you going?'

When Esme emerged on the other side of the island, she scanned the tidal shelf, searching for signs of life. There he was: her father, Aaron, marooned like Odysseus on Calypso's isle.

'Dad!'

He was gaunt and unshaven, hunched over on a boulder beside the portal to Spindrift. His hands gripped the rock as if it were a raft on the high seas.

Esme flung her arms around him. 'You're here!'

He didn't respond. He just sat there, mumbling incoherently.

'It's my dad!' The others, carrying Meera's art supplies, were coming out from amongst the trees. 'He finally made it over! But … he's not himself.'

She took a shaky step back toward her friends.

'Neither were you when you first showed up.' Daniel steadied her. 'Give him time.'

Aaron held up a hand and stared at it as if he wasn't quite sure who it belonged to. He patted his face with the same vague expression, then looked off into the distance, frowning, like he was trying to remember how he'd ended up here.

'Hello, Mr Silver,' said Lillian.

Aaron flinched. Reuben jumped into his arms. He held the cat close, squinting suspiciously at Esme's friends.

'Dad.' Esme squeezed his shoulder. 'Do you want to go and see Mum?'

'Esme?' He shook his head. 'Of course … why wouldn't you be here? This must be where all the drowned people end up.'

'You didn't drown,' Esme reassured him.

He kept clutching Reuben as Esme helped him to his feet. She and the others guided him away from the rock pools, through the foliage, to the north side of the island. He looked more and more dazed with each step, and when he reached the beach he started muttering.

'It's not real. It's not real.'

Across the water, sunlight glistened off the city's spires. Scions wheeled overhead. Esperance didn't look real, but it was.

Esme took his arm again. She led him gently to the water's edge, where *Talia* rocked in a slight swell. 'This is my friend Daniel's boat.'

He clambered into the boat and gingerly lowered himself onto the rearmost cross-bench. Then he lay back, staring at the sky. 'No use trying to make sense of this,' he mumbled. 'No use at all …'

After Esme and the others crowded in, *Talia* set off.

'Maybe get him to talk about home,' Meera whispered. 'Might help.'

Esme nodded. 'What's the last thing you remember, Dad? What happened after I left home?'

Her father sat up straight. 'You mean, after you *ran away* from home?' he spluttered, sounding a bit more like his usual self. 'I just got you back, and then you were gone! I searched everywhere for you—*again*.'

He screwed up his face and massaged his temples.

'I thought you might be hiding up in the lighthouse. That's where I found your bag, and—and ...'

'The bank statements,' Esme said softly.

He choked.

'I was sitting on the front steps, trying to make sense of things, when Mavis showed up. She told me she suspected her sister was up to no good. Then I showed her the bank statements. We went to my parents, and ...' He swallowed. 'They confessed to everything.'

His voice grew hoarse. 'The marriage was a sham. Everyone knew it was arranged, except me and Mavis. I don't know whose idea it was—Penelope, or my parents—but Penelope wasn't planning to stick around after I'd started in the family business. Six months, tops. Then you vanished. That really threw a wrench into things.'

'I'm so sorry, Dad.'

He leaned out the side of the boat and gazed glumly at the water rippling by. He looked—and sounded—so wretched that all Esme wanted to do was turn *Talia* back round, return to Picton, and throttle her grandparents and Penelope.

'Mavis idolised Penelope even more than I did,' Aaron continued. 'When she found out the truth, she was beside herself. She went to her sister, told her she'd blacken her name if she didn't leave Picton right away. So Penelope's gone now ... gone to prey on some other gullible fool like me.'

'You weren't a fool, Dad. You were lonely, and she took advantage of you.'

'At least Mavis was on my side. She helped me move everything back into the lighthouse keeper's cottage. Then she moved in, too.'

Esme sprang back so fast the boat rocked. 'She *what*?'

'It's only temporary, she says. Until she gets on top of her new job.'
'What new job?'
'Mavis is running my parents' fishing fleet.'
'*What?*'
'When I said I'd never take the role, Mavis nominated herself. And after a trial, they realised she was perfect. They needed someone who was tough and bossy, not someone like me. So they got what they wanted all along. The business is in safe hands now. They can retire and travel the world. Good riddance.'

'Forget about them,' said Esme. 'You're here now. I'm so glad you followed my instructions.'

The flash of anger in her father's eyes stopped her short. Reuben, sensing Aaron's ire, sought refuge with Daniel.

'Your instructions were a load of bunk! Dive into a rock pool and come out in another world? What do you take me for? I only went to Spindrift this morning to get away from Mavis—she's impossible to live with. Reuben came with me. As soon as we got to Spindrift, he bolted off to the rock pools.'

He scowled at the cat lounging in Daniel's arms.

'He kept yowling and putting a paw into the water, and I thought—well, animals often sense things humans don't. Maybe there was some hidden cave in there and that's where I'd find you. I went in to check, fearing the worst, but there was nothing there. Just some weeds and a shell.'

His eyes clouded over.

'I can't remember what happened next. Maybe there *was* a cave in that pool, and I'm floating in there, beside you. The fish are probably feasting on our eyeballs right now.'

He glanced down and noticed the oars tucked into *Talia's* sides.

'Er … how is this boat moving?'

'It steers itself,' said Daniel. 'It's enchanted.'

Hiding his face in his hands, like a hungover man blinded by the sun, Esme's father curled up in *Talia's* stern. 'I'm taking a nap,' he grumbled. 'Wake me up when we reach the pearly gates.'

Chapter Twenty-Nine

When *Talia* reached the Keeper's Quarter, the group split up. Daniel, Meera, and Lillian went to deliver the nightshade to Augustine, while Esme guided her father to the Anais.

The city sights that Esme had grown so used to—a dragon soaring over a rooftop, a water-walker crossing a canal, a wind-waver magicking the leaves off a porch—were all too much for her father. He started gabbling all over again.

'It's all a dream … It must be a dream.'

He was weaving all over the place. Only the reassuring presence of Reuben, clutched to his chest, seemed to save him from tipping headfirst into a canal.

At the Anais, Esme half-carried her father up the steps.

'Where are we going?'

'Mum's in here. It's a—sort of hospital.'

'A hospital? For the dead? What do they need one of those for?'

Esme braced herself as they neared her mother's room, but nothing could have prepared her for her father's reaction upon walking through the door.

At the first sight of his former wife, Aaron dropped to the floor in a dead faint.

A healer revived him, pronounced that he was suffering from shock, and gave him something to help him sleep. Soon he was laid out on a stretcher in the corner, in blissful oblivion. Reuben dozed beside him.

Esme couldn't blame her father for feeling overwhelmed. Ariane was barely there, only a whisper away from leaving them all.

At least we're all here, together, after so long, Esme thought.

Her joy was torpedoed by the sinking knowledge that this reunion might not last long. One recipient of the Elixir of Severance had lived. The other had died. By morning, Esme would know whether Ariane would be added to the count of the former, or the latter.

Death was a regular occurrence here at the Anais. Several times, Esme had seen wrapped bodies leaving on stretchers, but she had always managed to put them out of mind. Now, at this penultimate hour, it was difficult to think of anything else.

A rising tide of panic engulfed her. She was glad when Daniel and Lillian arrived, wearing fresh, warm clothes, and carrying a set for her.

'We dropped Meera home,' said Daniel. 'She's going to come visit tomorrow.'

'Is she okay?' Esme asked. 'She must be so torn up about Seth.'

'She's holding up better than Miranda,' said Lillian.

'Miranda?'

'I thought Mum deserved to know everything,' Lillian explained. 'I told her what we've been up to these past few months; how dangerous it's been, getting the ingredients for the elixir, who Seth really is. Luckily, she's so relieved at the thought of your mother waking up, she forgot to be mad at us. That might come later.'

After Esme had changed, Augustine arrived, Willow floating in behind him.

'The staff were right to sedate your father,' he said. 'It's too much to take in, all at once. We'll wake him when the time comes.'

'Is that the elixir?' Esme breathed, her eyes on the small glass bottle in Augustine's hand.

He nodded. 'It's finished. The Elixir of Severance.'

Augustine set the bottle down on Ariane's bedside table. The liquid inside was the colour of a pale moon, with a layer of deep red at its base.

'Your friends told me what transpired in Mare's laboratory,' he said. 'I am sorry to hear about Seth's duplicity, but at least the auroral nightshade he provided is genuine.'

He crossed to Ariane's bed. She was more shadow than substance, washed of all colour.

'Let's not delay a minute longer.'

Esme was about to crack into pieces. It took an enormous effort to stay as calm as Augustine was. Her hands twisted together. Daniel folded one of them in his. Lillian took the other.

Augustine gently shook the elixir. The red sediment flew up through the moony liquid, turning it the colour of claret.

'Let's prop her up,' said Augustine. 'It will take some time to administer.'

With the help of her friends, Esme manoeuvred her mother into a seated position, against a tower of pillows. Augustine filled a dropper and began to dispense the potent brew—a few drops at a time—into Ariane's mouth.

He repeated the process a dozen times over the next half hour, waiting a few minutes between each dose.

On the periphery were Esme's worried friends' faces, Augustine's focused features, the pictures on the walls, nurses coming in and out of the room. Esme barely noticed any of it. All her attention was on the limp figure slumped against the pillows, her feather-thin breath, her clammy skin, her silent fight to remain on this plane.

When Augustine had administered the last dose, he stoppered the empty bottle with a satisfied sigh.

'Willow, come here.'

The divining rod hovered over Ariane, communing silently with the keeper.

'Good,' he murmured. 'It's taken. Now we wait. It will be a long night. If anyone requires rest, the nurses have made up beds in the neighbouring rooms.'

Miranda soon arrived, laden with food and drink, overflowing with tenderness toward Ariane and Aaron, and bearing surprisingly little resentment toward Esme and Lillian.

'You two kept an awful lot from me,' she complained as they finished off the breyberry bread.

'Because you never would have let us do any of it,' Lillian said.

'Of course I wouldn't have. You fought karkavores and snuck into a criminal's secret laboratory! What kind of parent would I have been if I'd *let* you go?' She paused. 'But at the same time, I can't be too mad at you. Not if it means my old friend will finally wake up.'

She took a resigned sip of coffee.

'I always knew there was something fishy about Celia. Basil and I are debating whether to leak her and Mare's relationship … and their son's existence. We're just not sure whether it will make things better or worse for Bernice.'

'How could it possibly make things worse?' Daniel spluttered.

'A lot of people disagreed with Mare's conviction, remember. They still think he's innocent of all those charges. This sort of news could end up working in Celia's favour.'

Miranda didn't want to leave, but after nodding off more than once, she went home, promising to return early the next morning. Daniel and Lillian were the next to succumb to fatigue. Lillian retreated to a room across the corridor, while Daniel simply fell asleep on his chair, his mouth lolling open.

Esme couldn't sleep. She was too wound up and strung out to do anything but watch over her mother. The tide of panic from earlier had subsided, but it had left behind a shore pebbled with anxiety.

By midnight, the moon's silver glow had stolen into the room. At first, Esme thought the sheen on Ariane's forehead was a lunar reflection. When she looked closer, she saw that it was in fact bathed in perspiration.

Her mother was burning up.

She went at once to fetch Augustine, who'd gone for a quick nap. Moments later, he was bending over Ariane, his tongue clicking against the roof of his mouth.

'A fever.'

His voice was grave.

Fear gnawed at Esme.

'Can we give her something to bring it down?'

'I'm afraid not. The components of the elixir are designed to work perfectly in concert with each other. Adding anything else will disturb the balance.'

He and Esme took turns mopping Ariane's forehead with a damp cloth.

'Is this what it was like last time?' Esme asked. 'With Mortimer? Did he get a fever?'

He raised an eyebrow. 'So you know.'

Esme nodded. 'He told me the day he stole the elysium.'

'Mortimer developed a fever too. Eventually, it eased. So I left him with Nathan for a short while, thinking the worst was over. When I came back, Mortimer had passed away. Nathan told me that Mortimer's fever had spiked again, moments before he drew his last breath.'

Hours passed—hours in which Esme, half dead with exhaustion, felt as if she herself were in a fever dream. Her father snored softly on his stretcher. Reuben slipped in and out of her lap. Shadows grew, flitting along the wall, creeping into corners, moving along the floor, like Hades' shades preparing to spirit her mother away.

Esme woke with a start. Her head was resting beside her mother's hand.

'I fell asleep! Is she all right?'

Augustine was still right beside her.

'Don't worry. The fever is gone. Now we just have to pray it doesn't come back.'

The moments ticked by so slowly, it was like time had forgotten to advance. The red of dawn filled the room, birds sang outside, the red withdrew. Morning was upon them. Still they waited, Esme and Augustine, joined once more by Daniel, Lillian, and Miranda.

Without warning, like a warm breath on a cold day, mist dispersed from Ariane's mouth and dissipated.

Augustine's eyes brightened. 'I suspect that was her Gift leaving her body.'

After a quick check with the divining rod, he confirmed it.

'Yes. Willow assures me that Ariane no longer possesses a Gift.'

He stayed Esme's relief with a wave of his hand. 'This is a very good sign, but it's not over yet. She's been gone for such a long time, her aura has almost vanished. Let's bring her back to us, by whatever means we are able.'

He drew a small pouch from his case and lay smooth stones at Ariane's head and feet. Then he muttered spells under his breath, using every incantation he knew to draw Ariane home. Lillian sang the song she'd sung to call Esme up from the deep the day before. Esme simply stroked her mother's hair, held her hand, and willed her to return.

She watched intently—they all did—for any movement or sound.

Ariane was as silent as a falling star.

Gondolas rocked outside. Voices floated in from the corridor. Nurses came in with warm cups of tea. The tea was drunk, the cups collected. Daily life resumed for everyone except the little group and the silent figure in their midst. They all sat there, or stood there, frozen, suspended, waiting ... waiting.

It felt like someone had tied a cord around Esme's heart, and was pulling tight.

Then Ariane drew a deep, gasping breath.

Her deep blue eyes opened. They roved around the room, glassy, confused, shadows stalking them still.

'Esme?' she said uncertainly. 'Is that you?'

A great, shuddering sob escaped Esme. She threw her arms around her mother.

Ariane smiled, then fell into an exhausted sleep.

The tension in the room exploded like a firework.

'It worked!' Esme cried. 'The elixir worked!'

Her heart was loosed from its bonds. Now, she felt like it might burst with happiness. Relief bubbled up inside her, streaming through her limbs, fizzing out like champagne. She hugged Daniel, Lillian, and Miranda, and all dissolved into tears.

'You did it!' Esme sobbed to Augustine. 'You brought her back …'

Augustine's eyes glistened at Esme. '*We* brought her back.'

Chapter Thirty

The next time Ariane woke, Aaron was there at her side. His grizzled visage hovered over the love he thought he'd lost forever. Esme was beside him, watching, waiting, hoping. So much hinged on this moment.

'Oh, Aaron,' Ariane whispered. 'My darling Aaron.'

He went as white as Ariane's bedsheets. Esme thought he was going to faint again, but he managed to keep himself together. Bending forward, he brushed a hand against Ariane's cheek.

'Ari? It's you, isn't it?' His face crumpled; he choked on his words. 'I'd given up on ever seeing you again, but you're here. You're really here.'

She was gazing at him the way Penelope never had, and it was clear to everyone in the room that the feeling was mutual. Their love, sequestered away for so long, had come back stronger than ever.

Behind Esme, Miranda let out a sob. Esme took a step back and looped her arm in Miranda's. Lillian beamed on Miranda's left.

'Aaron …' Ariane gave a halting smile. 'I thought I'd never see you again.'

She reached up to his bristly face. He bent closer.

His lips met hers in a tender kiss.

Witnessing this reunion, watching those eyes open at last, hearing words come from those long-silent lips, was a panacea as potent to Esme as the Elixir of Severance had been to Ariane. Tears of exhaustion and relief spilled down her face. Daniel put a comforting arm around her shoulders. She leaned into him, and the worry she had worn like a second skin for so long began to slough away.

'Aaron … Esme …' Ariane slurred. 'I'm so sorry …' Her eyes fluttered shut before she could say any more.

Aaron kept his hand clasped tight around hers and murmured, 'I'm sorry, too.'

Esme slept until late afternoon. Upon waking, she heard the door to Ariane's room creak open and went into the corridor to see her father emerge. He vaguely acknowledged her as they traded places: he, seeking out somewhere more comfortable to sleep; she, slipping into her mother's room.

Ariane was upright against the pillows, eating a slice of apple. She stared out the window, looking preoccupied in a pensive sort of way. It wasn't hard to figure out why.

He's told her about Penelope.

'You've grown so much, Esme,' her mother murmured.

Esme embraced Ariane for so long that by the time they broke apart, both were in floods of tears. Esme scrabbled for some tissues and they dried each other's faces, half crying, half laughing.

'You look exactly the same as you did when you left us,' said Esme. 'You haven't changed one bit.'

'You have … according to your father. You're acting like a teenager now. I hear you objected at a wedding.'

'I wasn't planning to!' Esme leaped to her defence. 'My hand just … raised itself. It was so painful, sitting there, saying nothing. I got in so much trouble afterward.'

A wry smile had crept onto Ariane's face. 'Your father also told me you ran away and spent weeks here, looking for me. Then you ran away again and spent *months* trying to wake me up. He said that I'm safe now, because of you—and so is the pearl.'

'He told you all that?'

Then he's been reading my letters, all along.

'I thought he didn't believe a word of what I wrote to him.'

'Oh, he doesn't. But he'll come round.'

Esme regarded her mother curiously. She seemed calm—too calm.

'Are you okay? After hearing about Penelope? After losing your Gift?'

Ariane said nothing for a long moment.

'I'm still taking it all in,' she admitted. 'I'd rather your father have waited for me, of course, but ...' Her smile turned mischievous. 'I'm just glad he picked someone awful.'

Esme gaped.

Ariane speared another piece of apple off the plate on her lap and offered it to Esme. 'I was gone a very long time. I would have been lonely, too, if our roles were reversed. You could have ended up with an evil stepfather.'

Esme almost choked on her apple.

'And as for losing my Gift ...' Her mother gazed out the window once more. 'I won't miss it. I've spent enough time living in the past.'

'Seven years,' Esme mumbled.

'And I felt every minute of it. Sometimes, it wasn't so bad. I saw incredible things, history in the making, all over Aeolia. I can't wait to tell Professor Sage. But most of the time, I spent thinking about you and your father ... and it was agonising.'

A tear rolled down Ariane's cheek.

'What? How?'

'When I held the pearl in my hand, I realised it could link me into every part of Aeolia's history. So I tried to gather evidence against Nathan Mare. My Gift showed me a house burning in the night, voices shouting, blackened bodies being carried outside. It was horrific. I was so shaken, I forgot that my Gift had started giving me trouble. I'd been finding it hard to return to the present if I lingered too long in the past. But I stayed by the ruins of that house for ages—far too long.'

She reached for a tissue.

'Then I couldn't get back. Every time I tried, my Gift flung me to another time and place, at random. I'd completely lost control. It was like the pearl wanted to punish me for using its power for myself.'

'That's not it,' Esme insisted. 'You weren't trapped because of the pearl. The pearl sees you as its guardian—its protector. I know, because it granted me its power to save you.'

'Then …' Ariane laid down her fork. 'Why couldn't I leave?'

'Because Nathan Mare tampered with your Gift. He was trying to make it more powerful, make it so you couldn't just witness the past, but interact with it. He was trying to turn you into a time traveller.'

Ariane froze, all the colour leaving her face. Then the blood returned in a rush. Hurt, betrayal, and disgust crossed her features in quick succession. 'That man should be in *prison!*'

'He was. For a while. There was a trial.'

Ariane closed her eyes and clutched her temples. 'A trial? Oh, Esme, I've missed so much. This is making my head spin.'

'Then let's start at the beginning,' said a voice from the doorway.

The keeper strode into the room and set a tray down on Ariane's bedside desk, laden with tea, biscuits, and a blue box decorated with a gold ribbon. 'Truffles. From the city's finest chocolatier.'

He stretched out a hand to shake Ariane's. Augustine Agapios, the Keeper of Esperance.'

After tea had been poured, Augustine said, 'I'm very sorry I had to remove that marvellous Gift of yours. But it was beyond repair.'

Propped up against several pillows, swaddled in her blanket, armed with a cup of tea and a biscuit, Ariane grimaced. 'It was working fine before Nathan Mare came along.'

'How did you first meet Mare?' Esme asked.

'He helped me while I was pregnant with you. Without Nathan, I could have lost you. So when I first heard rumours about his wrong-doing, I wouldn't hear a word against him. My loyalties ran deep.'

She sipped some tea.

'It was Professor Theodore Sage who swore to me that Mare was up to something. He'd never liked Mare, and one day he told me that Nathan had started limiting the patients he saw … to those with intriguing Gifts.'

Ariane fidgeted with the blanket, wrapping the hem around her finger, unfolding it, folding it again.

'What he'd said nagged at me. Nathan had always been fascinated with my Gift, you see, and I'd started having problems with it, problems I didn't link to him. Like headaches, and difficulty returning to the present.

'I was thinking of going to see you, Augustine. I knew you were an expert on Gifts, but Nathan advised against it. He said you might make things worse.' She paused mid-sip. 'He really doesn't like you, does he?'

Augustine pursed his lips. 'I wish you *had* come to see me. Perhaps all of this could have been avoided.'

'I should have.' She hung her head. 'I was so naïve.'

Her eyes glazed over.

'You can tell us the rest later, if you're tired,' said Esme.

'No, I'm fine. It's just a painful tale, that's all. Broken trust isn't easy to stomach.'

'Chocolate is,' said Esme, passing her the blue box.

'I betrayed you, too,' Ariane lamented, after a truffle. 'You, and your father. For so many years. Telling you I was going off to paint … and coming here. You must be furious at me. I don't blame you.'

Esme felt a faint stir of old anger, but it didn't last. Perhaps it might resurface later. Her younger self, jealous and neglected, wasn't ready to forgive and forget. But for now, Esme was just grateful to have Ariane back in her life. Sheer euphoria overpowered everything else.

'I decided I couldn't do it anymore. Stretch myself so thin. One last exhibition, I decided, to celebrate the publication of Professor

Sage's compendium. Then I would return to Picton until you were older. The day after the exhibition, I headed to the university to say goodbye to Nathan.

'I heard voices inside his office. He was talking to Dr Quigley, a biology professor. The door was ajar, and I was about to knock when I heard my name.

'"*Ariane visited the Merle Fountain the other day,*" Dr Quigley said. "*She went underwater and didn't come up for an hour. Then she went to her studio and painted a very interesting picture: the Pearl of Esperance, in a hidden chamber.*"

'What Mare said next floored me. "*Go there tomorrow. Find the chamber's entrance … and bring me the pearl.*"

'I felt sick to my stomach. Mare kept talking, saying more and more unbelievable things. The way he spoke about the pearl, about me …' Her eyes flashed with rage. 'I barged in there, told him he was despicable. I told him I'd heard all the rumours about him. I swore I'd use my Gift to expose him for the charlatan he was.'

'Ah,' said Augustine. 'That explains the attempted break-ins.'

Ariane gasped. 'The *what?*'

'Someone tried to break in through that window—twice,' said Esme. *Probably Seth*, she added to herself. 'Mare didn't want you waking up and exposing his secrets. So … what are his secrets?'

Ariane buried her face in her hands. 'I didn't get the chance to find anything out. I went to Spindrift to recover from the shock, to try to work out what to do. I spent all night worrying about Nathan, and how catastrophic it would be if he got hold of the pearl. So the next morning, I went straight back to the chamber in the Merle Fountain.

'I swam as silently as I could, to the pearl atop its pedestal. Then Quigley showed up, but he didn't know he had to be quiet. He didn't know about the creatures in the water.'

'Stygians,' Esme said with a knowing nod.

'When Quigley reached the isle, he was covered in blood. He tried to grab the pearl from me, but I fought him off. He slipped and fell into the pool … and I didn't look back as I escaped. I don't know what happened to him.'

Esme shook her head. 'Nothing good.'

'Then I took the pearl to one of the places I'd painted for the compendium. I was going to leave it somewhere Mare would never think to look.'

Esme clasped her mother's hand. 'The Isle of Mists.'

Ariane gazed at the artworks on the walls. 'I suppose you know the rest of the story. You've drawn it. The isle, the sirens, the rock shaped like a wave … I always knew you'd grow up to be a talented artist.'

'I've got even more things to draw now. The slopes of Mt Asha— that's where we found the bloodstone for the elixir. And the temple where we found the karkavore fossils …'

A proud glint shone in Augustine's eye. 'Your daughter roamed all over Aeolia to find the ingredients for the elixir. It wasn't an easy task. I had to make sure there were no mistakes this time.'

Ariane frowned. 'Mistakes?'

'The last patient I used it on … didn't recover.'

'No, he didn't. And he haunts him to this very day,' echoed a familiar voice.

Mortimer glided down through the roof, floating a foot above them all.

'Mortimer?' The keeper glanced up at him. 'How long have you been hiding there?'

'Since yesterday,' Mortimer drawled in monotone. 'And as I hid, I relived my own demise. I, too, lay in wait for the elixir to take effect. I, too, developed a fever. It passed …' His translucent eyes drooped toward Ariane. 'Just as hers did.'

He swooped down to the keeper's level, and hissed, 'Then you left me alone with your assistant. He fed me the last few drops of the elixir, and my fever returned in a violent assault. With my last breath, I cursed your name.'

Augustine gave the ghost a blank stare.

'Mortimer, there was no more elixir to administer. I instructed Nathan to give you water, and only if you requested it. I never knew he gave you anything else.'

Mortimer's nostrils flared. He clasped his bony hands to his gaunt cheeks, then unhinged his jaw in a rage-filled scream. Several nurses came running, then stopped in the doorway, shrinking back at the sight of the ghost.

'So it wasn't your fault—*it was the boy's!*' Mortimer howled. 'Nathan Mare poisoned me! *I'll haunt him for the rest of his days!*'

Mortimer didn't bid farewell, or apologise for his years of tormenting the keeper. He just shot through the roof in a blinding silver blur, like a shifter about to go on a rampage. But Esme didn't have time to reflect on the ghost's change of heart—or rather, victim.

Because a real shifter had just landed on the windowsill.

The speckled sea eagle gave a loud *caw*, preened its feathers, and peered inside the bedroom. It warmed Esme's heart to see the shifter safe and sound. Then, with a chill, she thought of Seth. Had he made it out of that lab alive?

'Oh! My old friend,' Ariane cried, spotting the shifter. 'You've come back!'

She tried to rise, then collapsed against her mound of pillows.

'Don't push yourself,' Augustine instructed. 'You're still in shock. You need rest.'

Tucking Ariane back in, he gave one of those benevolent smiles that Esme had come to know so well and treasure so much.

'You're a remarkable woman, Ariane Silver.' Augustine poured her another cup of tea. 'And so is your daughter. If we could bottle resilience such as yours, it would be a powerful elixir, indeed.'

For the following days, the Anais was witness to new beginnings instead of sad farewells. Esme took time off school and greeted the constant stream of visitors to her mother's bedside. Many of them Esme knew: like Professor Sage, who spent an hour with Ariane, flipping through the compendium. Meera, Vince, and Fern came often, Daniel and Lillian even more so.

Despite her busy schedule, Miranda visited every day, catching Ariane up on the events of the past seven years. She was the one to tell Ariane that the pearl's removal had caused earthquakes so destructive, the Keeper's Tower had fallen and a whole district had slid into the lagoon.

'But if Mare had gotten hold of the pearl,' Miranda reminded her distraught friend, 'things would have been worse. Much worse.'

On one of Daniel and Lillian's after-school visits, Daniel handed Esme a stack of paper. 'We brought your homework. Although I don't expect you'll do it.'

'And Rank granted you an extension for your history essay,' Lillian said. 'Reluctantly. After we explained why you weren't at school.'

'Rank?' Ariane frowned. 'Who's Rank?'

'My history teacher,' said Esme. 'He's the worst. I can't wait for him to read my essay.'

'Neither can I.' Lillian sniggered. 'All that stuff you discovered about Mann … It's going to make his textbooks obsolete.'

There was a tap on Esme's shoulder.

'I'm afraid I have to get going.' Miranda had just finished changing the water in all the vases. 'Debate prep. There's only one more debate before the election, and Bernice can't afford to lose.'

'There's an election?' Ariane asked.

'It's all over the news,' said Esme's father, appearing at the door.

Under his arm, he carried several copies of the *Aeolian Eye* and *Esperance Daily*.

After days of wandering around in a haze, Aaron had finally, grudgingly, begun to accept that he wasn't dead. He had started to make himself useful around the Anais—tending to the garden, helping out in the kitchen, and delivering newspapers to patients.

Only when Maria floated into the clinic did he temporarily revert to a state of numb shock.

Ariane sometimes relapsed, too. She had been trapped in the past for so long that her mental wellbeing had suffered. She would often wake in a cold sweat, not knowing where she was—or when she was.

'Can you help me?' she would whisper, over and over, tears wetting her cheeks. It was heartbreaking to witness her descent into those dark days. Sometimes she would even drift off in the middle of a conversation and not respond for minutes at a time.

Fortunately, for the most part, Ariane was very much her old self, ecstatic to be back amongst her family, always ready for yet another hug from Esme or Aaron. The following weekend, the keeper declared her fit enough to be discharged from the Anais, and she moved, along with Aaron, into the very crowded house at No 8, Nestor Street.

By Sunday, Ariane was well enough to enjoy a gondola ride through the city. Esme took her to revisit countless places, including Akitsu's, Sofia Square, and the art studio on Conte Canal. The water, dappled by the winter sun, allowed them smooth, safe passage as they drifted along on a sleek blue vessel on their way to the Arts Quarter.

To their left and right, ancient dwellings rose into view before falling away. Around the next bend, tantalising aromas wafted from boats slung together to form a market. Ariane, rugged up in a blanket, tipped her head back to watch a dragon soar overhead. Esme, meanwhile, fell into a reverie.

The events of the past few months drifted through her mind like the slow, sensuous currents either side. Her first trip through one of Meera's portals. The dragonling, hatching and sneezing fire. The sunken city of Pallas, the smoking bowl of Mt Asha, the stark branches of the thrallbark tree. Mare's lab … and Seth's stolen kiss. In her relaxed state of mind, it all felt as if it had happened to someone else.

Except for that kiss.

All at once, Esme knew whose lips she would rather have touched hers.

Suddenly she was jittery and awake, and tingling all over. It had been there for a while, this soft knowing, hidden beneath the quest to save her mother and the trials she and her friends had endured. It tugged at her heart, persistent as a pulse. She was happy and curious and anxious, all rolled into one.

'What is it?' Ariane, colour in her cheeks, a sparkle in her eye, was observing her.

'I'm sixteen now, Mum,' Esme said lightly. 'Time to keep some things to myself.'

The Conservatorium came into view. The gondolier let them off at Esme's request.

'I've got a surprise for you,' she said, taking her mother's hand. 'Vivolino's. They do great hot chocolates.'

'Now that's one place I've yet to see,' said her mother.

'Really? I bet you've been there before. It's been around for centuries.'

'Yet to see with you,' her mother confessed with a smile. 'Come on. Lead the way. Let's make up for lost time.'

Time.

Time had almost swallowed Ariane, and Esme, too. The time they had spent apart … the time Ariane had spent trapped in the past … those years were gone, and there was no getting them back. But the present was theirs to savour. Pale afternoon light softened the cityscape, and each cherished moment together soothed their hearts, healing the sorrow that had been there for so long.

They wandered into Allegra Square and admired the sirens and muses adorning the Conservatorium's exterior. Melodies, old and new, wafted from the open windows. Esme and Ariane stayed a while, talking of Melisande, of songspells, of islands swathed in mist. The symphony of Esperance swept on, and Esme and her mother disappeared down a narrow lane, into the depths of the timeless city.

Acknowledgements

I survived! This was a tough novel to write, and my utmost gratitude goes to those who supported me throughout. My son and chief editor Chris again went above and beyond, pushing me to make this book the best it could be. Thanks to my readers for waiting so patiently for Book 2. Shealea Iral deserves a special mention for her unflagging enthusiasm for all things Esme, as do Chelsea Taylor and Katherine Liu. Thanks, too, to the early readers—Chelsea, Katherine, Julian Barr, Jean Rabeau, my son Nicholas, and my daughter Lucy—for their on-point advice. And finally, thanks to Michelle Lovi of Odyssey Books, for all her help in bringing the *Esme* series out into the world.

About the Author

Elizabeth Foster grew up in Brisbane, Australia, and now lives in Sydney. Apart from writing and reading, which take up most of her time, she loves swimming in the ocean, walking, and playing the piano (badly). As a child, she was called Dizzy Lizzy—which she regarded as an insult all her life, until she started writing. Now, daydreaming is a central part of what she does. Reading to her own kids reminded her of how much she missed getting lost in other worlds, and once she started writing stories, she couldn't stop. *Esme's Gift* is her second novel.